We
Are
The
Fool

Paperback published by Long Midnight Publishing, 2025

copyright © 2025 Douglas Lindsay

All rights reserved. No part of this publication may be reproduced or transmitted in any form or by any means without permission of the author.
Douglas Lindsay has asserted his right under the Copyright, Designs and Patents Act 1988 to be identified as the author of this work.
All the characters in this book are fictitious and any resemblance to actual persons, living or dead, is purely coincidental.

ISBN: 979-8293075157

www.douglaslindsay.com

By Douglas Lindsay

The DCI Jericho Series:

We Are The Hanged Man
We Are Death
We Are The Fool

The DS Hutton Series

The Vikström Papers

The DI Buchan Series

The Barney Thomson Series

The DI Westphall Trilogy

Pereira & Bain

Others:

Lost in Juarez
Being For The Benefit Of Mr Kite!
A Room With No Natural Light
Ballad In Blue
These Are The Stories We Tell
Alice On The Shore
The Arlington Revenant
Song To The Moon
Cold September
Santa's Christmas Eve Blues

WE
ARE
THE
FOOL

DOUGLAS LINDSAY

LMP

For Kathryn

I

This is where Robert Jericho's search would end. In an apartment on Barbarastraat, three blocks from the beach, in Noordwijk aan Zee. A cold day in early March, low grey cloud, the North Sea a grim, sullen calm, stretching far away to a solemn horizon.

The hangman's noose had been perfectly tied. The police would surmise Isabella Bishop had learned how to tie the knot from the internet, and had practised on a weighted dummy. The dummy itself, of the variety used in resuscitation lessons, had been left sitting on a sofa, facing the victim. The eyes of the dummy would have been one of the last things she saw, as she twitched on the end of her rope.

The bottom floor of the maisonette was open, with a kitchen leading to a dining area, merging with the spacious sitting room. To the left, a wide staircase led up to the first floor, with a wooden balustrade around the landing. It was to one of the ornate rungs that the rope had been attached.

Bishop was five feet, six inches tall. The rope was long. Her feet were only six inches from the ground. Six inches or six yards, it hadn't made any difference. The calculation had been made and her feet were never going to touch the polished, wooden floor.

Her face was blue when the housekeeper found her body. Agnieszka Korczak stood and stared at the corpse for several minutes.

Korczak could tell she'd been dead for some time. She'd

watched enough detective shows, had seen enough films. She walked forward and stood beside the body, no more than a couple of feet away. This close, the smell of death, which she'd noticed the moment she'd entered the apartment, was strong.

Bishop's eyes were open, staring blankly at the resuscitation dummy. There was no blood, the discolouration aside no obvious marks on her face, no sign there'd been a struggle. The death presented clearly as suicide, but Korczak knew a thing or two about the life of Bishop. People like her did not commit suicide. They did on occasion, however, get murdered.

There was often, thought Korczak, a beautiful hush in this apartment, something that was more than the sum of all the silence. The thick walls, the triple glazing that kept out the windiest day on the North Sea coast, that blocked out the planes approaching Schiphol and the birds in the trees; the expensive refrigerator that never hummed; the noiseless clocks; the floorboards that never creaked; the under-floor heating from which no sound ever emerged; the music system that was never played, the CDs that never left their boxes; the television that was never turned on.

The silence was thicker today. Korczak couldn't have said what it was that was missing, because she couldn't think of any sound that had been there before. Perhaps there had just been the echo of sound. The walk across the room, the quiet footfalls, the brush of cotton trousers, the placing of a cup on a kitchen worktop, the opening and closing of a door, and the remnants of those scant noises lingering in the stillness. But there had been no movement in here for several days, and the body hanging there had swallowed up whatever might have been left, old sounds with a half-life of no more than a couple of seconds, reverberating over time inconsequentially into stillness.

Korczak had never seen a dead body before, and she wondered about touching it. She got as far as reaching out, her fingers no more than a couple of inches from Isabella Bishop's right hand. And then she shivered, and the shiver was like a voice, and she pulled away, finally stepping back.

Only then, having been in the apartment for almost ten minutes, did she take out her phone and make a call.

2

The Swiss Embassy in The Hague is located on Lang Voorhout, between the embassies of Malta and Spain, a four-storey, white townhouse.

Ilsa Badstuber was leaving the office at 6:33 p.m. She had locked up at the end of another day, turned the combination lock on the outside door to the small box room that held her and one other member of staff captive, and was walking past the offices on the first floor on her way to the stairs.

'Ilsa?'

Badstuber stopped, hesitated a moment, and then took two steps back, looking into the office. There was a name plaque on the door that read, Nora Odermatt, Consul.

'That explains why you didn't pick up,' said Odermatt.

'What's up?'

'Close the door.'

'You want to go upstairs?'

'No, we're good.'

Badstuber walked into the office, closed the door behind her, but did not sit down. She glanced past Odermatt's head at the early March evening outside. Flecks of white against the streetlights, but no one was expecting much of a snow fall.

'We've got a body,' said Odermatt. 'A woman named Isabella Bishop, her cleaner found her dead this afternoon. Had hung herself from the banister in her own apartment. Or someone had hung her, and tried to make it look like suicide.

'I'm going down to the mortuary now to take a look, then

I'll probably head over to the police offices, get everything we can. She had four passports.'

She'd thrown the last few words into the mix as though that was all part of the ordinary turn of events, but that was the reason she was bringing the matter to the attention of Switzerland's Federal Intelligence Service in the first place.

'One of them was Swiss,' said Badstuber.

'Swiss, British, American, and the Vatican.'

'There's a different name on each passport?'

'Yes.'

'Are any of them Isabella Bishop?'

'No. The police got that name from the cleaner.'

'What nationality is Isabella Bishop?'

'We don't know.'

'So the chances that this woman is Swiss are minimal.'

Odermatt nodded.

'This is not good,' said Badstuber, with typical understatement.

Odermatt, familiar with Badstuber's dry delivery, smiled.

'The Dutch police would not have wanted to involve the Americans if they could avoid it,' said Badstuber. 'They wouldn't go anywhere near the Vatican, and then... they tossed a coin between us and the British?'

'That may well have been their thinking,' said Odermatt. 'The main thing is that none of the others are present when we get down there, because that'll be a shitshow. But I'm led to believe it'll just be us.'

'That is good. You are heading there now?'

'I am. You OK to join me?'

'It is this or *Tosca*.'

'Oh, sorry, were you–'

'It is fine. I was due to go alone. I am not a fan of *Tosca*. One sits bored for three hours waiting for *Nessun Dorma*, then it's over in two minutes.'

'That's *Turandot*.'

'That settles it then,' said Badstuber, absolutely deadpan, leaving Odermatt wondering, as ever, whether or not she'd been joking.

3

There were four of them around the corpse. Badstuber and Odermatt, Detective Inspector Bakker of the Dutch police, and the pathologist, Doctor Janssen. They had been standing for at least a minute in silence, looking down at the blue-blotched, naked corpse of Isabella Bishop.

The eyes of the corpse were open. Green surrounded by muddied white, the right eye bloodshot. She had greying hair, clipped short at the sides and back. The hair of someone, thought Badstuber, who regularly wore a wig. She hadn't seen the slew of passports yet, but she would have dramatically different hair in each one. Possibly the wigs would be in a cupboard at the apartment, or perhaps she would have had a lock-up somewhere – possibly in another country – where she stored her various disguises.

She had been in her mid-fifties, around sixty kilos, guessed Badstuber, and she'd never had children.

Of course, she knew a lot more about this woman than what she could discern from looking down upon her pale corpse. She recognised her, and she wondered how much of a coincidence it was that she herself was now standing here.

'Do we think suicide?' asked Odermatt, finally cracking the silence.

A conversation between the Dutch and Swiss could have been conducted in several different languages, but they had inevitably settled on English.

'As you know, we found four passports, with multiple

identities.' said Bakker. 'Whatever we find here tonight, looking down at this corpse, I think there will be a story to tell, and I doubt it ends in suicide. But you never know.'

Bakker was young, or at least seemed young to Odermatt and Badstuber, and spoke English with a distinct American accent.

'There are no indications that it wasn't suicide,' said Janssen, the first time she'd spoken since they'd arrived at the mortuary. She was older, her accent neutral. 'There is, indeed, very little to say about her. I have not yet opened her stomach, as you can see, but her cause of death was unquestionably asphyxiation through hanging, and there was nothing in her blood to indicate any intoxicants.'

'Not even alcohol.'

'No alcohol,' said Janssen.

'Any indication she'd been with anyone?' asked Odermatt.

'You mean, sex?'

Odermatt wasn't entirely sure that was what she'd meant, but she nodded.

'No. There's nothing on the body to indicate any recent contact, sexual or physical, with anyone. Your people will be able to tell if there are any signs on her clothing,' she added, glancing up at Bakker.

'How long has she been dead?' asked Badstuber, the first time she'd spoken since they'd arrived.

She didn't like cadavers, and there was a time when she'd have barely been able to stand here for more than a few seconds. Likely, that still applied to cases where the corpse had been badly mutilated.

'I'm not sure who you are,' said Janssen in response, indicating that she at least already knew Odermatt's identity.

'Embassy consular,' said Badstuber. 'I work with Frau Odermatt.'

Janssen held her gaze for a moment as though considering whether or not this might be true, then looked at Odermatt as she answered.

'Three days. You'll understand that I can't give you an exact time, but I would speculate Friday afternoon. There are a few more tests to run, and we may identify the last thing she ate. There's a small chance that gives us some clue as to her whereabouts on the day.'

Bakker nodded, then looked at Badstuber and Odermatt.

'We are finished here, I believe. You have any other questions? No, then we shall leave.'

She turned abruptly away. Badstuber and Odermatt both acknowledged Janssen, though she wasn't looking at them, then followed Bakker from the room.

The three women stood in the corridor outside. Very long, white, antiseptic, recently visited by pungent disinfectant. There was one poster on the wall, A5 in size, showing a picture of hands beneath a tap, and the legend *was je handen of deel uitmaken van de ziekte*.

'I am going home now and will return to this business in the morning,' said Bakker.

'Do we know next of kin?' asked Odermatt.

'We do not.'

'Has it been released to the press that a Swiss, British, American, Vatican joint national has been found dead?' asked Badstuber.

'It has not. Nothing has been done bar bringing the body here. No one has been notified, as there is currently no one to notify.'

'Did she own the apartment she died in?'

'Again,' said Bakker, 'we are in the dark. We will resume the investigation in the morning. With a full day ahead of us, I am confident we will make progress.'

'Is there anyone currently at the property?' asked Odermatt.

'We considered placing a car outside the building, but it is an apartment block with twelve units. It did not seem worthwhile.'

Odermatt and Badstuber exchanged a look.

'You want to go round there now?' asked Odermatt.

'I have other things to do,' said Badstuber.

'Sorry, *Tosca*.' Odermatt checked her watch. 'Might make the second act.'

Badstuber had no intention of going to *Tosca*, but Odermatt didn't need to know what she was going to do.

'I will go in the morning,' she said. 'You will –'

'Morning's fine with me,' said Odermatt, cutting her off.

They looked at Bakker, Bakker made a small gesture to indicate her satisfaction. She would have shown no emotion about it, but she was glad the Swiss had not wanted to run ahead of themselves, and spend the entire evening on the case.

And so, with a perfunctory nod, Bakker turned and was

walking quickly towards the far end of the corridor.

Φ

Forty-five minutes later.

Odermatt was walking in through her front door, her fifteen-year-old son glancing at her from a slouched position on a sofa just inside the sitting room, her ten-year-old sitting on the stairs, his head lowered to a book Odermatt knew he probably wasn't reading.

Bakker, having said she was heading home, was back at the police station. She had three staff reports, which she'd not yet begun even thinking about, to complete that week.

And Badstuber, having rushed home and packed a rudimentary bag, was on her way to Schiphol Airport.

4

Robert Jericho was sitting at the table in his kitchen in Wells, Somerset, doing a jigsaw of Hendrick Avercamp's *Winter Landscape with Skaters*.

Not long before midnight. On the table to his left the remnants of a glass of white wine. His fourth of the evening, the taste had long since soured, and had been poured long enough ago that its temperature had warmed considerably.

He'd spent about an hour at the jigsaw intending to get up and make a cup of tea, and now it was too late, and he was getting tired and about to go to bed.

When he'd left the Police Service ten years previously, he'd given himself a year to crack the mystery of the secret organisation that called itself the Pavilion, regardless of the fact that his wife Amanda had been trying to crack it for many years longer than that. He didn't doubt her abilities, it was more that he thought he'd made enough inroads into the organisation, and had learned enough information, that a breakthrough would come more easily.

At the end of the first year, he'd given himself another. By the end of the fourth year, he'd started giving himself two more years.

When he entered his tenth year on this fruitless task, he'd declared to the few people who were still interested in his existence, that this was it. Ten years and done.

And he'd meant it.

New Year had come and gone, and he'd had to admit he'd

been no nearer learning the truth. And as the world had spiralled into a hellscape of misinformation, conspiracy theories, lies and distortion, what had all those stories of the Pavilion, and its pernicious place in society over the previous one hundred and eighty years, actually amounted to?

Just another conspiracy theory. And the longer he'd gone on, the more people he'd talked to and confronted, the more he'd begun to sound like a deranged conspiracy theorist.

The last year had been long, and possibly the most fruitless of them all. He'd even begun to think that perhaps the Pavilion didn't exist anymore. Maybe that awful night in Oslo had been the beginning of the end. The longer it had gone on, the less he seemed to find.

And then, just like that, the year had come and gone, and Jericho had known he was done. He'd lost.

And now he was just a sixty-one-year-old man, sitting in his home at midnight, doing a jigsaw, and wondering what the hell he was going to do with the rest of his life. He had his pension, he walked in the Mendips and the Quantocks, and he went to four gym classes a week at the local leisure centre, where a young woman named Ellie shouted at a ragged group of twenty or so, while they did push-ups and abdominals and jumps and skips and runs, and Jericho clung to the last vestiges of fitness before the inevitable atrophy and descent towards the end.

This is me, he sometimes thought, this is all that there is. The Jigsaw Man.

There was a knock at the door.

Jericho didn't move, staring at a jumble of pieces he was trying to sort out into a grey, cloudy sky. Midnight on a Monday, he thought. Who was going to be calling at this time?

'Nope,' he muttered quietly to himself, unable to think of who it might be.

At one stage it would've been Detective Sergeant Haynes, but Haynes had got married and moved to London, and now he was a detective inspector in the Metropolitan Police, and he lived with Professor Margot Leighton in a townhouse on Clapham Common, and they had two children, and his life was a million miles from the one Jericho had led.

Another knock at the door. Not insistent, not too loud. Just right.

Jericho could see the outline of a woman through the glass,

and opened the door.

Ilsa Badstuber, in a light grey coat, a small bag thrown over her shoulder, was standing just beneath the awning, out of the light March rain.

They'd neither seen each other, nor had any contact, in the ten years since they'd travelled to Oslo together. The last time Jericho had seen her, she was being attended to by a paramedic because she'd been shot in the neck.

Nevertheless, in those ten years, the days when Jericho had not thought about her had been few.

'Hello,' he said, which didn't seem like very much for ten years of longing.

'Good evening,' she said.

She did not smile. Jericho was still too surprised by her arrival that he didn't immediately invite her in.

'I have bad news,' she said.

Jericho couldn't begin to think what that might be, and now his manners made a belated arrival to the conversation.

'Come in, sorry,' he said, stepping back, and holding the door open.

Badstuber nodded, stepped into the house, and immediately bent to remove her Louboutin ankle boots, then they walked through into the sitting room with the small dining table.

Billie Holiday was playing, Leonard Bernstein's *Big Stuff*, the volume low.

Badstuber approached the table and took it all in. The jigsaw, approximately one-third completed. The unfinished glass of wine. The small plate with toast crumbs.

Jericho watched her back for a while, then found the words, 'It's nice to see you.'

Badstuber turned. Her face softened a little.

If she was ever to allow herself to be honest – with herself or anyone else – she would admit that the slow disintegration of her marriage had begun when she met Jericho. That, nevertheless, was something she preferred not to think about.

'I'm sorry, I have bad news,' she said again, her voice a little gentler, now they'd got past the first hello, and she felt she could let her guard down a little.

'You said,' said Jericho. 'You're all right?'

'I work for the Swiss security services now, based in The Hague.'

'I heard,' said Jericho.

Badstuber took a moment. She had kept track of Jericho's movements all these years, as best she could, but had not for a moment thought he might have done the same with her.

She hesitated, now that it came to it. She'd never been good at delivering ill news when she'd been in the police force. Too cold, she'd been told often enough.

'Best just to say it,' said Jericho, trying to take the tension from the moment.

'I was called to view the corpse of a Swiss national this evening. She'd been found hung in her apartment on the Dutch coast. She was also in possession of passports for the UK, the US, and the Vatican.'

Another hesitation, though this time it did not matter. Jericho knew where it was going.

'It was Amanda?'

Badstuber nodded.

That news, thought Jericho, was not the shock it might once have been.

Twenty years now his wife would have been living this peculiar itinerant life, no roots, no home, fighting an invisible evil. The great global conspiracy, that Jericho hadn't got anywhere near being able to understand. But she was no superhero. She didn't have powers of indestructibility. If there were enough people in the world who wanted you dead, eventually it was going to happen.

'You had seen her since Oslo?' asked Badstuber.

'One time,' said Jericho. 'Six years ago. You want a tea or coffee, glass of wine? We should talk.'

'You have green tea?'

'Maybe.'

'You do not know if you have green tea?'

'Might be some buried at the back of a cupboard.'

'Thank you. I am tired. We will talk briefly, then I must sleep. It is OK if I stay here for a few hours?'

'Of course. You can st –'

'I am on the six-thirty-five flight to Schiphol tomorrow morning. I would be grateful if you could join me.'

Jericho had left his brain at the door two and a half months previously. And now, out of nowhere, his old life had suddenly come crashing in on him once again.

'You do not have to, if you would rather not,' she said, in her familiar, formal manner.

'I'll come,' said Jericho.
'That is good. Make the tea, then we should get some sleep. We are not so young anymore.'

5

April 2019, Jericho was in New York, looking at a painting in the Whistler Gallery. A William Hart Melville, painted in 1853.

He'd learned about the painting the previous week, coming across it in a late-nineteenth century manuscript he'd uncovered in the chained library of Wells Cathedral.

It seemed absurd that after all his chasing around the world, there might be something worthwhile sitting right there on his doorstep, but he'd been nothing if not desperate by then, clutching at every tiny lead he could find.

He could, of course, have examined the Melville online, but according to the museum's website, they'd only been in possession of it for a couple of years, having received it upon the death of a private benefactor.

Jericho wanted all the details, and had been happy to tell himself that turning up to ask a question was far more likely to produce results than an e-mail or phone call. But really, he'd just gone to Manhattan because he'd needed something on which to focus.

On any given day, the Melville did not draw a particularly large crowd, and Jericho had been able to devote a lot of time to studying the painting, getting to know it. In this regard, he did not make a huge amount of progress, as he already knew the painting inside out from studying it online.

He'd arranged a meeting with Dr Ella Horsted. He himself had travelled to New York under the name Dr Iain Bennett. It was not an alias he'd used before. He had no idea if the precaution had been necessary, but he'd taken to travelling under a different name every time he ventured out of the UK, or indeed, made any kind of new contact.

Only rarely would he reveal his real identity. In ten years, not one person had ever looked at him with any kind of awareness, something else which had, over time, slowly added to his sense of ridiculousness.

He had sat and waited outside Horsted's office for ten minutes. Her PA, the keeper at the gate, had offered coffee. Jericho, suspicious of the quality of what he might receive, had refused. They sat in silence while he waited, and the PA studied her monitor.

'You can go in now, Dr Bennett,' she said suddenly, giving him a quick smile.

He walked into the office. Dr Horsted was at her desk, head down over some hard copy paperwork.

'I'll just be a minute,' she said to Jericho, 'if you'd like to take a seat.'

She didn't look up.

Jericho had stopped just inside the door, after closing it behind him. Horsted had long dark hair, and was wearing large-rimmed glasses, a garish red to purple ombre through the frame. But it didn't matter. She could have been wearing a gorilla suit and a bag over her head, Jericho was going to recognise that voice anywhere.

He'd first met his wife when they'd both worked for the Metropolitan Police. At some point, however, she'd tired of the police, and taken a job with Zurich Insurance. It had allowed her to use her skills, without having to confront domestic abusers and knife-wielding drug addicts. And, particularly once they'd discovered just how good she was, they'd paid a lot more.

Ultimately, though, she'd still been dealing with criminals, though it had become people in suits trying to defraud an insurance company. And then she'd stumbled across the story of a Japanese expedition to summit Kanchenjunga, all the members of which had mysteriously died, and that had led her into the mire of the Pavilion, and she'd never escaped.

'Amanda,' he said.

She didn't immediately lift her head, and then slowly she looked up.

'Damn.'

'How are you?' he asked.

'I did not see you coming,' she said.

'That's not good. What if I'd wanted to kill you, rather than ask you questions about the Melville in two-ninety-eight?'

'How'd you find me?' she asked.

'I didn't. What we have here is one of those happy accidents you get in life. Though I'm not sure either of us is looking all that happy.'

'You want to have dinner?'

'So forward of you, having avoided me for fourteen years,' he said, drily.

'We can talk.'

'We're talking now.'

She rested her chin in her hand, she stared across the desk.

'You don't trust I'll be there if we make plans for seven o'clock this evening?'

'I won't trust you if you say you need to use the bathroom.'

She smiled, she nodded.

'Did Becka offer you coffee?'

'I said no.'

'It's great coffee,' she said, 'reminds me of the espresso we used to get on a Sunday morning at that little place on the other side of the heath. You remember it?'

'You insult me,' he said.

She pressed the intercom through to the outer office and said, 'Two coffees, Becka, please. And a plate of the amaretti Giancarlo left on Monday.'

'No problem,' said Becka.

And then Amanda removed her glasses, and she and Jericho looked at each other for the first time in four years.

Jericho noticed the silence in the room. No sound from outside, no sound from anywhere else in the building. A quality to the silence that was like standing in a wood, in the middle of nowhere, after heavy snowfall.

'What did you see in the Melville?' she asked.

Easier, thought Jericho, to talk about that, rather than the great big glaring thing that sat between them. She'd gone missing, he'd spent years searching for her, she'd turned up in Oslo to save his life – as well as the lives of Haynes, Badstuber and Leighton – and had immediately disappeared again.

'There's the familiar Pavilion symbolism. The two-headed eagle, the unicorn, the goat, the griffin, all carefully woven into the narrative of the painting. The painting was commissioned by

Prince Ludwig IX of Saxony, and given as a gift to Caroline Augusta of Bavaria, later the wife, then widow of the Duke of Milan. She was an unwitting recipient. It hung in the corridors of Sforza Castle, and she had no idea of the message it sent to members of the Pavilion.'

'And what was that message?'

'I don't know. Quite possibly, there wasn't one. It was little more than a wave. Boasting. Placing their marker, like a bear rubbing itself against a tree in a forest.'

She smiled.

'We could've been working together all this time,' he said, abrupt and out of nowhere, bringing the conversation back to the thing they were determinedly not talking about.

She didn't have an answer at that moment, and she hadn't had an answer that night at dinner.

Φ

They fell asleep in bed together in his hotel room. He was determined to stay awake, knowing that if he fell asleep, she'd be gone when he woke up.

But they'd talked long into the evening. They'd drunk wine, they'd eaten their fill, they'd returned to his room and they'd made love.

He wondered if maybe she'd slip something into his drink to make sure he fell asleep, but she hadn't had to. She had his jet lag on her side.

They lay in bed at one in the morning, New York time. Jericho had been awake too long.

'I failed you,' he said.

The last thing he would ever say to her.

Staring at the ceiling, trying to keep his eyes open, and losing the fight.

She squeezed his fingers. She might have said something, but he never heard it.

6

'What is your life now?' asked Badstuber.

They were somewhere over the English channel. There hadn't been much conversation, something unknown in the silences between them.

'I don't know yet,' said Jericho.

'You have not found purpose?'

'I hadn't given it any thought, and now I'm retired, and I don't know what to do.'

'That is common. Perhaps, more so, when you had such purpose previously and failed in your assignment.'

He glanced at her. She was staring blankly at the headrest in front. He couldn't help the faint smile at her familiar bluntness.

'You have friends in Wells?' she asked.

'No. You have friends in The Hague?'

'I have colleagues, at least, though I'm not sure I would call them friends. I briefly had an affair with a French diplomat, but I only started it because I knew he was leaving for a posting in Santiago.' She sat on that for a few moments, then added, 'He asked me to go with him, and I ended the relationship shortly afterwards.'

Jericho could imagine the emotional brutality with which Badstuber ended any relationship.

'How shortly afterwards?' he asked, glancing to his left.

There was a pause, then she said, 'In the next sentence. We had an agreement, and he broke it.' Another pause, and then,

'He began to pester me. I believe he possibly thought he was being romantic, but it was anything but. I told him I knew of the passport scheme he'd run out of Bogota ten years previously, and that if he did not leave me alone, I would inform the Quai d'Orsay. I have not heard from him since.'

Jericho had more questions, but thought that would be getting close to prying. He'd noticed the lack of a wedding ring as she'd drunk her cup of green tea the previous evening.

'You do jigsaws all day?' she asked.

Jericho thought about his day, and how it would sound. But Badstuber was not someone he felt he had to lie to. Perhaps he wouldn't lie to anyone, but with others he could certainly slide into obfuscation and avoidance.

'I get out of bed at seven. I eat breakfast while listening to the radio. BBC Radio 3. Four days a week I go to exercise classes at the leisure centre. Once a week I go to evensong at the Cathedral. I walk in the hills.'

'The hills?'

'The Mendips.'

'They are hills?' she said.

She amused him more than she had before. Then she said, 'You are not religious,' though it wasn't a question.

'I like the music.'

'This is all you do?'

'One weekend last month I drove down to the south coast and spent the night.'

'You do not talk to anyone?'

'I get my haircut every three weeks. I talk to the barber. She remembers me from being the officer in charge when a school friend of hers was arrested for murder fifteen years ago. In January I went to London and spent the evening with Sgt Haynes and his wife. You'll remember Professor Leighton?'

'Of course. They are well?'

'Yes. They have two children. And the sergeant is now Detective Inspector.' A moment, then he added, 'They seem happy.'

She didn't say anything, and he gave her a quick glance. Her face expressionless, she stared directly ahead as before.

Maybe that struck a little too close to home, thought Jericho.

'Your children are OK?' he felt the need to ask, and in asking immediately feared something awful might have happened.

'They are good. My eldest is at university in Leiden. I see her often. The others remain at boarding school in Switzerland. I see them every four or five weeks, and they have many holidays.'

'Good,' said Jericho.

There was a slight jolt, and Jericho looked out of the window. Far below the endless beach of the Dutch North Sea coast.

He wanted to ask what had happened with her husband, but the words remained unspoken.

7

And there she was. Amanda Raintree, Jericho's wife, dead on a slab in a mortuary. A slit down her gullet, skin cold and colourless. Bruising around her neck. A healed wound in her abdomen that he'd never seen before. Old bruising on her shins, a scar on her ankle.

He felt nothing.

'These scars,' he said, indicating the abdomen and ankle, 'they're from operations or... otherwise?'

'The one on the ankle I think is from an Achilles operation' said Dr Janssen. 'This scar in the side is another matter. It looks like she was perhaps stabbed, and the wound was stitched up unprofessionally. She was in the military?'

Jericho didn't answer. Badstuber, a couple of paces behind him, answered with something of a look at the doctor, though neither of them necessarily knew what the look said. Whatever it was, it was enough.

'You identified the last thing she ate?' asked Badstuber.

'Moules et frites,' said Janssen. 'That would be a tough one to narrow down to a specific establishment around here.'

DI Bakker had left them to it this morning. Odermatt had already seen the lay of the land, and recognised whatever this was, it was far above her pay grade. It could be left to the security services.

'You know this woman?' asked Janssen.

'No,' said Jericho. 'It's not who I thought it might be.' He lifted his eyes from Amanda's cold, dead face, and looked at

Janssen. 'I'm sorry. I can't help you.'

'You came a long way for nothing,' said the pathologist.

'That's…' began Jericho, but then, as regularly happened, the rest of the sentence, the rest of the words waiting to spill from his lips, seemed unnecessary, and he waved them away, gave Janssen a small nod, glanced at Badstuber, and unwilling to betray himself, he turned away without taking a last look at Amanda.

Φ

They walked in silence through the corridors, and then the reception area of the large municipal building, and then they were outside in a cold, grey morning in March.

'You lie well,' said Badstuber, as they walked to her car. 'I understand why, though I think perhaps it would've been better if you hadn't.'

'Why?'

'If you are to help with this investigation here in the Netherlands, your involvement makes more sense if it's in relation to a case on which you previously worked, regardless of your actual relationship with the victim. I'm not sure how I get you in the room with me when I am interviewing, following leads.'

He didn't say anything. They walked in silence to the small, red Mitsubishi ASX, she clicked the doors, they got in. They settled into their seats, they fastened their seatbelts, they stared straight ahead. Badstuber did not start the car.

After a few moments they turned to look at each other.

'You are not intending to work with me,' she said.

'No,' said Jericho. 'I don't like asking you to lie for me, but you did it by not mentioning Amanda after what happened in Oslo, you obviously did it by not mentioning her last night, and you just did it in there when I showed my fake ID. Really, I think you'd be –'

'This is OK,' she said, cutting him off. 'We can assume Amanda's death was at the hands of the Pavilion. Nevertheless, the less it is talked about, the less they know that we know, the better. But if we are to presume their omnipotence, the long reach of their tentacles, they will likely already know you are here.'

'Possibly,' said Jericho. 'Nevertheless…'

He had more to say, but chose to let it go. Badstuber, blunt to the point of crushing conversational convention, was happy to say it for him.

'You do not want to get me involved, in case I get hurt again,' she said. 'You do not want the same thing to happen to me as happened to Amanda.'

Jericho answered with a familiar blank face, a silence that agreed with what she'd just said.

She lifted her hand and touched him softly on the side of the face.

'Thank you.'

He still had nothing.

'I am involved, nevertheless. I have spent some time on the Pavilion in the past ten years, though it has felt increasingly fruitless.'

She reached into her pocket, and brought out a single unmarked USB stick.

'Last week I received this,' she said. 'It contains a series of passwords. That is all. They are, in themselves, entirely useless, not without knowing the accounts or systems to which they apply.'

Jericho frowned.

'In your line of work, that could be a hundred different things, couldn't it?'

'Possibly. Nevertheless, the strangeness of it speaks of the Pavilion. I have taken the time to memorise the passwords, believing that the other half of the riddle would make itself known. I think Amanda's death… it may not be the half I was looking for, but it is part of it.'

'You think she sent these to you?'

'Yes. She must have known she was in imminent danger. Perhaps, after all this time, she was just getting too close to the heart of it, and they had to eliminate her. Or perhaps she had made a mistake, and her whereabouts and identity had become known to them.'

Jericho stared at the USB stick as she placed it back in her pocket. He thought of asking if he too could take the time to memorise the details, but that wasn't him. He had never memorised a single one of his own passwords. He had trouble with his five-digit credit card pass code for his phone.

'We are involved together, whether we like it or not,' said Badstuber. 'You will go your own way, and I will work as I can through official channels and within the agency of the Federal Intelligence Service.'

She started to raise her hand towards his face again, and then stopped herself with a silent admonishment.

'There will be time,' she said, and a sad smile edged its way on to her lips.

'Yes.'

The moment was over, and they both turned and stared forward.

'Where would you like me to drop you?' she asked, as she finally grasped the morning.

'Is Amanda's apartment OK?'

'Yes. Then I will return to the Hague.'

She started the engine, and slowly moved off, out of the carpark and into light, mid-morning traffic. The drive would not be long.

'How did you get the job in the first place?' asked Jericho.

'You mean the move from the police to the security services?'

'Yes.'

'I understand the question,' she said. 'You wonder about the possibility the Pavilion were involved in my move, for some nefarious purpose of their own. I have considered it previously, but I do not think it suspicious. I was not recruited. I was restless for a while. I decided I would like to move overseas, to travel. This…' She hesitated, as she was about to go into the circumstances of the break-up of her marriage, and then she let that go. 'It was me who drove the move, that is all. I was a good candidate. There is no reason to think my position within the service was compromised from the moment the recruitment process began.' Another pause, and then, 'Although of course, that does not mean it was not. We must be wary, but it can be counter-productive to see demons in every shadow.'

Damn, thought Jericho. *Counter-productive to see demons in every shadow…* A perfect way to put it. Sadly, ever since this damn thing had started all those years previously, he'd been seeing demons in every corner, in every face, in every cup of coffee, and every grain of sand.

They drove the rest of the way in silence.

Badstuber parked two blocks from Amanda's apartment. She did not turn off the engine when she stopped. They'd had their moment, back there in the hospital car park, they'd faced the mutual concern and had almost allowed themselves to face the attraction, and now it was time to get on with the job.

A glance from Jericho, a look passed between them, and then he was out of the car, and walking quickly along the road. Badstuber watched him for a few moments, and then checked her mirror, and moved off slowly into the late morning traffic.

8

Jericho sat in the middle of the sitting room staring at the fifty-six-inch television screen. People change, he thought, but his Amanda would never have cared for a television that size, and he didn't believe all her time chasing ghosts would have made any difference to that. She would have been renting this apartment, and he was going to find nothing of her here.

Even on the off-chance Amanda had brought anything of herself to this place, the people responsible for her death would have taken it away. Consequently, could the police believe anything they found here? What did the four passports even signify?

That Amanda would have had four passports, none of which were in her name, was entirely believable, but they could just as easily have been planted.

These people who had been giving him the run-around for so long, they seemed to have endless resources, were able to produce fake documents on a whim, and for the most insignificant reasons.

'You can talk,' muttered Jericho to the room, sitting there with three fake I.D.s in his pocket.

But there was nothing here, as he'd known there wouldn't be, just as he'd known he wasn't going to learn anything from looking at Amanda's body. These were acts of closure, that was all.

There was the sound of a key in the front door, and Jericho was straight to his feet. Most likely it was the police, and though he had his cover story in place – and had straightened it out with Badstuber on their way over here – this would be a bad start to getting anywhere with DI Bakker.

When Agnieszka Korczak walked into the sitting room, Jericho was already out of sight. A few quick, soft footfalls, and he was in a side room, the door half-open, looking through the gap.

Korczak stood in the middle of the room, taking a moment, looking around, Jericho wondering if she sensed his presence.

He didn't recognise her, but there was something about her that said she wasn't a player in the drama. Not an active one, at any rate, though he couldn't have put his finger on what it was that made him think that.

She stood for a moment, then walked through to the kitchen. Jericho had to move in order to see her, and now stood inside the doorway, took out his phone, camera on, and put it just around the corner, so that he could see what she was doing. Very low-key, and rather obvious surveillance, he thought.

Korczak opened a cupboard door, took out a bucket and mop, and placed them on the floor. And then she removed another couple of cleaning products and set them on a countertop.

Jericho withdrew his phone.

The woman had turned up yesterday to clean the apartment, and instead she'd had to report a death. Now she was back to do her job. He wondered if the police had already declared the potential crime scene no longer active, or whether she was just unthinkingly doing what she was paid to do. The police, at least, had not closed the place off.

Jericho had had enough lurking in the shadows, and quickly discarded the idea of exiting the property without her realising he'd been there. Accepting there was no way to announce his presence without scaring the living daylights out of her, he just walked quickly through into the open-plan.

Korczak dropped a plastic bottle of bleach, her hand going to her mouth.

'Jezus!'

'Agnieszka Korczak?' said Jericho, and she answered with a nod, her hand now hovering over her chest, coming down off the rush of the shock.

'Detective Inspector Cole, London Metropolitan Police,' said Jericho, holding forward his ID. It was a perfect forgery, though its elegance in deceit was lost on Korczak, who was nowhere near close enough to read it in any case.

'Agnieszka Korczak?' he asked again, and this time she looked a little more relaxed.

'You scared me,' she said.

'I'm sorry,' said Jericho. 'I needed to see who had come in, and it would've been impossible to then emerge without scaring you.'

'You could have coughed,' she said, and Jericho couldn't help the smile.

'Would you mind if I asked you a few questions?'

'Do I have choice?'

'Yes,' he said. 'I have no jurisdiction here. I'd be grateful, that's all. Perhaps we could step out, and I could buy you a coffee.'

'There is coffee here.'

'This place is haunted now,' he said. 'Let's have coffee in the café across the street.'

She looked a little troubled at the mention of the word haunted, and then reluctantly nodded.

9

They sat in a window seat, Jericho with a view across the road to the front of the apartment building. He really didn't know who any of the players were going to be, so had no idea who exactly it was he was looking for. Except sometimes in this game, the players stood out a mile.

Two coffees, a croissant each. Korczak was eating hers with some sort of indefinable berry conserve.

'You're employed by the owners?' asked Jericho.

'I am unsure why I answer questions from you,' said Korczak. 'Though I like coffee. This was good choice.'

'The woman who died was British. I'm from the British police. The death of a foreign national can be complicated, and the Dutch police are happy to wave this off as a suicide. Suicides are not complicated.'

'You think it is complicated?'

'I don't know yet.'

'You think Ms Bishop was murdered?'

'I don't know yet.'

'I thought she was Dutch. She spoke Dutch very good.'

Jericho stopped himself correcting her English. Perhaps she recognised the look on his face. She lifted her coffee.

'How long had she lived there?'

'Two months. Before that nice couple. I also think they were Dutch, but now I am not so sure. They left as they were going to have baby. They needed to move somewhere cheap.'

He took a drink, watched as a woman entered the apartment

building.

'I just need you to tell me anything you can about Ms Bishop. How often did you see her, what kind of impression you had of her, did she ever have any visitors…?'

'I do not have much to tell you,' she said, 'though there was one man.'

'A regular visitor?'

'I do not know. I only saw him once. But sometimes he had been at apartment. As a cleaner you know signs.'

'They'd had sex?'

She looked slightly surprised at the bluntness of the question, then said, 'Yes, they had sex. Although I meant sometimes two dinner plates or two wine glasses or two coffee cups.'

'Did he leave things at the apartment?'

'What kind of things?'

'Clothing.'

'There was jacket. I think maybe that was his.'

'Can you describe him?'

'I only saw him once.'

'There's potential that could be enough,' said Jericho.

She stared blankly at him. He imagined she was picturing the man, trying to think how to describe him, though she could possibly have been contemplating lying.

'Like you,' she said.

'He looked like me?'

'Yes.'

'Facially, or height, hair, age…?'

'Same height, similar age. Maybe better looking. Yes, he was better looking. You look tired. You look like you have given up. He did not look like that.'

'Hair?'

'He had hair.'

'What colour was his hair?' asked Jericho, drily.

'Greying like you, but more of it. He looked like someone. George Clooney.'

'You just said he looked like me.'

'You do not look like George Clooney.'

'I know.'

'He looked like you, and he looked like George Clooney. I cannot explain this.'

'Did you see them together, Ms Bishop and this man?'

'They came in together one time when I was there. Ms Bishop said I could go home.'

'When was this?'

'Four o'clock in afternoon.'

Jericho stared drily across the table. Korczak drank her coffee, then tore off a piece of croissant.

'Was it recently?' asked Jericho.

'Two weeks. Maybe three.'

'The other times there had been evidence of other people in the apartment,' asked Jericho. 'How d'you know it was the same man?'

This was not something she'd previously given any consideration.

'I do not,' she said. 'Perhaps you are right.'

10

DI Bakker had a desk in a corner of a busy office. There was a bustle and urgency about the place that was a complete contrast to the station in Wells where Jericho had last worked, and a million miles from the past ten years, when Jericho had plodded around the world at his own pace, only rarely jutting up against drama and anticipation.

Bakker was on the phone, dealing with another matter, as she had been since Jericho had arrived, and they'd had a brief exchange.

'How'd the Met get to hear about it so fast?' Bakker had asked, and Jericho hadn't answered, as the only things he could think of would've been glib, bordering on rude. He'd spent most of his career trying not to come across as rude, and invariably failing.

She'd indicated for Jericho to sit down in the cramped space at the side of her desk, and had handed him a clear envelope containing the four passports.

After leaving Amanda's apartment, he'd quickly abandoned the idea of travelling around the small area by train, and had hired the first car he could get his hands on in Noordwijk, a small, white Mazda CX-30.

Jericho skimmed quickly through the passports, looking at each of the four images of his wife. In Switzerland, she'd been Isabella Bühler; the USA she'd been Elizabeth Barnes; in the UK, Elizabeth Blake; in her Vatican passport she'd been Isabella Blackwell. As well as the four passports, the envelope also contained a Netherlands ID card in the name Isabella van der Berg, which had not been mentioned the previous evening. The European passports had neither entry stamps nor visas. The US passport had multiple stamps, enough indeed that it would take more than a cursory look to reveal any pattern of movement.

There was no ID to support the name Isabella Bishop, by which she'd been known to the cleaner.

Bakker hung up the phone, took a moment and a long exhaled breath, and then turned to Jericho.

'You have looked at the passports.'

'Yes,' said Jericho. 'I wasn't aware there was a Dutch identity card.'

'One of my men discovered it in a coat pocket. I didn't learn of it until I returned to the office.'

Jericho took a measure of the woman, before making the false offer.

'I had a brief word with my Swiss counterpart. Given this identity card, would you like me to stand down? Obviously I can't make the same offer on behalf of the Swiss.'

'At this stage there is nothing to indicate that she was definitely Dutch. You can certainly stand down if you like, but we're more than happy for the help. As you can see...' and she indicated the office, and the explosion of files and paperwork across her desk.

'Can I take these?' asked Jericho, indicating the bag.

'No. I will give you copies. The details have been with records since late yesterday afternoon, and we can go...' and she paused while checking the time, 'yes, we can go now and speak to them. Maybe they'll have something for us. Then, depending on what we have there, it may be that I leave you to it, or that it gets passed on to our intelligence division. I feel the chances are on the latter.'

She rose quickly from her desk, and began walking through the office, out of a door to the left, and along a bright corridor, windows all along looking down onto an empty courtyard. The sky overhead was now a pale blue, and somewhere behind the five-storey building opposite, there was a feeble sun.

Up a flight of stairs, and then through into another large office, a similar size, with a similar feeling of bustle, to the one where Bakker worked. To the far end, and Bakker stopped beside a desk that was the polar opposite of her own workstation. A monitor and keyboard, all the paperwork neatly collected in an old-fashioned in/out-tray, a photograph of a young man in a small frame next to the white telephone.

'Birgit,' said Bakker, 'this is DI Cole from the Metropolitan Police Service.'

Birgit did not acknowledge Jericho. She seemed young, he thought. Mid-twenties, perhaps. Twenty-five got younger and younger, the further away from it he became. A small ring through her nose, the only statement against convention. She was smartly dressed, her long hair neatly tied in a ponytail.

'The report is almost ready, I'll send it in five minutes,' she said.

'You can tell us the basics?'

'Of course. Each of these five women has an identifiable story and history going back to their birth, including social security numbers and health service records. Records would indicate that these are clearly five different people, therefore it's currently impossible to say which, if any, of them is the real person.'

She glanced at Jericho for the first time, a look that said there was little need at this stage to be involving the British, any more than anyone else.

'Do any of them have a next of kin listed?' he asked.

'They all have next of kin listed, and I've run checks and verified them all. They all exist. Or, at least, records of them exist.'

'Home addresses?' asked Bakker.

'Again, yes. There is everything. I'll send it through.'

'You have an overall impression?' asked Bakker.

'This is good quality cover. I would presume she was working for someone. A national intelligence organisation or a global crime syndicate, any number of things in between.'

'You have the name for the Dutch next of kin?' asked Jericho.

Another quick glance, then Birgit turned to her computer screen, pressed a few keys and brought up an older woman by the name of Mila van der Berg, and said, 'Her mother. She lives on this side of Amsterdam. It should not take more than an hour at this time in the morning.'

'And the victim had employment here?' asked Bakker.

'Isabella Bishop, I don't know about. Isabella van der Berg worked at the International Criminal Court.'

A moment, and then Bakker said, '*Godverdomme.*'

'You'll have the report by the time you get back downstairs,' said Birgit. 'You'll be interested to know that she also worked at the UN in New York, and at an NGO in Lausanne. Good luck.'

She said the last with no tone whatsoever, and then once more turned her back. Jericho and Bakker shared a glance, and then began walking back through the bright office, past the three large potted Japanese peace lilies, and out into the corridor.

II

Jericho was waiting in the reception area of the ICC. He'd not been shown through security, nor allowed access to the building or shown into an office. There were seats in reception, but he was standing to the side, reading the descriptions on the wall of the ICC's relatively short history. He'd read through the condensed Rwanda files, and had moved onto Yugoslavia.

The reception area was bright, and he could see the bulk of the area behind him, reflected in the lamination of the boards. He didn't turn as he watched the woman approach from behind.

'Detective Inspector Cole?'

Jericho turned.

Here he was again, only a couple of months after having given up the chase, back in the game. Badstuber had arrived at his door, and like an alcoholic presented with a 30 year-old Macallan, he'd folded instantly. And how many conversations like this one had he had in the last ten years? Pretending to be someone he wasn't. Lying through an interview, not entirely sure what it was he was hoping to uncover. Thinking he would recognise *the thing* when he stumbled across it.

Jericho nodded, the woman said 'Janne Halscolm,' and they shook hands.

'You don't mind meeting out here,' she continued. 'We have a busy day today, security is in overdrive. The verdict on Muhajir ibn Khalid is due.'

'It's fine,' said Jericho.

He'd noticed the security detail on his way in, and during

the twenty minutes he'd been standing in reception. No different, he thought, from how it had been the previous twice he'd had cause to visit the ICC over the past ten years.

Halscolm led him over to a low table with three padded armchairs, offered the seat to Jericho, and then followed him in sitting down.

'So, how can we be of help?' she asked, clasping her hands together, leaning forward.

Jericho passed over Amanda's Dutch ID card, in the name of Isabella van der Berg.

'You're familiar with this woman?'

'Of course,' said Halscolm, a stitch in her brow. 'Bella works in our research department.'

'Her body was found in her apartment yesterday afternoon.'

The soft buzz of the ICC reception area continued around them, although time seemed to pause on Halscolm's face. She held Jericho's gaze with the kind of vacant stare with which the police are so familiar. The processing of information behind a blank canvas.

'What d'you mean?' she asked finally.

'She's dead.'

'How?' Face still expressionless.

'There's a police investigation.'

'What? Was...'

The question drifted off into confusion.

'Ms van der Berg was found dead in her home yesterday afternoon,' said Jericho, slowly, clearly. 'We need to establish her movements prior to her time of death.'

'Where are the police?' asked Halscolm, as her brain finally seemed to come into focus. The flick of the switch.

'They are busy on other things.'

'The Metropolitan Police are making initial enquiries?'

'Ms van der Berg was a UK passport holder.'

'I don't think so.'

'We've seen her passport. This is why I'm here.'

'It would have been revealed in her background check,' said Halscolm.

'You might want to take a look at your procedures.'

She looked unimpressed, then waved that particular worry away.

'What authority do you have here?' she asked.

'None,' said Jericho. 'I'm informing you of the death of an

employee, you're under no obligation to answer any questions. I'd be grateful, however, if you could be of assistance.'

Playing the game, having to hope he'd have made some progress before the Dutch authorities worked out that Detective Inspector Cole of the Met was a fraud.

'Bella worked for me two days a week. Thursday and Friday.'

'She was here on Friday?'

A pause, and then, 'She was off last week.'

'Planned leave?'

Another vacant look. Perhaps she didn't know.

'She was off,' said Halscolm, and left it at that.

'What did she do for you?'

A pause, the forever calculation about how helpful to be to a stranger.

'I can't tell you.'

No calculation whatsoever, as it happened, just refusal. Jericho recognised the tone. The ICC had a clear set of countries and conflicts they were investigating, well reported and acknowledged. It was hardly far-fetched to think there would be other investigations taking place, out of the spotlight, as they tried to establish momentum before making their intentions public.

'You can't tell me which area she was working on?'

'No.'

'You know what she did the other three days of the week?'

'I had no oversight of that.'

'How long had she worked for you?'

Another pause, although this time she made the decision to answer.

'Just over two months.'

'And the terms of her employment haven't changed? Two months working two days a week, investigating the same issue the entire time?'

'Yes to the first part of that, I can't answer the second.'

Her tone was getting colder.

'Would you know of any reason why Ms van der Berg would want to kill herself?'

This time Halscomb couldn't keep up the deadpan look. She even moved her hand towards her mouth, in what Jericho might have considered a staged movement.

'That's…' began Halscomb, then her words ran out. She

looked like there was another sentence she wanted to form, but this one stalled with her mouth slightly open, concern and fear in her eyes.

'There's a police investigation, and the likelihood is that the local police will need to speak to you,' said Jericho. 'In this first instance, I'm just trying to get a little ahead of the curve with the potential circumstances surrounding the death. Did she seem stressed, or particularly worried about anything at the moment? I need to go and speak to Ms van der Berg's mother, and obviously she will have questions. If there's anything I can tell her about Isabella's state of mind these last few days and weeks, that'd be very helpful.'

'No, no... Bella didn't say much, kept herself to herself. I don't think any of us ever saw her outside of work, we never saw her around town. She never came to any, you know, work events, that kind of thing. She came to work, that was all, she did her job, she turned in reports when they were needed. And she was good.'

'Is it possible she was killed because of what she was investigating?'

'What?'

Another look of surprise, as though she'd begun to get used to the idea of suicide, and now murder had been tossed unexpectedly onto the table. Jericho didn't speak, letting the question work its way through the shock with which Halscomb was still struggling.

'You think she might have been murdered?' she managed to say eventually.

'We have no idea. We do know it wasn't natural causes. With any apparent suicide, there's always the possibility that the death was staged, framed to tell a false narrative. It'd be a good start if you could let us know the case she was working on.'

Finally Halscolm turned slightly, beginning the process of disengaging from the conversation, and looked down at the ground.

'I'll need to speak to some people,' she said, her voice already sounding more distant than it had half a minute previously.

Jericho recognised the change in tone. Halscomb had no need to answer any of Jericho's questions, and the decision had been taken.

'Can you tell me anything about Isabella?' asked Jericho.

39

'D'you know if she had a partner?'

Halscomb was glazing over, too many questions having been asked, needing to go away and process this information in private, or with people she knew, and not under interrogation.

'Not as far as I'm aware,' she said, her voice distracted. Jericho wasn't entirely sure she was being honest now.

He watched her for another few moments, and then made the decision. It was time to get on with this, and sitting here watching this woman's face go through various stages of confusion and grief wasn't going to get him anywhere.

'So, you can think of no one outside the office with whom Isabella was acquainted, and neither was she especially close to anyone in the building?'

'That's… yes, that's correct. You're making me realise how little I really knew her.'

'And the matter she was working on at the Court was not one of your regular, public investigations?'

'That's corr–… No, that's not what I said. That's…'

Her words, clumsy and with little aforethought, stumbled to an uncomfortable halt.

'Thank you, Mrs Halscomb. The local police will be in touch, I'm sure.'

Jericho got up, and walked quickly from the building, back out into a chill March wind.

12

Where was the jurisdiction going to lie?

That's what Jericho was wondering, as he sat in the Mazda, on his way across Amsterdam. As far as the Dutch were concerned, they had a woman of indefinite nationality, who'd been working for the International Criminal Court, on a subject inevitably involving a foreign power, and one that by the very nature of the ICC's involvement, was a disputed political arena.

Amanda's death was likely to get political very quickly, and the chances were that the Dutch security service, AIVD, would be involved before too long. When AIVD heard there was a detective from the Met asking questions, the call would be put through to London, and Jericho's access to official circles would be brought to an end.

He'd long had a system in place with his former sergeant, now DI Haynes. He would be a point of contact for him, a low level of cover if needed, prepared to lie for Jericho, to an extent that far exceeded Jericho's wish to cause him any trouble. Here, though, he was not going to be sending anyone in Haynes's direction. If the AIVD went to the Met, it would be without Jericho's input, and they would learn quickly enough that DI Cole was a rogue player in the game.

He hit the Amsterdam ring road, the traffic quieter than expected, and was off the road and into the Oud-Zuid district a little over an hour after leaving The Hague.

He was heading to the address listed as the Dutch next of kin for Isabella van der Berg, but whoever this was, it wasn't going to be anyone related to Amanda. Not a blood relation at any rate. Mila van der Berg was going to be a cover for someone, or something, and he had no idea what.

He came to a row of two-storey, post-war terraced townhouses, a solid row of cars parked down one side of the road, a double red line on the other. The satnav informed him he'd reached his destination, and he pulled the car into the side of the road, up onto the pavement on the prohibited parking side, leaving enough room for traffic to pass down the middle.

He locked the car, looked the length of the street, only one person around, an old woman pushing a shopping trolley about fifty yards away, glanced up at the cold sky, and then walked round the car, across the cycle lane and the broad pavement, and rang the bell of number forty-three Vijfde Flinckstraat.

The door was oak, a frosted glass panel at head height. He stared at it for a moment, waiting to see if there was any movement behind, and then turned and looked back along the road. The minute anyone came within talking distance, they would be complaining to him about his parking, and the chances were that by the time he emerged from the house, there would be a policeman standing by the car, writing out a ticket.

The door opened. A woman, late thirties perhaps, an apron tied around her waist, wearing a pair of bright yellow Marigolds. Her light brown hair was tied back, a strand having fallen across her face.

'Hey,' she said, eyes wide.
'I'm looking for Mila van der Berg.'
A pause, then the woman smiled.
'I don't know that name, sorry.'
'You live here?'
'Yes.'
'And you don't recognise the name?'
'I'm afraid not. Can I help you?'
'How long have you lived here? We had this listed as Mila van der Berg's residence until very recently.'

It didn't take much sometimes. The flicker across the eye, the very slight rearrangement of facial muscles, the movement of the lips.

'Who is *we*?'
The strain in the tone of voice.
'I'm with the British Embassy,' said Jericho. 'Consular services. We have information on a relative of Mrs van der

Berg's, and we'd like to speak to her.'

'I'm afraid she's not here.'

'Would you know why she might have been listed as living at this address?'

It could have been, of course, that Amanda created an imaginary next of kin, plucking an address at random out of the phone book.

'There was likely some mistake,' said the woman. 'Perhaps the house number is incorrect. This is a long street.'

She glanced up the street, as if indicating its length, and then smiled stiffly at Jericho.

'That's possible,' said Jericho nodding, deciding it was time to move this on to the next stage of the conversation. The awkward stage. 'Look, my phone ran out of charge when I was coming over here. D'you mind if I use your phone to make a call? Sorry, I know, massive imposition, but I'll be quick.' He paused in response to the blank face, then added, 'I won't call the UK.'

They stared at each other over the threshold. The age-old, unspoken conflict. Both fairly sure the other was lying, the silent stare while they measured their opponent and made the call on how quickly this would escalate.

As ever, Jericho was going on his gut instinct. This woman's denial felt wrong, and therefore it probably was.

He knew the moment was coming a split second in advance, so that he was moving his foot forward at the same time as the woman began to slam the door shut. The edge of the door cut against his ankle and the side of his foot, and in the same instant he was thrusting his shoulder against wood panelling. The pain shot up his leg, as the door gave a little at the push of his shoulder. He thrust as much of his body into the gap as he could manage, and now the door was jammed against his arm, and the top of his leg.

They pushed against each other for a second, Jericho with the slight advantage, and then he felt a little more give in the door. He knew what it meant, and quickly began to withdraw his arm, but too late, as his adversary grabbed his wrist, and then twisted his arm brutally as she completely gave way inside the door, and Jericho fell forwards into the house.

As he crossed the threshold, he twisted his body to move with his twisting arm. With the movement, he pulled his wrist free, fell further into the room, rolled over and sprang back up, now inside the house, a few feet from his assailant.

The woman kicked the door shut, and now they faced each other, a couple of yards apart. The front door led straight into a sitting room, with a small kitchen off the back of the room, and a narrow flight of stairs leading up from Jericho's left.

When was the last time he'd actually done something like this?

Two years, more or less. That idiotic fight out of nowhere in a hut in the small jungle town in Laos. Temperature over forty degrees, monsoon season, large spiders scurrying across the matting on the walls, Jericho and some dumb French bastard throwing punches at each other, at the end of which, when somehow Jericho had come out on top, the man had bitten into a suicide pill, like he'd been determined to pull out every damn cliché he could find, and Jericho hadn't seen it coming.

'Do you know why we're fighting?' he asked, his quiet, relaxed voice a counterpoint to the tensed muscles, his body ready for the scrap. 'I mean, I have absolutely no idea. I'm just here to deliver a message.' He smiled, another skill he'd been working on the past ten years. 'If you've got a gun tucked in that apron, you are literally going to shoot the messenger.'

'Really?'

Jericho turned off the phony good humour, allowed himself a moment, a glance up the stairs. Trying to get a feel for the place, a sense if there was anyone else in the house. Presumably if there had been, they would already have made an appearance. Unless they didn't want to be seen.

Since this wasn't the address of a next of kin, who was it likely to have actually been? A contact? A controller? A courier? Impossible to begin to even fathom, particularly since he had no idea what Amanda had been doing in the Netherlands.

'We need to talk about Amanda Raintree,' he said. 'I mean, we can stand here all day if you like, but –'

The woman moved faster than Jericho had thought she would. Her open palm caught him on the side if the jaw, Jericho's defensive swing of the arm too slow, too late. Then her foot was clipped round Jericho's leg, and another open-palmed punch sent him reeling back onto the floor, his head missing the stone stanchion at the foot of the stairs by a couple of inches. He had no time to regain his balance before the woman was over him and kicking down hard on his groin.

He moved his hip marginally as the foot descended,

lessening the impact of the kick, but still pain shot through him, and he groaned loudly. But he was in the middle of the fight, and the pain was for later, and he forced himself up onto his elbows. Now, however, with his face lifted off the ground, the woman punched him again, close-fisted this time, a solid hit to the chin. Jericho's head snapped back, cracking off the floor.

His attacker lifted her leg, preparing the brutal kick to the midriff. He knew that being badly winded, followed by hands wrapped around the throat, was a killer combination. He took his last chance. A swivel on the hips where he lay, a sharp kick, and as the woman brought her foot down, Jericho caught her flush on the back of the knee on her supporting leg. Her leg buckled, and she fell back, a loud, vulgar exclamation escaping her lips.

Jericho leapt off the floor, the pain in his testicles and on the back of his head ignored, and he was on top of the woman, his hands automatically going for her throat. He grabbed her neck, he squeezed, his thumbs pressing hard into the windpipe. The woman's body squirmed and fought beneath him. For a moment she tried to prise Jericho's hands from her neck, and then she switched to attack, her fists frantically punching his head, as Jericho ducked and pressed his head down at the woman's chest, to make it harder for her to land a solid punch.

What are you doing? Jesus! Don't kill her!

He was in the fight. He'd been here before. There wasn't going to be a more relaxed stage to this encounter, where he had dominion over the woman, and he could ask her who she worked for, and what she'd known about Amanda, and what exactly was going on. Half a minute previously, the woman hadn't stood over Jericho contemplating offering a coffee and a chat to sort out their differences.

As ever, as Jericho had learned in his dealings with the Pavilion – and he had no doubt this woman worked for the Pavilion – fighting was a zero-sum game.

The body spasmed beneath him, the last frantic fight for breath, the legs kicking uselessly at the air, the fists landing desperate, ineffective punches.

'Fuck it,' muttered Jericho, and he leaned into the death clinch, pressing his fingers even more firmly into the woman's throat. The last, hopeless, flailing kicks became weak, erratic paroxysms, death throes, and then they were done.

Jericho looked down at the open, dead eyes. He held his fingers steady and tight on the throat. His heart was thumping, his breaths coming heavily, forced from deep within his chest.

He turned suddenly and looked up the stairs, spooked at the idea that someone might be watching him, but the stairs, with a mirror reflecting the first floor landing at the top, stared back at him, empty and silent.

Finally, Jericho let go of the woman's neck, and slumped back against the front door.

13

Jericho stood in the bathroom, looking at himself in the mirror. He'd bled from his bottom lip, there was a large bruise on his lower jaw, the jawline looking puffy around it, and there was a cut on the side of his eye. He must've been caught by a ring in the woman's final, clawing, throes of desperation.

He'd been through the house, and had little more than what had been in the woman's small black handbag. An iPhone and her purse, containing several credit cards and a Dutch ID card in the name of Greta Yossarian.

There was a painting above the fireplace in the small sitting room. A William Hart Melville. A winter scene in the style of Bruegel. Some elevated farmland in the foreground, a few dwellings, the land giving way to a large, frozen lake, upon which there were people skating, and playing sports. One of those, all human life is here paintings. In the foreground, in amongst a small flock of sheep, a goat. In the bottom left-hand corner, a couple of horses, munching on a large stack of hay. On closer inspection, however, one could note that one of the horses, its head buried in the feed, actually had a horn protruding from its snout. Not a horse, but a unicorn. In the distant sky, a large bird, an eagle, painted to give the impression of its head moving, surveying the land beneath. Except, that was not the right impression. Instead, the eagle had two heads. And a flag flying from the small town hall, placed to the right of the lake. Yellow, with a red griffin, the flag folded over in low wind, only one eye and the claws of the griffin visible, but a griffin, nevertheless.

In amongst these four, a thousand other images, any of which could have been a clue to *something*. Regardless, the Melville painting was at least confirmation. He was in a Pavilion safe house, which was an odd address for Amanda to have listed as a next of kin for her false identity. Nevertheless, at least the woman now lying dead on the floor hadn't been an innocent, desperately defending her property from some random guy who'd barged his way inside.

He sat in a wing-backed armchair beside the fireplace, the chair turned a little so that he could see the front door. The door, and the body of the woman he'd just killed.

The smart thing to do was to walk out of here and leave the body where it was. Someone would find it soon enough. And when she was found, and word got back to Bakker that there was a body at the address she knew Jericho had recently learned, the Dutch police were going to be coming for him.

He would've preferred a little longer without the police on his tail. That was something that had happened too often since this madness had all begun. This, however, was not normal for him. He'd just killed someone, acting entirely as a private individual. No police back-up, no safety net, no official cover.

He had no idea whether the house was likely to be bugged, but it was hardly beyond the bounds of possibility. He contemplated stepping outside, but was just as wary of the place being watched.

He activated one of the phones he'd picked up that morning. One of four he'd purchased.

Badstuber picked up after one ring.

'You are OK?' she said, by way of hello.

'Yes, fine. I got a list of the next of kin of each of Amanda's alias's. I came to the Dutch address. You got a pen?'

'There is a Dutch address?'

'There was also a Dutch ID card, with yet another name. I came to the address of the next of kin.'

'Tell me.'

He gave her the address, she noted it down in silence.

'There was a welcome committee. We got into a fight, she died. Do you have a wolf operation?'

'You mean a clear-up team?'

'Yes.'

'We are Switzerland,' she said.

'That means no?'

'That means no.'

'You don't have a contact with an independent operator?'

He sensed her hesitation, and immediately felt bad about calling. She had a life to protect. A job, and presumably, a job that was paying for her children to be put through school. He couldn't be asking her to get involved.

'I will send you a name,' she said, before he could withdraw the question.

'It's OK, I shouldn't have called. Sorry, I'll –'

'I will send you a name. He will not expect you to tell him how you got the contact. Use the code Zbigniew.'

She hung up. Jericho stared at the phone, and felt the discomfort of what he'd just done. If he was to call her again, it could only be to say that everything was all right, the job was over, and did she want to have dinner.

A message came up on the small screen. A name, a telephone number. He replied thank you, thought of expanding on that, and decided he had to be practical in the face of this madness. He sent the message, waited thirty seconds for a similarly brief reply, then when none came, he made the call to the fixer.

'Oui,' came the short reply.

'Henri Quatre?' asked Jericho.

'Oui.'

'I need a body removed. Forty-three Vijfde Flinckstraat.'

'Who are you?'

'Zbigniew.'

A short pause, then he said, 'I will send bank details. Ten thousand euro now, five thousand after the job is complete.'

'Roger,' said Jericho, feeling foolish that that word had even appeared in his mouth, though he said it often.

The phone went dead, and now Jericho was committed to sending ten thousand euros of his own money to a completely random bank account. And he was going to have to get out of here right now, and could hardly wait around to see if the job would ever be done.

He trusted Badstuber, and she'd given him the contact, and so he had to trust the contact.

Deep breath, and he logged into his bank account.

When he'd done everything that was required at that moment, he took another look at the phone number, tried to memorise it, that wasn't happening, and so he found a pen and wrote the number on the inside of his arm, reversing the digits after the initial code, removed the phone's SIM card, placed the phone on the hard kitchen floor, and stamped on it a couple of times, before lifting it and putting it in his pocket.

14

Jericho needed to call Haynes, but first of all he needed to get as far away from this house as possible. He'd already decided he should get back to the UK, and was thinking through the best way to go about it. He had, at least, other documents he could use to cross the channel.

He walked to the side window, and looked down onto the street, in either direction. He was aware that if there was anyone down there, they'd see him looking out for them. That part didn't matter anyway. If there really *was* anyone out there, they'd already know he was here.

His eyes moved quickly over the scene. Every parked car, every shrub, every reflection in every window. There was no sign of anyone, bar a single man across the other side of the road, heading slowly towards him, head down, earphones in, staring at his phone. It would be a toss of a coin whether he was a non-combatant.

The pedestrian aside, there was nothing to note. He stepped away from the window, intending to look back in a minute, to gauge once more all the mundane details, to note if there had been any changes. Now he walked out into the hall, into the rear bedroom and looked down on the back of the property. This looked down onto a car park, bounded by similar two-storey houses on three sides, a road at the bottom. Bare trees, uniformly around eight feet high, separated each car parking space. There were six cars, none of them obviously occupied. There was a man with a pushchair, containing a sleeping infant, on the far pavement. There was no one in sight in the windows of any of the other houses.

He looked over it all, then stepped away from the window. Phone out, looked at the time. Glanced around the room. A sparsely furnished spare bedroom. The bed was not made up. Plain mattress with a single duvet folded on top of it. A chest of drawers, with a small, simple painting of a Dutch landscape on top, propped against the wall. A lamp by the bed. A pair of ladies shoes on the floor beside an old wooden wardrobe. On the back of the door, a winter coat, red, size ten.

That was it. Nothing to indicate that anyone really used this room at all. A peculiar set-up.

Back out into the hallway, into the bathroom. Toothpaste and a toothbrush by the sink. A small shelf beneath the mirrored cabinet with a woman's deodorant, some face cream. A single bottle of shampoo, a bar of soap, neither conditioner nor shower gel by the bath. A quick check of the cabinet. A turquoise and white razor, three other creams, an almost-empty packet of sanitary towels, cotton buds, tweezers, a bottle of ibuprofen, a small plastic tub of antibiotics, which a quick shake indicated only had one tablet left inside.

He closed the cabinet door, turned and looked around the bathroom. The shower wasn't spotlessly clean, but there was no dampness in the air, no splashes of water. It hadn't been used that day, maybe not for a while.

Back through to the main bedroom, which didn't look much more used than the smaller room at the back. No clothes dumped, no bags. The bed was made, but not especially neatly. Jericho pulled the duvet back, touched the cold sheets beneath. Then he walked to the wardrobe, pulled the door open. The cold, musty emptiness of an old wooden cupboard stared back at him.

He closed the door, turned back to the window. Something different. A reflection in the glass across the road had changed, that was all. He couldn't see anyone, but something had moved. The sun was hitting a spot in the room that it hadn't been hitting before. Whatever had been blocking it had now moved.

He studied the window, and what he could make out of the dull scene in the room within, and then cast a quick look around the rest of the street.

A flicker of movement, and it was gone, rushing out of his line of vision. So quick, so strange, almost as if he hadn't seen it.

He stepped away from the window, took another blank look

around the room. Assessing the situation, knowing he had a decision to make that would largely be made on gut instinct.

This was not the fixer who called himself Henri Quatre, not this quickly. And if there was someone else coming, then he'd possibly just flushed ten thousand euros down the toilet.

The money meant nothing to him. Getting out of here, and being able to get on with the business at hand, was all that mattered.

'Dammit,' he muttered to himself, as he moved through to the rear bedroom, 'get a bloody move on.'

He stopped on the threshold of the room. The slightest noise from downstairs. A suspicion of sound. He cursed quietly, standing absolutely still for a moment.

Silence.

He didn't breathe.

Tick. Tock.

A footfall on a floorboard.

Jericho moved quickly now, to hell with the noise he made. Wasn't like they didn't know he was here.

Into the rear bedroom, and he opened the window. A quick look, seemingly nothing had changed. There would be someone, though, and he'd just have to deal with it when it came.

He glanced down below, just one floor, braced himself, and then jumped. No more than fifteen feet, softened his legs, fell to his side into a small hebe, taking the shock of the landing through as much of his body as possible. He was going to have to run, and a busted ankle would be the end of the chase before it had begun.

He didn't even glance back up at the window. Whoever was up there wasn't going to be the immediate problem. He scrambled along the ground, keeping low, until he was behind a silver Ford Puma, then glanced up over the bonnet.

'Dammit,' he muttered again. Still no sign of anyone, which he didn't for a second think meant that there was no one there. He'd just have to move and take his chances with whatever came his way.

Round the car, he didn't glance back, eyes scanning the road ahead, and then he was running full pelt towards the intersection. Reached the next road unmolested, allowed himself a glance behind. Nothing.

He began to run quickly to his left, what would be away from the centre of this small area of the city. A one-way street, cars parked down both sides. He looked for the easiest car to break into, something old, where the lock could be more easily picked.

He had to lose his pursuers first though. No point in stealing a car if they were going to know which one he'd taken. The getaway would be made when he'd given himself a little space on foot, and then could slowly drive off, blending into the traffic.

There was no one up ahead on his side of the road; the man with the pushchair, who he'd seen earlier, was on the other pavement, walking away from him. He allowed himself another glance over the shoulder.

No one.

Despite himself, despite the automatic need to run, he started to slow. Eyes all over, ahead, behind, in the homes and cars past which he ran.

Had there really been a noise? Had there been a footfall at the bottom of the stairs?

He looked over his shoulder again, as he slowed to a jog. Breaths heavy, heart still pounding.

A car door opened in front. Head turned, he didn't notice. One pace, two, and then he ran into the door. No warning, unable to brace herself, he let out a yelp of pain as the door edge jabbed into his side, and then, juddering to a halt, he fell in a rough, ugly tumble to the pavement.

15

At some point, filling his time, doing something he thought might be useful, he'd done a month-long boot camp, run by an ex-SAS staff sergeant. He supposed his fighting skills had improved, he'd got fitter than he could ever recall being previously, and he'd lost close to twenty-five pounds. It had suited him perfectly at the time, though he'd never done it again, having resolved to do it once a year.

Nevertheless, he'd never forgotten those words from the miserable Welsh staff sergeant. When you're in a fight, you're in a chase, you're in a rush; as long as you've got a clear head, then throw the punch, move, run. Forget the pain. Your body will compensate. Your body will let you ride it out. It'll hit you later, but you can worry about that later too.

He'd been running, he'd been ready for the attack, and now he rolled quickly away from the car, out of the reach of the extended arm in a black jacket, and then jumped to his feet.

'Get in the car.'

The voice was utterly devoid of tone. However, the Glock 17 in his hand gave his words a certain quality.

There was no one else in the car, no one else in the street that he could see, bar the man and his pushchair, away up on the other side. The Glock had its suppressor, and there really was no one else around to hear the shot. He had no reason not to shoot Jericho. Unless, of course, they didn't want him dead.

What other reason could there possibly be for him not just putting a bullet in Jericho's chest right now?

They wanted to know what he knew.

'No,' said Jericho.

The guy got out of the car, took a quick look around, then, holding the Glock close to his side, aimed it at Jericho's knees.

'Get in the car,' he repeated, his voice the same dull monotone.

There was no ignoring the pain of a bullet in the knee. Adrenaline could only go so far.

'I don't want the mess,' said the guy dully, 'and I don't want the drama. But you've got two seconds, then your knee explodes. Get in the fucking car.'

Jericho lifted his hands above his head. Head down, breaths back under control, defeated expression. The guy backed off to keep his distance as he approached the vehicle. Now Jericho could feel the pain in his chest where he'd hit the side of the door. *Too damned early for pain*, he thought. *Not yet!*

The guy would be waiting for a move, and Jericho would just have to hope his pretence at defeat gave him the fraction of a second he'd need.

He stepped towards the car, wincing at the pain in his chest. He paused for a moment, and then, hands on the roof, bent to get inside.

The distraction of normality.

His next movement was sudden. Weight pushed forward through his hands, then he swung back, extending his body, kicking out with his right leg. He felt the gun against his shoe as he connected, and as he whirled round he saw it bounce off across the pavement.

He came at him, fist raised, but Jericho was kicking out again in the same movement in which he'd turned. Toe of his shoe brought sharply up into his testicles, and then, as he bent forward, an uppercut to the throat. The gun, the balls, the throat. Three perfectly timed hits, and the guy was down.

Jericho didn't wait to see if he was going to get up.

Into the car, door slammed shut and locked, then he was pressing the ignition, and he was off.

Checked his mirror as he drove along the road, no great acceleration yet, no gunning of the engine or screeching of the tyres. There were no cars behind him on the road, and the guy was hidden immediately from view behind other cars.

Then, as he got up to thirty mph, the end of the road a hundred yards away, the other man he'd been waiting for made his play. The only pedestrian he'd seen on the road in the past couple of minutes, the man with the pushchair, turned towards the road, then when he was halfway across, left the pushchair, and quickly retreated.

Jericho had a split second to make the call. He couldn't presume the guy would be faking it, that there would obviously be no real baby in the chair. Jericho had come up against people all his life who would happily put a baby in the line of fire.

Cars parked down either side, nowhere else to go. The rapid-fire process of options. The risk. The blood that would be on his hands. Kill a child so that he could evade capture.

He slammed on the brakes, the desperate squeal of tyres, dropped the car into first, lifted the brakes, steered into the side of the road, dented the door of a Peugeot as he slowed, full brake pedal, and then the car juddered noisily to a halt less than a foot away from the pushchair.

Jericho glanced down into the chair. A small child stared back at him. His eyes wide at the noise, that slightly confused second or two before the kid was about to burst into tears.

'Jesus,' muttered Jericho.

Four shots fizzed into the tyres of the car on the passenger side, and then with a quick, single step up onto the bonnet and down the other side, the man who had happily left a small child in the middle of the road in front of a speeding car, was putting a bullet in the tyres on the driver's side.

Like the pain in his side that had completely vanished, Jericho wasn't going to hesitate over burst tyres or a complete bastard with a gun. He slammed the car into reverse, and started accelerating backwards.

The shooter now let off several rounds at the windscreen, the bullets pinging off, barely seeming to leave the slightest mark.

'Dammit,' thought Jericho.

This was no ordinary car he'd just hijacked, and he could feel the power of it beneath his right foot.

He could ignore the guy in front of him, receding quickly into the distance. He looked in the mirror as he reversed in a perfectly straight line. The first guy, kick to the balls, punch to the throat, had brought himself out into the middle of the road, and was standing, slightly doubled over, aiming at the car, letting out quickfire rounds, the bullets pinging off the chassis and the windows, as Jericho's wheel rims ground noisily into the tarmac.

Jericho did not slow, and the guy leapt out of the way at the last second.

Jericho came to the junction, hand brake, sharp tug at the wheel, out of gear, the car swung round ninety degrees, full brake, and then into third, heavy on the clutch and he accelerated away from the angry fizz of the twin Glocks.

He thought of the pushchair, still in the road, and here he was, the hero of his own damned story, speeding away from a crying child, leaving him in the care of a bastard who'd use his life as a prop in a gun fight.

'I couldn't take the kid,' he muttered to himself, voicing it out loud, trying to get rid of the thought and the accompanying guilt.

There was a clear road for three blocks, a red light in the distance. He floored the accelerator, the car cursed, the wheels ground and scraped along the tarmac, and he moved away from his pursuers. A bullet struck the back of the car, another glanced off the roof.

He streaked across two junctions without slowing, trusting to the quiet roads, and then was preparing to bust the red light up ahead and take the consequences, when it changed to green and he flew through, turning right onto the main road and accelerating noisily, heading away from the centre of the city.

16

Jericho had a safe house in London that he'd never had to use in anger, something he'd bought when he'd left the police.

It had felt unnecessary, bordering on ridiculous, but he'd always thought it might be needed, now that he was working solo against a secret, sometimes seemingly omnipotent organisation, whose tentacles reached into every corner of the great world order.

He hadn't been to the house in three years. He'd asked his sister to contact the non-family member she trusted the most in the world, to go to the place twice a year to make sure it was ticking over OK. No leaks, no squatters, nothing untoward, though he'd stopped short of asking them to sweep for bugs.

He'd never been undercover in his life as an officer, he'd never had to lie, never had to be incognito, that brief period of being on the run from the press and the police in the midst of the *Britain's Got Justice* absurdity aside. The safe house was just one more thing to induce the feeling of imposter syndrome.

Now, at last, it was needed.

Φ

In Amsterdam, he'd abandoned the car seven blocks away. He'd walked quickly three further blocks, and then jumped on a tram. He'd changed tram three times, then found his way to the train station. Along the way he'd activated the second of his four phones to send a message to Henri Quatre, before erasing the number on his arm. It wasn't about getting his money back, but the man was no longer necessary, and Jericho didn't like the idea of throwing the contact Badstuber had given him into the middle of the firestorm.

He received no reply, though he did notice, sometime later, that the money had been returned.

He ditched the second phone, then activated the third to call Haynes once he was on the train to St Pancras from Amsterdam.

Haynes had a phone that he kept on at all times, just in case. Jericho always knew the numbers of Haynes's burner phones, but never the other way round.

'Boss,' said Haynes, picking up after three rings.

'One day you can stop calling me that,' said Jericho, and he could imagine Haynes's smile at the other end.

'What's up? Thought you'd retired?'

'Why'd you keep the phone active?' said Jericho, and Haynes laughed.

'Good point. You in the city?'

'Heading there now. Will be a couple of hours yet. Sorry to trample all over your home life, but can you meet me somewhere at ten o'clock this evening?'

'Somewhere?'

'I have an apartment.'

'Right. Sure I can't invite you round for supper?'

They smiled silently together at either end of the phone.

'I'll message the address,' said Jericho.

'Boss,' said Haynes.

And they hung up.

17

'Holy shit,' said Haynes, looking down on the Thames from the eighth floor. 'This is a nice place, boss. How much did this set you back?'

'An amount,' said Jericho.

He started to approach the window, and then thought better of it.

'Tea?' he said, as the kettle rumbled.

'Sure, thanks.'

There was a kitchen at the rear of the sitting room. One bedroom, one bathroom. A small apartment, but the location doubled its value.

Beneath the bed, two long metal boxes with combination locks. Inside, six Nokia 3310s; seven fake passports; five envelopes containing cash – yuan, dollars, sterling, roubles, euros – with around five thousand pounds worth of each; three hats; ten pairs of spectacles of various styles; two reversible Macs in bags; pepper spray; a Walther PPK and twenty-four rounds; a toilet bag.

'Close the curtains when you're done,' said Jericho.

He had a line about how obvious Haynes was making himself standing in the window, but Haynes was now a senior Detective Inspector in the Met, and he didn't want to lecture him on basic protocols. Perhaps it also sounded overly dramatic, the idea that every movement of his life was being watched.

He placed the two mugs on the small table, alongside a packet of milk chocolate digestives. Haynes sat down opposite, having closed the curtains. They lifted their mugs, they made a cursory cheers gesture, they drank. Jericho pushed the biscuits towards Haynes, and he opened the packet and took out a couple.

'So, a safe house is pretty next level, boss.'

'Thank you,' said Jericho, drily.

'Do you have a stash of weapons and money and disguises and a selection of twenty false IDs to choose from?'

Jericho stared blankly across the table, and Haynes smiled and ruefully shook his head.

'Wow,' he said, 'that's amazing. You are James fucking Bond, man. You've got to have that as one of your aliases, right?'

'Sure,' said Jericho, 'because the purpose of every fake ID is to draw attention to yourself.'

'Ha. Well, this I did not expect. I thought maybe you were asking me to an Airbnb.'

'How are the kids?' asked Jericho, to get the subject off himself.

'Pretty decent. Margot's got their reading level up to roughly twice their age, and she's like a Nazi controlling TV and iPad time. She's terrifying.'

'What about you?' asked Jericho.

'Does she control my TV and internet time, or am I like a Nazi with the kids?'

Jericho smiled ruefully.

'Not sure, to be honest,' said Jericho. 'Both, maybe.'

'Yes and no,' said Haynes with a smile.

They each took a bite of biscuit, silence settled slowly upon them.

It hadn't been so long since they'd seen each other – Jericho had stayed one night with them at the beginning of the year, as he'd officially, for his own purposes, ended his quest. Nevertheless, there was a melancholy in their meetings, reminders of a close working relationship, a simpler time, which had never been going to last, but which they both fondly remembered.

'So, you're back in the game,' said Haynes. 'That didn't last long.'

'Thought I was done,' said Jericho. 'Got a visit last night from Ilsa Badstuber.'

'Damn, really? How's she? You haven't heard from her in

all this time, have you?'

'No. She's Swiss security services now, based in The Hague. She was called to look at a corpse of a woman who had four passports, one of them Swiss, as well as a Dutch ID card.'

Jericho left it at that, took another drink. Swallowed. It was harder to say than he'd been anticipating.

'Damn,' said Haynes, picking up on the hesitation. 'Amanda?'

Jericho nodded.

Haynes reached out his hand, but stopped short of actually leaning forward and squeezing Jericho's arm. Jericho watched his hand, his brow creased a little.

'I went over there with Ilsa this morning.' He thought of the day he'd had, the whirlwind of interviews, lies, death and gunfire. 'It was eventful,' he said, to sum it up.

'There's certainly evidence of that on your face' said Haynes.

'I think I'm going to have to tell you a little more than I'd like to. I killed someone – they were trying to kill me, it was one of those – and I'd like you to make some enquiries, see if it's being officially talked about. You got a notebook?'

Haynes took it out of his pocket, passed it over, and Jericho wrote down the name Greta Yossarian, the woman's description, and the address, then pushed the notebook back across to Haynes.

Haynes read the details, then lifted the pen, and couldn't help the smile when he looked up.

'So, how did this work? You just randomly killed someone? You've changed.'

'Funny. Before I started having to avoid the Dutch police, they shared some information with me.'

'You pretended to be from the Met?' asked Haynes, eyebrow raised.

'Nobody knows,' said Jericho, and Haynes nodded an acceptance of the question avoidance. 'Their cyber whiz girl, she was not happy sharing anything with me I don't think, but she had a DI there giving her the nod. She'd found next of kin details attached to all five of Amanda's identities. So, I did the obvious thing.'

'You went to the address of the Dutch next of kin.'

'Yes.'

'And she tried to kill you.'

'Admittedly, in the first instance, she tried to slam the door on me, and then I barged my way in, and things escalated. That was how it went.'

'What did you find there?'

'Didn't really find anything, though there was a William Hart Melville at least.'

'That guy. The painting had the…?' and he made a gesture to indicate the animals.

'It did,' said Jericho.

'So, it was a Pavilion house?'

'Yes.'

'You think the other four next of kin addresses might also be Pavilion houses?'

'There has to be potential,' said Jericho. He took another drink of tea, set down the mug and continued, 'I'm going to check out the London house later, and we'll take it from there.'

'Later?' said Haynes.

'Yes.'

'I don't suppose you could let me get into work tomorrow morning and do some checks, then you can take a look?'

'Striking while the iron's hot,' said Jericho.

'You want me to come with you?'

'One hundred per cent no. This,' he said, indicating the two of them sitting at the table, 'this is partly to let you know the game's afoot again, and partly to ask you to check some things for me. I admit, with Amanda dying, there's a new urgency, but the rules with you and me are no different from before. This is my fight, not yours. You have too much to jeopardise. So, I'd be grateful if you could run some basic checks on all these addresses. I presume the names that go with them all will be fake. The names are not the thing, the addresses are what we're looking into.'

'I can do that,' said Haynes, and he pushed the notepad back over to Jericho. Jericho brought the names and addresses up on his phone, and started writing them out, minus the London address.

Haynes watched him in silence for a while, half reading the names upside down.

'You doing all right?' he asked. 'I mean… that's a long time you were looking for Amanda, and out of the blue like that. Must be difficult.'

Jericho paused for a moment, and then resumed writing

quickly, before answering.

When he finished, he checked through, making sure he'd got all the details correct, then he passed the notebook back over.

'I think I'd given up on her after Oslo. It was wonderful to find her alive, except… I couldn't believe I was seeing her. I couldn't believe she'd just disappeared like that. Like she couldn't trust me. That she'd just left me hanging all those years. And…'

He'd given this far too much thought, all of it in isolation, never sharing, never talking it through. The fact that she'd shown up at his house, and the fact that his reaction had been one of deep psychological disfunction. Nevertheless, that had only been as the drama picked up around the stolen Book of Lazarus. For years previously, she'd left him alone in his desperate, lonely ignorance and loss.

They looked at each other across the table, Haynes perhaps a little uncomfortable that his old boss was being far more open than usual.

Jericho took another drink, then waved away all that he'd said.

'More than that, I think, was that having reinserted herself in my life like that, to save me, to save all four of us, to then say, OK, got to go. See you around.' He shook his head, let out a heavy sigh. 'I've resented her ever since,' he said. 'It's been hard to shake. Not that she wasn't around, I realise she had bigger fish to fry than me. But she couldn't let me know?'

'She'd have been doing the same thing you're doing with me. Keeping you out of it.'

'I was already knee deep in it,' said Jericho. 'You're not, and you've got a wife, and children and a bloody good career. You have everything to lose. I only had one thing to lose, and it was already gone.' He took another drink, scowling a little this time, laying the mug back on the table. 'She made her choice. And it might not sound like it, but I've accepted it. She went off doing whatever she was doing, and when she finally turned up I couldn't handle it. I entirely blame myself for that, so you know there's guilt and self-loathing as well as annoyance at her. And maybe that was enough for her to think, my husband's nuts, I should leave him out of it. But, you know, I also saw her six years ago in New York, and it… it was like old times, I was literally there doing the same thing she was, and… she shut me out again.'

He was nodding to himself by the time he finished.

'I think maybe that was it, that was the moment when I really emotionally closed the door. But also…' He let out a long sigh, rubbed his hand across his face, stared off into nothing across the room. 'We had dinner, we talked about a thousand things, we made love, and… it was sad, that's all. Whatever had been there before, just wasn't there any longer. We were two strangers, passing in the night, something to share, something in common, but that was all. The day dawned, and we'd gone our separate ways. Except, of course, she made the choice without further consultation.'

Haynes nodded, a little wide-eyed, then momentarily hid behind his mug of tea.

'You thought I'd just say I was fine, didn't you?' said Jericho, and Haynes laughed ruefully.

'Like I said when you confessed murdering some random Dutchwoman in her own home, you've changed.'

'Piss off, sergeant.'

'Funny.'

Haynes looked through the list of names and addresses.

'She likes the name Elizabeth,' he said.

'She always did.'

Then Haynes winced as he read the Vatican details.

'Ouch.'

Jericho glanced over, saw what he was referring to, and nodded.

'Odd that these people are listed as next of kin, but then it was a Pavilion house. You think this was Amanda's way of planting and passing on information?'

'Yes,' said Jericho, 'it's a possibility. We'll find out a little more tonight.'

'What's the address?'

Jericho smiled ruefully, didn't answer.

'Fine,' said Haynes, 'I can't say I wouldn't turn up this evening if you told me. You'll let me know how it goes, assuming you haven't been kidnapped, arrested or killed in the night?'

'Agreed,' said Jericho.

Haynes took another look at the list, then folded the piece of paper and slipped it into his pocket.

They drank tea. Jericho lifted another biscuit.

18

Another townhouse, cut from the same cloth as the house in Amsterdam, on a quiet square in the west of Pimlico. In the middle of the square, a private garden, the gate locked overnight.

Jericho stood and looked at the gate for a few moments, thinking of Amanda. For a while she'd called these gardens whoops-a-daisy gardens after the scene in *Notting Hill*. At least she had done until she'd heard of someone else who did the same thing, and then she'd stopped, as she didn't want to be like everyone else. And Jericho had teased her for it, and they'd laughed. That was such a long time ago now, and he was surprised he remembered it.

He turned, he walked on. The house was at the end of the row. All Jericho had was a Crowne Z 23 lockpick, and a small pair of pliers. Industrial age crime tools in this modern world, he thought, and utterly useless in the face of an expensive alarm system.

One a.m., the square deserted, the four-storey townhouses blocking out the bulk of the noise of the city at night.

There were a few lights on, the odd sign of life, but mostly the square was asleep.

He came to the house at the end. Number seventeen. Home of Mr Jeffery Blake, supposed father and next of kin of Elizabeth Blake.

No lights on, nothing to suggest the house was currently occupied. But then, at one o'clock in the morning, why should there be?

First rule of surreptitious crime committal? Don't look surreptitious.

Jericho walked up the three steps to the front door, Crowne Z-23 out of his pocket. Two locks – a mortice and a Yale – and he got to work. The light wasn't great, but then he didn't need the light. It was all done on feel.

Ten years ago, when he'd left the police, this would have taken him ten minutes, perhaps longer. He'd had a lot of time to perfect a variety of skills in those years, skills that he long since thought completely pointless. And now, out of nowhere, he was getting to use them.

The mortice lock was done almost instantly, as though he was using a key, and then he moved to the Yale lock at the top. Slightly trickier, but it did not take long. The lock turned, he paused for a moment before opening the door, deep breath, and then he edged it slowly inwards, in case it was about to judder against a chain.

No chain, and the door slowly opened.

He pushed it further open, then stepped quickly into the house, closing the door almost shut behind him. A look around, trying to see if there was any sign of sensors, or an alarm. There were no pinpricks of light in the darkness.

Softly he closed the door behind him, a hand on both locks to make sure they clicked shut with the minimum of sound, then he turned back to the silent darkness of the hallway. Small torch out of his pocket, and he turned it on and first of all shone its light in quick succession to the stairs directly in front, then to the doorway to the right, and the hallway leading away to the side of the stairs.

There was no one there, no one standing watching him, waiting to make themselves known.

He went through the first door, the light held low, into what was a large sitting and dining room. A table by the window, a pair of two-seat leather sofas around a fireplace in the other half of the room. In the corner, a floor-standing globe. On the far wall, a huge painting, the type one might only usually see in a gallery or a stately home, stretching the length of the wall to a closed door that would likely lead to the kitchen. A battle scene, nineteenth-century perhaps.

On the left-hand wall, shelves of books, and an old-fashioned drinks cabinet. Above the fireplace, a large, gold-framed mirror.

The room had a look of country house pastiche, thought Jericho.

He turned off the torch and slipped it into his pocket, and then walked to the window. He didn't want to shut the curtains, but he also obviously couldn't be so bold as to turn on the light, despite the square looking dead for the night.

He walked to the other end of the room, and sat down in one of the sofas, facing the door, letting his eyes become accustomed to the darkness.

There would be three more floors, and he had to go upstairs. Hope there was an office of some sort, with a desk he could go through. Again, it would all be in darkness, and it was too early to say that there wasn't someone here. Perhaps still fast asleep.

Two more minutes, he thought, while the house got used to his presence and settled back down, while his eyes got used to the darkness as much as they could, and while he became acclimatised to the sounds and rhythm of the house. He could leave the torch in his pocket, apart from when he was sitting at some grand desk in a third floor room, going through paperwork.

He glanced over his shoulder at the magnificent painting on the back wall. Should he examine it closely for signs of the Pavilion code? Should he do that with every painting in the house, if he didn't find it here?

There would be a lot of paintings, he surmised, as he'd already noticed several lining the stairs. Nevertheless, he could stop when he'd found what he was looking for.

Perhaps all he needed was confirmation for himself that this was a Pavilion house, then he could get out, and get a camera set up somewhere across the road, within the evergreen bushes of the park. Wait and see who came and went. He could stay in London, and be in a position to tail them when the time came.

Though wasn't there something about this house that said it wasn't lived in? That it might go months, or even years, without anyone staying here? A safe house, like his safe house, and like a million other safe houses.

Maybe there was someone upstairs. Maybe the place was owned by a sanctioned Russian oligarch, and had been lying empty for three years. 'Maybe,' muttered Jericho to himself, 'all sorts of shit.'

A floorboard out in the hall, a spike of adrenalin surged through him, then the door opened, a figure appeared in the darkness, and then the overhead light was on, the room brightly illuminated, and a woman in a rich maroon dressing gown was scowling at him.

'You didn't want to turn the lights on?' she said with annoyance, shaking her head, and then going to the window and closing the curtains.

She turned back, pulled the gown a little closer to herself, even though it was already tied, then stood by the other sofa, looking down at Jericho.

'Seriously?' she said. 'I hate it when you fucking guys come in here and creep around in the dark. And you know there's a doorbell, right?'

She was American. North-east coast, thought Jericho.

'It's late, I didn't want to disturb you,' he said.

She laughed, rolling her eyes.

'Sure, pal. You want a coffee or something? I can make you something to eat if you like, but it's one o'clock in the morning. You're too old to be eating at this time of night. Not that you should be drinking coffee either, but that doesn't stop most of you idiots.'

'Coffee would be great,' said Jericho. 'Make it a latte to take the edge off.'

'That'll make all the difference.'

She walked past him, through the other door, turning lights on in the kitchen as she went. Jericho got up and followed her through.

A large kitchen, very modern. An island in the middle, windows at the back that would likely look onto a tiny courtyard. A dark green Rayburn, a double sink, everything neatly arranged around the kitchen as though they were about to do a photoshoot for Country Life, or film a new Nigella Lawson series.

She glanced over her shoulder as she took the milk from the fridge, and got a jar of coffee grounds from a shelf.

'You know I'm the staff, right?' she said. 'You guys don't usually follow me around.'

'How long have you worked here?' asked Jericho.

She stopped, she stared curiously at him.

'Really?'

'Look, it's been a long, lousy day,' said Jericho.

'You look a little rough,' she said.

'I'm tired, just wanted a little human interaction, that's all.

Sorry, I'll leave you to it...'

He began to turn away, stopping in the doorway when she spoke.

'Seventeen years.'

He turned back, held her look for a few moments.

She was early fifties maybe, a look about her that drew him in, glasses that leant her face a seriousness that maybe it wouldn't otherwise have had.

'You ever get to leave the house?' asked Jericho, smiling.

She took the joke, nodding and returning the smile, as she turned away.

'Yeah, yeah, once a year at Christmas. Haven't seen the sun since two thousand eight.'

Jericho eased his way into the more relaxed mood, and then walked back into the kitchen, and pulled out one of the high chairs at the island.

'You going to join me?'

'You're nuts,' she said. 'I'd really like to be able to get back to sleep in the next few hours.'

She glanced over her shoulder. Jericho gave her a look to suggest that maybe neither of them had to go to sleep. Or maybe he meant something completely different.

She set the coffee going, and the sound of the machine ground its way through the middle of the dark night. Then the glug of the milk from the bottle, the whoosh of sound as it was steamed, and then she poured the shot of coffee into the milk, and set the cup down in front of him. Then a bottle of water from the fridge, she poured two small glasses, and sat down opposite.

'Where've you come from?' she asked. And in the fraction of a second when he hadn't answered, she shook her head and said, 'New York, right? You're not one of those fucking guys, are you?'

Jericho smiled.

'I'm here from New York,' he said, 'but I'm not one of those fucking guys.'

'I'll bet,' she said, smiling.

She looked around, a glance at the fridge, and Jericho recognised the consideration of getting a glass of wine. He took a drink of coffee, made a small gesture.

'Nice,' he said.

'So, what's it like over there?' she asked. 'There are so

many rumours flying around at the moment, it's insane.'

Jericho took another drink, taking the moment, hiding behind the small mug.

'You know, I'm sorry,' he said.

'Can't talk.'

'It's nuts, that's all,' he said, and she nodded in agreement.

'No one knows whose side anyone's on anymore,' said the woman, and then she shrugged lightly and added, 'And that goes for you and me, so we should probably just shut up, right?'

Jericho nodded. Took another drink.

'Thinking of getting out anyway,' said Jericho. 'Too old for this shit.'

She looked a little surprised, and he thought, damn, said the wrong thing. Mouth shut until he saw which way the wind was blowing.

'Well, I guess I know what side of the bed you're sleeping on,' she said, and Jericho nodded ruefully, and took another drink of coffee.

'Any chance that wasn't a euphemism,' he said, and she smiled.

'Look, good luck to you. I mean, maybe this is all going to work itself out, but the way I hear it…,' and she let out a low whistle. 'Every time you turn on the goddam news, you just never know. Like this whole thing in Sudan. Goddammit, that is some bad-ass shit, you know? Those people are dying in the hundreds of thousands, it's a fucking hellscape, and you're looking at that, and you think, wait was that *us*? Because I just don't know anymore.'

Jericho shook his head.

'Sudan's not us,' he said. 'Some things don't need any help.'

She let out another low whistle, another head shake, then lifted her glass of water and downed it.

'Look, I got to get to bed. You mind if I show you to your room?'

'Please,' said Jericho.

'You got a bag, a change...?' she began, then at his head shake said, 'I'll put you on the top floor. There's an en suite, everything you'll need up there.'

'Thanks,' said Jericho.

He downed the coffee, placed it by the sink, and followed her from the kitchen, turning the light off as he went.

Φ

Ten minutes later, when he emerged from the bathroom, she was lying in his bed. Leaning on her elbow, head rested on her hand, the white duvet pulled up to her chest, but revealing the first curve of her breasts.

There was a bedside light on, casting low shadows into the far corners of the room. This, Jericho had thought when he'd first come in, was like a two-grand-a-night boutique London hotel.

'Couldn't sleep,' she said. 'Was thinking maybe you couldn't sleep.'

Jericho paused for a moment, but since he'd already considered knocking on her door after he'd had a shower, there wasn't a lot of thinking to do.

'What's your name,' he asked, and she laughed lightly.

'How wonderfully old-fashioned,' she said, then she smiled suggestively at him, as though needing to give the question serious consideration.

'Eve Kendall,' she said eventually.

Jericho stepped forward, and placed his hand gently on the side of her face, then took hold of the cover, and flicked the duvet off. She was naked, and made no attempt to hide herself now that Jericho had revealed her.

'How trusting of you,' she said, smiling. 'Don't worry, I'm not working, I'm not here to spy on all you agents as you pass through.'

She shifted the bedding a little further off her body, and stretched her legs, so that they parted a little.

'You wouldn't leave a girl hanging, would you?' she said, coyly.

Jericho sat on the edge of the bed, and leaned into her. As their lips met, he rested a hand gently on her side, and then moved it slowly across her skin until he was cupping her right breast.

19

Jericho lay in bed waiting for her to fall asleep. In the first instance, he'd waited for her to leave, but that hadn't happened, and now they were lying together, her arm lightly draped over him, as he listened to the sound of her breathing.

This, he thought, was sub-optimal. He was going to have to search the house while she slept, which meant the entire operation would have to be conducted in silence, while he looked over his shoulder, waiting for her to appear.

He needed a plan B. Plan B was likely just going to have to be industrial. Subdue her, silence her, tie her up. But what if they got into a fight like the one he'd had in Amsterdam? He didn't want to be killing someone every time he visited a house he suspected of belonging to the Pavilion. The casualness of the sex he'd just had suggested a sixties spy novel, but he really didn't care for that level of casual death. Not to mention, of course, that he was a literal lone wolf, with no wider organisation to fall back on.

The blinds were drawn, but streetlight crept in around the edges, and it had been dark for long enough now that he could clearly see the whole room. He was just going to have to take her out where she lay, waking her abruptly from a deep sleep as he bound and gagged her.

'I can practically hear your brain whirring,' she said softly.
Dammit.
'Shouldn't have had that coffee after all,' he said.
He didn't look at her in the night.

And then, in the silence of the room, the metallic click of the cocking of a small pistol, then the cold metal of the gun barrel pressing against his head.

'You killed Greta,' she said.

Jericho took a moment. Time to play the game, he thought. Time to slip into someone else's skin.

'Did I? Friend of yours?'

'You strangled her. That must have felt good, I suppose. Killing a woman with your bare hands.'

'I don't remember,' he said, continuing to feign ignorance, with a lightness in tone that suggested that of course he knew exactly what she was talking about.

'I'm surprised you didn't kill me when you had me here, naked and vulnerable. Men like you like that.'

He started to move his head a little to look at her, and immediately felt the gun pressing more firmly.

'No movement,' she said, coldly. 'Nothing. The slightest hint of it, you're dead.' A pause, then, 'You'd better hope you don't have to cough.'

'It's all right for me to speak, though, right?'

He felt the press of the gun.

'Tell me,' she said.

'I'm in the dark here,' said Jericho.

'I checked, cowboy. No one's due here this evening. No one knows who you are. Except, wait a minute, folks, yes, they do. You're the former cop, Jericho, that's who. This morning you killed Greta, and now up you damn well pop, like a bad penny, at another one of the houses. And you need to start talking, because I'm not known for my patience.'

'What would you like to talk about?'

'Where did you get the addresses?'

Jericho automatically began to turn his head, so that he could raise his eyebrow at her, and she jabbed him with the gun again.

'No one's going to miss you if I have to pull the trigger,' she said. 'Start talking.'

'You know the rules,' he said.

'Sure, I know the rules, and you're on the list. Start talking.'

'Can I...?' he said, trying to turn his head, and she leant up now, the gun thrust against his skull, pushing him further back against the pillow.

'No. You can talk, that's it.'

He took another moment, crept a little further into the new skin.

He sighed.

'You know what we're like now. Used to be one hand didn't know what the other was doing. Now, no one knows what anyone's doing. It's a shitshow, everywhere you go. So, I wouldn't expect you to know, and I'm not sure I should even be telling you.'

'Know what? And just so you know, so far, buddy, whatever this is you're trying here, I'm not buying it.'

'I spent seven years trying to track down the Pavilion. Then I got brought on board. We stopped fighting. I mean, me and the Pavilion, we stopped fighting, which didn't amount to much, given how one-sided it'd been. I've been the Pavilion's man in The Hague for the last two years. I killed Amanda Raintree five days ago. Looks like I killed Greta today, but Greta was trying to kill me, so we all do what we have to do, right?'

'Raintree was your wife.'

'Yes.

'And you killed her?'

'I hadn't seen her in ten years. Turned out our reunion didn't go so well.'

Silence.

She was thinking it over.

Jericho too, for that matter.

She'd likely got an image of him from a security camera somewhere on the property, and the check wouldn't have taken long to run, but she must have done that before she came to his bedroom. Which meant she knew exactly who he was, but hadn't called it in.

'OK, here's what we're going to do,' she said. 'I'm going to get up and turn the light on. Then I'm going to get dressed. Then you're going to get dressed. Then we're leaving. If you attempt anything at any stage, I'll kill y –'

'Why the sex?'

'What?'

'You must've found out who I was two hours ago. Yet you didn't call it in. You came to my room, we made love, we lay here in bed, waiting for the other one to fall asleep, and then you finally cracked because I didn't fall asleep first. What's your game?'

She moved quickly, off the bed, then had hit the light switch and was standing naked at the side of the bed, the KelTec P-32 aimed at Jericho. The room was cold, the goosebumps showed on her skin.

'Like I said,' she said. 'Any unexpected movements, you're dead.'

He lay where he was, his head turned slightly towards her. She looked beautiful, standing there naked and cold, he thought.

'What?' she said, at the slight smile he hadn't been able to hide.

'You look amazing,' he said.

'Oh, fuck off.'

She glanced at the door.

'Ah,' said Jericho, 'you hadn't thought this through, had you? You came to bed naked, clothes in the other room. So either you let me get dressed first, or we both walk through there, or is it back downstairs, together naked. It's all a little awkward.'

'Get up and move,' she said, gesturing towards the door with the gun.

'You could just come back to bed,' said Jericho.

'Get up.'

'We could have breakfast tomorrow, then we could go wherever it is you want to take me. Think about it,' he continued. 'If I'm on the inside, then you take me somewhere, we all get to lay our cards on the table. But if I'm the Jericho you think I am, I'm still not going to try to get away. I want you to take me somewhere. I want you to take me into the heart of your operation.'

'How d'you know I'm not just taking you into the woods to put a bullet in your head?'

'You'd kill me now, then you'd get a disposal team to come and remove the corpse,' he said. 'I know how we operate.'

'*We*,' she said, with an eyeroll.

She was annoyed at herself, he could tell. This was the first time in a long time she'd actually had something operational, something beyond the mundane passage of an operative through town, and she was making a mess of it.

She was bored with her life. That was why she'd slept with him. That was why she hadn't called it in straight away. That was why she'd created this little drama.

'Fuck,' she said in a low voice, allowing her agitation to

show even more.

'Just take me where you want to take me,' said Jericho. 'I'll be happy to –'

A low alarm started to go off, she swung a look at the door, she said, 'Fuck!' far more loudly, and then a whoosh from the window, and a metal shutter slammed down, the sound of doors locking, and shutters closing around the property.

'What's happening?' said Jericho, although it was pretty obvious.

'You're fucked,' she said, as she lowered the gun, and headed for the door. 'You might want to get dressed,' she threw over her shoulder, as she left.

20

'How long have we got?' asked Jericho.

They met in the corridor, third floor, both dressed. She had the gun in her hand, and immediately pointed it at him.

'I've got all night,' she said, 'you've got about three minutes. Don't do anything dumb.'

'You think you've got all night?' said Jericho.

She noticed the change in his demeanour. Whatever it had been before – something in him that said he'd been enjoying the hunt – had gone. There was imminent threat, and it was much more imminent than her pressing a gun against his head.

'I have all night,' she said, forcing the certainty.

'If they're doing this, they don't trust you to bring me in. You're expendable.'

He left that there for a moment, let the words hang in the air, let her come to terms with the reality.

The muscles in her face tightened. For the first time, maybe, she looked her age. The same for all of us, he thought.

'Dammit,' she muttered.

The lights went out.

'Fuck,' from them both at the same time.

Total darkness.

They stood in silence for a moment, searching for sound.

Nothing.

'You know Jonas?' said Jericho, quickly reaching for a lie.

A moment, he could feel her shaking her head, then she said, 'No.'

'He's in New York. If we can get there, we'll be safe.'

'The fuck are we getting to New York?'

'I have a house in town they don't know about. I have money, we can lie low until we can get you papers. A day, maybe two, we can be out of here.'

She thought about it in the dark.

A rumour of sound from downstairs.

'You've got about half a minute,' said Jericho.

'Fuck.'

In the single syllable, the admission of defeat.

'You got any more weapons up here?' he said.

Another low curse, and he could feel her giving in.

The line about Jonas had been a lie, but otherwise, he wasn't wrong. He knew the Pavilion, just as she did, and she absolutely was expendable. Not only that, they were obviously paying attention to what she did in a way she'd never realised, and they hadn't liked the fact she'd slept with him, and they hadn't liked the way the conversation in the bedroom had been going.

They'd heard it all.

Another sound from downstairs.

The torch on her phone went on, aimed at the floor.

'Come on,' she said.

She turned, she hurried through to her bedroom, Jericho quickly behind her, his own phone torch now illuminated, aiming at her feet.

'Your name really Eve Kendall?' he asked, something in his tone shifting again, now that she'd come over onto his side.

'Seriously?'

'I've seen *North By Northwest*,' he said, and she didn't turn to look at him.

She came to a cupboard, slipping her phone into a pocket, her gun into the back of her trousers. He held his light up for her.

She opened the cupboard door, quickly parting the hanging clothes, revealing a small keypad. She tapped in the number, then pressed her thumb against a pad, and the door clicked. She pulled it open, revealing just the kind of thing Jericho had back at his place. Passports, money, two weapons.

She lifted a couple of passports, thrust some money into a pocket, took out the two hand guns, handed him one, and then took a cartridge for both, shut the door, clothes back in place, cupboard door closed, then she handed him a spare cartridge.

They stared at each other in the half-light of his lowered torch.

'You must've known this was coming one day,' said Jericho.

She'd grown complacent. They both understood the situation, and there was no need for any further discussion.

'Torch off,' she said.

'Where will they have come in?' he asked, pocketing the phone.

'I don't know.'

'OK. Let's try and stick close together, less chance we shoot each other,' he said.

'Sure,' she said ruefully.

He found her hand in the night, and squeezed her fingers.

'Jesus, you're not getting romantic on me, are you?'

'Stay close,' he said.

He didn't let go of her hand, as he led her back out into the hallway. He felt his way to the top of the stairs, then knelt down behind the wall, Kendall following, and now they crouched in silence, adjusting to the darkness and the night, waiting for whatever was coming up the stairs to meet them.

'What's your exit plan?' he asked after a few moments of absolute still.

'Turns out they know this place a lot better than me, and I've lived here for seventeen years,' she said.

'You have a way onto the roof?'

A moment, and then, 'Yes.'

'We've got to try,' said Jericho.

'Yes.' And then, 'Come on.'

She took his hand again, and led him quickly to the next flight of stairs, back up to the fourth floor where they'd been shortly before. At that moment, a fizz in the dark, they both knew what was coming, and then the smoke grenade went off, 'Fuck it,' escaped Jericho's mouth, and the burst of a series of bullets peppered around them, thudding into the walls.

And now that the attack had been unleashed, the sound of footsteps just below was rapidly following them up the stairs.

Up onto the fourth floor, Jericho turned and fired off a couple of quick shots into the void of smoke. Something to hold them back, that was all.

Into a small room, next to where they'd made love, Jericho let off another couple of rounds, bullets peppering the walls around them as he slammed the door shut.

A basic bolt across, which would barely delay them a second. Torchlight again, as Kendall shone the light against the back wall.

'This'll take a minute, if they haven't already shut it off,' she said. 'You get the door.'

Jericho was already poised. Kneeling behind a desk, waiting for the door to open, not entirely sure that it even would. It could just be the room would suddenly be filled with five hundred, unavoidable bullets.

KelTec in both hands, finger poised on the trigger, plenty of rounds left. Next to him, the sound of Kendall exerting herself, lifting something heavy, then the thump into the wall, followed by another, and this time the sound of the wall beginning to crumble.

'You know doors are a thing,' he said.

'Funny.'

Another loud thump, the wall gave way, then he glanced over and the lights of the city and the night very visible through a substantial hole.

'We're on,' she said, and she forced her way through the small gap.

Jericho was up and moving quickly to the hole, as the door burst open, the room instantly filling with the sound of gunfire.

He turned at the gap in the wall, the first figure in black was coming through the door, gun indiscriminately firing. Jericho took one careful shot to the head and felled him. The next man immediately dove for cover, and Jericho caught him in the chest, a single bullet, and he slumped dead onto the floor.

A pause, Jericho turned to go through the gap, just as the next missile was tossed around the door.

A controlled bang, the room filled with thick smoke, and then was lit up with a hail of bullets, as Jericho forced himself through the hole and outside.

He caught his side on a jagged piece of wall, a sharp pain, then he was out, and faced with the precipitous four-storey drop. Kendall was to his left, feet on the stone rail around the side of the building, holding onto the cornice, edging quickly away to the far end.

Heights.

Crap.

No alternative but to thrust the gun into his trousers, then he was out onto the narrow ledge, the sound of gunfire behind him, then he was up and grabbing onto the roof, as his weight fought to pull him backwards.

How long did they have?

From inside, the continuing avalanche of sound. To his left, Kendall found the spot, and pulled herself up onto the roof. Jericho had no more than a couple of seconds, and then they'd be at the hole in the wall, and he'd be a sitting duck.

His foot slipped, he grabbed the guttering more forcefully than it could take, and it pulled away sharply from the wall. He flailed.

She grabbed his jacket, leaning over, and yanked him back towards the wall, and then he pushed upwards, she pulled, then he was up onto the roof, and following her as she scurried quickly up the slight incline.

Ahead of them a long terrace of rooftops, illuminated by the city at night, and she broke into a run, Jericho on her tail, following her footsteps.

This was a route in and out of pipework and aerials and air conditioning units and vents that she'd already worked out. She may have been surprised she was being disposed of so easily this evening, but she'd known it was coming at some point. Maybe it was enemies of the Pavilion she assumed would come for her, rather than her employers.

Running low, around obstacles in the dark, and then they were at a bigger structure, obviously leading to a stairway, with a full-size door, and now she dived in behind it, and Jericho followed.

She took a moment, breaths heavy, and then allowed herself a glimpse around the corner of the building.

'Nothing yet,' she said.

'What's next?' asked Jericho.

'The tree.'

She said it without turning.

Jericho looked along to the end of the terrace. There was an oak, old and large and magnificent, shorn of leaves.

'We jump into the tree?' said Jericho.

He was breathing hard.

'Yes.'

'That's your plan?'

'Yes.'

'Seriously?'

'I always hoped if I needed to use this route, it'd be in the summer.' And then, 'Shit. Come on.'

She turned, then was quickly up and running away from the structure at a slight angle, hoping to keep it between them and their pursuers, Jericho close behind her.

As they neared the edge, he realised she was speeding up, and he forced himself to do the same. All or nothing.

The gunshots rang out as she pushed herself off the edge of the building, leaping into the heart of the bare branches of the oak, Jericho half a second behind.

Jericho reached out as he clattered into the branches. Kendall fell, a dead weight, a bullet hitting her in the back, exploding through her chest, killing her instantly.

Jericho came to a blunt halt, catching his side painfully on a large branch, then thudding into the trunk. He didn't manage to take hold, and he slipped, his feet and hands clutching at branches to get a grip, but he needed to fall as quickly, and safely as he could, and he let the clumsy descent continue. Branches caught him painfully, every part of his body, tearing his clothes, scratching his face.

A gun shot rang out, another, but outside like this, they were wary of raining bullets down.

His foot caught in a branch, he pitched to the side, he lost what control he had, then he was falling, and almost instantly he hit the ground in an ugly tangle of limbs.

He couldn't linger in pain. He pulled himself up, he looked at the fallen figure of Eve Kendall. Dead before she hit the ground, a branch at some stage impaling itself in the side of her face.

He took no more than a moment, and then he turned and started to run. His ankle immediately buckled, his right thigh screamed at him, but he pushed through. Five strides, six, seven, and then he was up and running, the pain ignored, and quickly in the direction of Victoria, where he could get lost in the maze of quiet, night-time streets.

21

He opened the door of his apartment, and stepped into the darkness.

There was someone here. He sensed the change.

A woman, but not someone trying to conceal herself. The scent was light, but if you were going to go crawling around someone's house in the middle of the night, you didn't wear anything.

He checked the blinds were still drawn, and then turned on the light. Badstuber was there, sitting in the dark on the sofa, waiting for him. As soon as she saw the state of him, she was out of the seat.

She touched the side of his face, her fingers soft on his skin. He hadn't realised how bad it was until he'd seen himself in the three-sided mirrors of the elevator.

'Mostly scratches,' he said, 'though I think I've been shot in the side.'

Her eyes went down to the dark red patch of his coat.

'How long ago?'

'Half an hour,' he said. 'Stuart told you where I was?'

'I followed you from Amsterdam,' she said. 'I took a week's leave. I chose not to track your movements tonight, but perhaps I should have done.'

'You shouldn't have come at –'

'I am here now,' she said. 'You should take a shower. We must not be prudish about this. I will clean your wounds, and make sure they are properly bandaged. You have a first aid kit?'

He nodded.

'You have anything we can use for stitches?'

'Seriously?'

'You have been shot. Would you have me use Blue Tac?'

'I don't think so,' he said.

'We will deal with that later. First you must get in the shower, and tell me what happened.'

'Yes, ma'am,' said Jericho.

Φ

He wondered if she was going to get into the shower with him, but she stood in the dry, examining his body, paying particular attention to where the bullet had passed harmlessly, if painfully, through his side, when he'd thought, at the time, he'd caught himself on the wall.

He told her the full story of the evening, leaving nothing out. By the time he was finished telling the tale, she had finished patching him up, seeming to take a certain pleasure in applying stinging antiseptic to the wounds as he detailed walking out of the bathroom to find Kendall naked in his bed.

Four a.m, and they were sitting at his kitchen table with hot chocolate. Jericho had been surprised to find that he owned hot chocolate, until she'd told him she took a supply everywhere with her.

'You intend now to visit these other safe houses?' she asked.

'That's the plan. Not sure if I'm getting any closer, or whether I'll just risk getting killed everywhere I go, but for now I don't have anything else.'

'Which one is next?'

'New York,' he said. 'Amanda was working at the UN, and I need to see what was going on there. I want to go there first, then take a look at the property. Looks like it's in Brooklyn.'

'I will come with you,' she said.

He hated the idea of her getting hurt, but he wasn't about to tell her that she couldn't. It wasn't as though she was really giving him any choice.

'Thank you,' he said.

'Though we should not travel together.'

'Yes,' said Jericho. 'This is it for me, though, I don't have anywhere in New York. I'll find an apartment somewhere, though I'll maybe wait until I get there, and be as under the wire as I can be in booking it.'

'I have a place we can use,' she said. 'We will stay there. It is in Two Bridges, not so far from the Brooklyn bridge. It will be walkable.'

'You have a place, or your agency has a place?'

'It is mine.'

'New York? You have any others?'

'I do not,' she said, 'but New York has proved useful.'

'When was the last time you were there?'

She stared across the table, and he wondered for a moment if she was thinking about it and couldn't remember, then she put the cup to her lips, and he realised she just wasn't going to answer.

He nodded to himself, and took a longer drink of the chocolate.

'Always thought this was for kids,' he said. 'This is damned good.'

'Yes,' she said, matter-of-factly, then tagged on, 'We should get some sleep. Finish your drink.'

He smiled ruefully, downed the drink, and licked his lips as he placed the mug back on the table.

'You can have the bed,' he said. 'I'll sleep on the couch.'

'You are squeamish about sleeping in bed with two different women on the same night?' she said, her tone just a little lighter than normal, and Jericho did not entirely know how to respond. She seemed to enjoy his awkwardness for a moment, then said, 'The bed is big enough. We will sleep. You need rest, not more sex. Maybe one day that will happen, but it will not be tonight.'

She stood up, lifting the mugs.

'The apartment in New York has three bedrooms, so there also, we will be able to focus on work.'

Jericho watched her as she went to the sink to wash out the mugs. He couldn't help the smile, and the last thing he wanted to do now was have sex with anyone, but he really wished he hadn't so easily given himself to Eve Kendall, to salve her boredom on what had turned out to be the last night of her life.

22

Thirty-one hours later. New York. Six forty-three am, the grey light of dawn in the apartment, as Jericho walked through into the sitting room and kitchen. A warm shower, followed by thirty seconds of an icy blast of cold water, two minutes with the electric toothbrush and a rinse with the most vicious mouthwash he'd been able to pick up at the airport, and the effects of travel had mostly been banished.

The room smelled of coffee, classical music was playing quietly in the background. Badstuber was already up, sitting at the breakfast bar, coffee and orange juice at her side, working on a MacBook.

Jericho poured himself a coffee and a glass of water, and sat down opposite.

'You're working already,' he said.

On their arrival the previous evening, Badstuber had cleaned the wound in his side again, and this time had been in a position to apply stitches. Jericho, sceptical at first, had been surprised by the softness of her touch. And then, when he thought about it, he'd accepted that he really oughtn't to have been surprised at all.

'I was awake at four a.m.,' said Badstuber. 'Amanda, as Elizabeth Barnes, worked as a coordinating manager in the office of the Economic and Social Council. ECOSOC as it's known in the language of these people.'

'Coordinating manager sounds wonderfully vague,' said Jericho.

'Yes. She worked one week a month, although not necessarily on five consecutive days. She last reported for duty three weeks ago. ECOSOC is not yet aware that she is deceased.'

'You've found what office she worked in?'

'Yes, of course,' said Badstuber.

Jericho was still enjoying her abrupt manner, and couldn't imagine tiring of it.

He turned and looked around the kitchen, noticed the basket with the paper towel lying over it.

'There are croissant, and there are pain au chocolat,' said Badstuber, without following his gaze. 'If you are helping yourself, I will take a croissant and apricot jam, please. And a top-up of coffee.'

Jericho got up, started sorting out breakfast. Despite sleeping in separate bedrooms, they seemed to have slipped into an easy domesticity, as though they were already a couple. Perhaps that's what came from spending the last ten years thinking about each other, even if they were yet to open up about it.

'What have you been working on recently?' asked Jericho, as he poured the coffee. 'I mean, before you found Amanda?'

'Mainly Russia,' she said. 'Everyone in Europe has spent the last two years working on Russia, which of course, has just opened doors for everyone else. It is, as you people like to say, a shitshow.'

'You know anything about the Russians that isn't on the news?'

He looked at her as he asked, and she finally lifted her eyes from the computer and stared blankly at him.

'I know many things,' she said, 'but nothing that breaks the mould of what everyone thinks. I feel, nevertheless, there is something going on beyond the madness of the dictator, but I do not know what it is.'

'The madness of the dictator,' said Jericho. 'We're all getting familiar with that.'

'Yes,' she said. 'Meanwhile, Islamic fundamentalism walks across Europe, having come in through the front door, while the right marches ever more brazenly against it.' She paused, then looked back at her computer as she said, 'It will end badly. Russia plays her games, China waits in the wings, America disintegrates, and we all wait to see what becomes of civilisation.'

At some point long ago, perhaps Jericho would've had something to say about that brief, apocalyptic vision, but no more. He agreed with her. Civilisation teetered on the brink.

He placed the coffee, and croissant with apricot jam on the side, next to her. Then he put a croissant and a pain au chocolat on a plate, topped up his coffee, and sat down opposite.

She took a moment, then closed her computer and looked across the table.

They stared at each other, something overwhelming in the look, and then he felt the need to snap it, and said, 'What's the plan?'

'You know people who work at the UN building?'

'No one.'

'That is good. I know several people, and my face will be known to security. You will go to the UN building?'

'Sure,' said Jericho.

'I have created a pass for you, and a keycard for Elizabeth Barnes's office,' she said. 'I believe she has her own room.'

'OK, I can do that,' said Jericho. 'What name have you given me?'

'George Harrison,' she said.

Jericho's brow creased a little.

'Really?' he said.

'It is a generic British name.'

'At least it won't attract attention,' he said.

'No one is going to think you were in the Beatles,' she said bluntly, and Jericho smiled. 'I have given you a note of the five passwords from the USB stick I was sent. If it was indeed from Amanda, then there is a chance that one of those passwords will get you into her computer.'

'It's unlikely to give me five attempts though, is it?'

'That is correct.'

'And I'm not going to know which one of the five to use.'

'No.'

They stared at each other in silence for a few moments.

'Shall I use the Force?' asked Jericho.

'You can try,' she answered, seriously.

'I was being facetious.'

'You will have a sixty percent chance of them opening her computer.'

'Don't we start fifty-fifty on whether or not *any* of the five will work, before we get to only having three chances.'

'That is statistically accurate, yes. You have a less than sixty percent chance. Nevertheless, we have to try. Three failed log-in attempts is unlikely to immediately bring security to the office door.'

'What are you going to do this morning?' he asked, abruptly changing the subject. He wasn't worried about it. The passwords would work, or they wouldn't, that was all. 'I'm thinking, park as close to the UN as you can, and keep the engine running.'

She smiled, which he wasn't used to, and he allowed himself to be lost in it for a moment, then she said, 'I will go to the Whistler Gallery. I will look at the William Hart Melville painting. Then, I will look at other paintings. The latter will not be for work, but for my own benefit.'

'Shall I meet you at the Whistler?' he asked.

'Yes, that is possible. If I have finished, perhaps we could meet in the park, or back here. Or perhaps some other avenue will be open to us.'

Jericho was nodding his way through his croissant. He'd grown used to working on his own, and this relationship they now had was a lot less formal than the one they'd briefly held previously, when they'd been detectives jointly working a case.

Silence returned, but he could tell from the look in her eyes that she was not comfortable with the intensity of it, so that her, 'May I be blunt?' question, was no surprise to him.

'Please,' he said.

'We did not work together long, but... but I fell in love with you. I allowed it to happen. And Valentin recognised the change in me, and our marriage started to fail from that moment.' She swallowed, took a drink of coffee, and made a small gesture to let him know she hadn't finished. 'After my marriage ended, I slept with four other men, and two women, which is perhaps why I am so sanguine with what you did last night. But now that we are here, working together again, I am happy to say that I love you, and I know you feel the same.'

'Yes,' he managed to squeeze in.

'But there is no time for romance,' she said. 'There is work to do. I do not know what this will look like on the other side, but I wanted to get the emotion stated plainly, so that we know where we are. We do not have time for foolishness.'

'OK,' said Jericho.

'We are happy?' she said.

She didn't sound happy.

'Do I get to say anything?' asked Jericho.

'Yes, of course.'

'I love you too,' he said.

She stared blankly across the table.

'This was already acknowledged,' she said, though her voice was a little softer.

23

Jericho approached the UN building with his head down, staring at an iPhone, looking like everyone else on earth as he walked along the street.

Badstuber had given him a shorter haircut, and a pair of thick-rimmed glasses. 'Clark Kent?' he'd said, looking over his shoulder at her in the mirror.

'You look different,' she said. 'I like it.'

He was reading a story about a tech billionaire in Switzerland who'd committed suicide. Badstuber had pointed it out to him. It wasn't news anywhere else, it was barely news in Switzerland. But it was, she said, just the kind of thing that seemed to be happening more and more. A random death of someone who might have been a player. No known connection to the Pavilion, of course, because no one had a known connection to the Pavilion, but that was how it was for people in this loop now. Whenever anyone died in even slightly peculiar circumstances, whenever there was a coup, whenever there was the merest hiccup in the great workings of the world, one now wondered if the Pavilion was at play.

'The world is collapsing around our ears,' she'd said to him. 'Perhaps every generation thinks it, and perhaps every generation says what I am about to say. But now, there does seem to be the kind of existential threat to life on earth that we have not faced. The madmen have more money and more power. The internet spreads idiocy, and the infantilisation of the west becomes unstoppable. The climate collapses, war spreads, the world burns. Where before communities or towns or perhaps regions might become caught up in a fever cult, now it spreads around the world. We are lost.'

The old Jericho, the man he'd been before ten years of travelling the earth, something malignant dying within him as he went, would have agreed with her, and morosely said nothing in response. This Jericho, the one who'd emerged from the other side of his failed search for the Pavilion, had simply said, 'And yet you can still get fresh doughnuts,' and Badstuber had accepted the joke with a sad smile and said, 'But for how long?'

He walked through the revolving door, having waited for a Japanese delegation to pass through, and then walked across the lobby of the United Nations, his phone still in hand. He was taking in everything around him, but there was little in the world now that made you blend into any surroundings like having your head bowed to your phone.

Up ahead he glanced at the procedure taken by those passing through security – a walkthrough scanner, bags run through an X-ray machine – coupled with having to show the pass to a guard on the other side, before running the pass across the scanner.

He stood for a moment taking a last look at the phone, as though sending a message, then looked up, smiled at the first guard, placed the phone, his keys and some loose change in a small tray, and walked beneath the scanner.

He collected his items on the other side, paying little attention to the security staff, and was immediately looking at his phone again as he walked on. Scanned his pass, handed it to the guard with a business-like smile, and then was on his way to the elevator. A short wait, and then he was into the elevator with eleven others, waiting his turn to press for the twenty-eighth floor.

He scrolled through a variety of news sites as they ascended, stopping every so often, people getting in and out, and then he alighted at his floor, and turned to his left, without having looked anyone in the eye. He was in New York, it wasn't like anyone would notice.

He walked along a corridor, head still down to the phone. There was a reception desk on this floor to his left, but he didn't look over. Through the waiting area, a set of double doors, and then a long, carpeted internal corridor, doors on either side. To the right the doors were all open, a long, open-plan office behind.

Most of the doors to the smaller staff offices on the left were closed, but there was an open one just ahead, not far from a water cooler. He passed the door head down, now only four doors from Elizabeth Barnes's office. There was no one else in the corridor.

'Excuse me?'

The voice from behind, in the office he'd just passed. He stopped without hesitation, turned back, put his head round the door, asking the question with his eyebrows.

There was a man who'd stepped out from behind his desk. Mid-forties, short, maybe only five one or two, dark hair and a thin moustache. Although his dark suit had a modern cut, there was something old-fashioned about him, as though he'd been with the building since its opening in 1951.

'You're looking for someone?' he asked.

Staring at your phone will only get you so far, thought Jericho.

'I'm going to Ms Barnes's office.'

'Beth won't be in today,' said the guy with the moustache, and he glanced at Jericho's pass. Jericho held it forward for him to take a closer look.

'I'm from WMO in Geneva. I was with Beth yesterday. She asked me to collect some things for her.'

'She gave you her keycard?'

There was something in the guy's tone that said she shouldn't have done it, but that he wasn't going to rugby tackle Jericho if he tried to use it.

'I can neither confirm nor deny,' said Jericho, with as close to a disarming smile as he could manage.

The moustache nodded, his eyebrow a little sceptical, then with a head shake, said, 'She always plays by her own rules.'

'That is certainly Beth,' said Jericho, sharing a moment of mild exasperation, and the guy made a gesture of agreement, said, 'Have a good day, Mr Harrison,' then turned back to his desk, waving Jericho on his way.

He walked on, came to the office door – room 2829 – and did not look round. Swiped the keycard and he was inside, the door closed quickly behind him.

He stopped, took in the office. Twenty feet by ten, a desk to the right, three large, potted plants on the floor, a small desk and three cabinets on the other side of the office, walls painted a light, greenish white, hung with several etchings of old port scenes, the far wall dominated by three large windows looking out onto the East River.

Jericho enjoyed the silence for a moment, then walked forward and looked down on the river. A cold morning, steam still rising from the water. Runners in the park on the far bank.

He turned round, placed his phone and the folder on the desk and took a quick look at the picture of the port scene on the wall behind. Port Moresby, 1871, a tall ship in dock, the rich, forested hills beyond.

Amanda had always wanted to go to Papua New Guinea. Back in the days when they used to work all their lives, and conjure up holidays they'd never go on, she'd talk of walking into the mountains without a guide, taking their chances with the weather and the wildlife and the people they'd find there.

At some point, when they'd met in New York six years previously, he'd thought to ask if she'd been to PNG on her travels, and she never had. Or, at least, she said she never had. He had long stopped accepting he could believe anything she'd ever told him.

He sat down at the desk, the top of which was completely devoid of clutter. There was the monitor, there was a plain, white telephone, there was a tray with one slim brown folder. He leant down and turned on the hard drive, clicked on the monitor, and while the Dell 5860 Tower whirred into action, he lifted the folder and took out the twenty-page document within.

Photovoltaic Cells: The Next Generation, Supply And Distribution In Sub-Saharan Africa – Changing The Continent By 2037. It was marked UN Confidential, and credited to Matteo Moretti, BSc, FBES, FIET.

He automatically closed the folder, and then immediately opened it again, and began quickly scanning through the document.

The log-in screen flickered on. Name. Password.

Even twenty years ago, Amanda had called herself a password extremist. She would never use someone's name, or a significant word or date. Her passwords were always a random series of upper and lower case letters, digits and symbols. Completely unguessable, and at least for her, as it would be for most people, completely unmemorizable.

He took out the piece of paper on which Badstuber had written the five passwords that had been included on the USB stick which had arrived randomly at her desk, and which may, or may not have come from Amanda.

Two of them looked like the kind of passwords Amanda used to create. The others featured five groups of three digits and letters, separated by hyphens.

'Nope,' muttered Jericho, looking at those three.

He quickly typed in the first of the two passwords he thought gave him the best chance.

Incorrect.

A moment's hesitation, then he tried the next.

Incorrect.

He stared at the screen, he stared at the list of passwords. More than likely he only had one chance left.

He shook his head, and put the piece of paper back in his pocket.

He pulled at the top drawer of the desk. Locked, but a simple cam lock. Nevertheless, he'd had to leave behind the lockpick he now carried everywhere with him. It wasn't something he'd wanted to be found with when passing through security.

He looked around the room, thinking that Amanda wouldn't have wanted to travel around the world, taking a small desk drawer key with her everywhere she went.

His eyes fell on the plants, three large green tubs sitting in matching basins.

'The one in the middle,' he said to Amanda, as though she might have been in the room.

He walked over to the plants, he pushed the pot in the middle slightly to the left, then to the right, and there was the small key lying beneath the pot, in the base.

He returned to the desk, wondering if Amanda had known he would end up here one day, and that he'd be able to get into the drawer without any problem. And as soon as the thought was in his head, he felt sure he was about to find the password hurriedly scribbled in a notebook.

He opened the drawer. Stationery. Paperclips, hole punch, stapler, pens, a pencil, a sharpener, an eraser, Post-it notepad, a ruler. A photograph. Amanda, perhaps ten years ago, round about the time they'd met briefly in Oslo, standing with another woman of a similar age, holding a pair of skis, a chairlift behind, beyond snowy mountains, a clear blue sky. They were both smiling and happy.

An untitled folder, which he took out and placed on the desk. Beneath that, a book, a small volume with a plain, dark blue cover. *Duplex Animo*. He opened it, looked at the publication date – 1923 – read the short inscription in pencil on the inside title page – *This is love, my love, Roderick, The Grange 23rd August 1924* – flicked quickly through the two hundred or so pages, reading none of it, then placed it back in the drawer.

There were other odds and ends scattered here, the perfect symbol for the odds and ends of anyone's life – a hair clasp, a pair of sunglasses, an iPhone charger, a CD of Arvo Pärt that would have been a gift at one point from an Estonian delegation – but no small note with a random and hurriedly jotted down row of figures.

He studied the drawer for a moment, then pushed it back in and pulled out the larger drawer beneath. This drawer was unlocked, and filled with a neat row of organised files and folders. Jericho didn't even look at them before he pushed the drawer back in. Operating manuals and procedures.

He had another rummage through the drawer, then rolled his eyes at himself and lifted the Post-it notepad, and flicked through it. Sure enough, written on a note near the bottom of the pad, a password in her old, familiar style. *hXy673$tTvV60+47zY*

He typed in the password, and this time the log-in page faded out, the screen went blank for a moment, and then the large ECOSOC logo appeared, and shortly afterwards Elizabeth Barnes's home page came up, featuring at its centre two thousand, three hundred and twenty-three unread e-mails.

24

A Friday evening in Tallinn, Estonia, some years previously. A warm day in August, the last of the daylight disappearing out to the west, as they looked down over the port from the window of the Horizonte Bar at the top of the Swissotel.

Jericho had wanted to meet Karpov in any of the dive bars in the Bermuda Triangle in the middle of the old town, but she'd travelled straight to the hotel upon arriving in the city and had insisted she wasn't leaving it again until she was heading back east the following day.

She hadn't spoken yet, but that wasn't so important. The part of the arrangement where Jericho got the measure of her wasn't dependent on her speaking.

The view of the Old Town from the Horizonte bar is, of course, blocked by the twin tower of the Swissotel, but there was the view over the port, and the sweep of Tallin bay round to Pirita, and on out past Aegna and Naissar, the islands that framed the passage to the Baltic.

Karpov wasn't taking in any of it. She was looking down twenty-three floors to the street below, as though she expected to see, at any moment, a phalanx of cars, windows blacked out, pull up outside the hotel and disgorge a team of masked, armed men.

Jericho had a gin and tonic, Karpov a vodka, no mixer, a single cube of ice. The waitress, with typical Estonian efficiency and reserve, had just placed a selection of salted snacks between them. Karpov held her glass, which was resting on the bar that ran the length of the large, floor-to-ceiling window, in her right hand, gently tapping the side of it with her index finger, her silver ring with a multitude of tiny diamonds occasionally clinking against the glass.

Jericho had already determined he'd sit there until Karpov decided to talk. Conversation wasn't going to be forced from the likes of her. Questions out of nothing would go unanswered. She would feel she had to control the discussion, and so Jericho was just going to have to play the situation, and let her think she was in charge.

Of course, she was, in fact, in charge.

Jericho took a drink – a large, round glass, with a tonne of ice – enjoyed the sharp taste on his tongue, the chill of the cold liquid hitting the back of his throat. Lifted a pretzel stick and took a bite, watched a ferry begin to slowly manoeuvre out of the harbour.

'I wish I could say I come to you at turning of tide,' said Karpov, her words suddenly appearing in the silence.

Jericho snapped from his reverie, and for a moment he felt discombobulated, as though he'd been asleep. Where had he gone? He hadn't thought it had been any further than the ferry.

He thought of the words that had broken the silence, tried to recall them, then reached up and plucked them out of the air, as though they'd been waiting there for him.

I wish I could say I come to you at turning of tide…

'When tide turns,' she continued, 'this becomes easier. Easier to find people who will talk, easier to find people who will cover for you. But now, there is only fear, and you people are being crushed by us every day. You are lost. You do not know what you are doing. It is not just… we know expertise has been lost, but it is beyond that. It is feel for game. The game.'

'You people?' said Jericho. 'You know I'm not –'

'All of you, whoever you are. MI6, CIA, FSU, like they have shit to give, police everywhere, and you, you and your ilk, lone wolves trying to save world.'

She shook her head, lifted her drink and took half of it, before placing the glass back on the table with a clank.

'What can I say?' she continued. 'We were in Washington DC. Three years, Yuri and I, before he left for that slut Maria. We played in softball league. I had friend at Russian Embassy, and we played with them. We were good. We beat Ukrainians, of course, we beat Latvians, we beat Chinese. It is easy game.

Simple, like everything Americans invented. But when we played Americans, the difference was clear. It was not that they were better, because often, not so much. Not so much better. They were fat, they could not run, they were over-confident. But they had it in blood. The game was in blood. You understand me? They did not have to think, they just did. Every move we made, every step we took, we had to think. Even after three years it did not come naturally, because we had not aged with it.

'This is where we are now in game we play. Pavilion has never stopped playing, it has never turned its back. The West? The BRICS? You have been playing tic-tac-toe while Pavilion plays three-dimensional chess. And now, suddenly, you realise you are in fight for survival.

'Russia is weak. The pieces they play are those of small power, enfeebled power. Internet trolls and little green men, flagless mercenaries worming their way into battle, unable to wage all-out war without embarrassing themselves. All the while, China rises and will one day crush you all. The west self-immolates beneath corporate greed, the young care more for human rights and three hundred different genders. There is no time for that, not while there is a war of ideology to be fought. It is too late.'

'Nice speech, Helena,' said Jericho, 'and I'm not going to argue with it. But being behind in the game isn't a reason to quit playing. We've arrived, and it doesn't matter whether it's a state agency, or Robin Hood, we're not going to get on the score sheet until we've got people like you on our side.'

Karpov snorted.

'You cannot begin to imagine places our people have been going,' she said.

'I can imagine all sorts of things.'

He held her gaze for a moment, then a cruel smirk came briefly to her lips. She shook her head, drained the vodka, placed the glass back on the bar and stared back out of the window. This time she stared far out over the bay, but she wasn't looking at the view.

'Glib comments do not sit well on you, detective,' she said. 'You are all same, all of you. As though every line from your lips is from Bruce Willis movie.'

'Tell me,' he said.

She didn't immediately answer. She lifted the glass again, accepted it was done, and placed it back down.

'Tell you what?'

'Give me an example of what it is I can't imagine,' he said. 'I mean, I don't want to sound like Bruce Willis, but really, my imagination's pretty good. I imagined you and me working together a lot earlier than you imagined it.'

Karpov smiled at him, as much with her eyes.

'You are sure you did not just imagine tits?'

Jericho looked her in the eye. She placed her elbows on the table, clasped her fingers and rested her chin on her hands.

'We will control world,' she said, 'it is inevitable. This is not question. The question is, who controls Pavilion.' A pause, her eyes turned away, out across the water. 'This is path you must follow. The guard is changing. People are dying. What once was set in stone, now crumbles. We near end, but whether it is end of an era, or end of all things, we do not –'

A bullet hole in the window, and the .300 Win Mag exploded in her forehead, removing the right half of her skull cap, and her body toppled backwards off the chair.

Jericho dived down, making himself flat to the floor.

As he did it, however, he knew he had little to worry about. If they'd been intending to kill him too, it would have already happened.

25

The Battery, a cold wind coming in off the water. A guy on a bike. A jogger. Two women pushing prams, talking animatedly, both clutching Styrofoam coffee cups. An old man slumped, asleep, on a bench. The Staten Island ferry kicking up froth, two minutes into its twenty-five minute journey.

Badstuber was sitting still and alone on a bench, looking out over the water. She had a coffee held in her hands. She wasn't wearing gloves, and looked like she was clinging to the cup for warmth.

The women with the prams made Jericho think of the man in Amsterdam, the pushchair so flippantly left in the middle of the road. His senses, frequently so sharply drawn, were now permanently taught. Every bum sleeping on a bench, every jogger, every mum with a cup of coffee, every random person walking along the street was a threat.

He sat next to Badstuber, didn't look at her, staring straight ahead at the water, watching the rear of the ferry as it churned up the waves. He felt hungry again.

'There is news?' asked Badstuber, her voice low, quiet, seeming to blend with the cold wind that whirled around the park.

'None, my lord, but that the world's grown honest,' replied Jericho after a while, and Badstuber looked at him curiously.

'I don't know where that came from,' said Jericho.

'And as true today as it was then in the state of Denmark.'

'Quite.'

'You made it in and out unmolested?'

'More or less.'

'Did you have to interact with anyone?'

'Three people in the end.'

Another two joggers came into view, side by side, a man and a woman, dressed for serious running, devices strapped to their upper arms, running in perfect, synchronized stride, as though it was something they practised. Neither of them had a backpack, their clothing, despite the weather, was skin tight. They could have no concealed weapons about them, but he watched them as they ran by all the same. They were not talking. The man looked like he might have been struggling to keep up.

Badstuber followed Jericho's gaze, and then looked at him.

'You are skittish?'

Jericho nodded, didn't speak, finally managed to take his eye away from them, and now he stared at the ground a few feet in front.

'Three people spoke to you?' said Badstuber.

'Yes. I told each of them I was picking up something for Barnes from her office, and they were all fine with it.'

'You think it was too easy?'

'It certainly felt too easy, and in the years I've been doing this, nothing has ever been easy.'

'They knew you were coming, and they allowed it to happen?'

Jericho looked out over the water, thinking it through.

'Possibly. You know, it did feel like Amanda's office. Large windows looking out on the East River. Etchings on the walls that are similar to ones we used to have in the house. There were the same houseplants she used to like. I don't think there are other specifics, though I might have missed them, but that didn't matter. Walking into the office was like walking back into her life.'

'The passwords from the USB stick were of use?'

'No,' said Jericho. 'But, as it turned out, the password was written in just the kind of place Amanda used to write them down.'

'Perhaps we should not read too much into the ease with which you gained entry,' said Badstuber. 'Amanda knew you would come one day, and she paved the way for you. Perhaps it was easy because she wanted it to be, not because the Pavilion wanted it to be.'

'Possibly.'

'I am cold,' said Badstuber, abruptly. 'Can we get something to eat while we talk?'

'Of course.'

Badstuber turned and looked back at the towering presence of the One World Trade Centre behind them.

'There is a restaurant with a view up there,' she said. 'We can be tourists while we work.'

Φ

Jericho had placed his phone in front of Badstuber, who was flicking through the images of pages he'd photographed, occasionally expanding one so she could read the text.

They were sitting at the window on the hundred and first floor, looking out over the Hudson and across the flatlands of New Jersey. The sky was a perfect pale blue, stretching to the distant horizon. They were drinking water, each eating a lobster salad. Jericho had automatically ordered the same as Badstuber. It saved him thinking.

He was trying not to look at her while she looked through the phone, forcing himself to look out over the land stretching into eternity to the west.

'Elizabeth Barnes had a renewables brief,' said Badstuber, though she may have been talking to herself.

'Yes,' said Jericho, regardless.

'Solar.'

'Yes.'

Badstuber raised her eyes.

'Is there any possibility that was a part-time job she undertook?' she asked.

'I doubt it,' said Jericho. 'I think we need to work on the basis Amanda was full-time going after the Pavilion. That was her life's work, and she was going to do it until she broke them down, or died. This, working at the ICC in The Hague, doing any of these other things she was working on, they must all have been related to different strands of her investigation.'

'Or the same strand,' said Badstuber, looking back at the phone.

'All this stuff here,' said Jericho, 'it's about solar power in the Third World. Building infrastructure, and ensuring the power created found its way to the right people, in particular people who wouldn't otherwise have been able to pay for it.'

'Free energy?' said Badstuber.

'Yes.'

'And if it's channelling the power of the sun, then we're talking unlimited free energy.'

'Yes. There's work being done here with NextEng, Solar Origin, InPhase. All market leaders. Brookheimer are talking about big upgrades, and there's funding for that coming from various agencies within the UN.'

'Nothing says global equity and fairness like the United Nations giving money to big business,' said Badstuber.

'Perhaps they would view it as payment being made, in order to make their continued existence as an energy provider obsolete,' said Jericho.

'That will never happen.'

'No.'

She ran her hand through her hair, tucking it behind her right ear, a movement Jericho found attractive, and he looked away, just as she did the same, and they both looked out over the flatlands.

'There would be a lot of people with money who would be threatened by that,' she said, her voice soft, as though she was still talking to herself. 'And while one might wonder which side the Pavilion would be on – helping people in order to get them onside, or trying to stand in the way of progress in order to protect established business and investments – organisations which hire assassins tend not to be on the right side of an argument.'

Jericho cast a quick glance her way, then turned back to the view.

Tend not to be on the right side of an argument.

He smiled to himself.

'You intend to go to the safe house in Brooklyn?' asked Badstuber.

'Yes,' said Jericho. 'Going to go back to the approach I made in the Netherlands, and knock, rather than creeping around in the dark.'

'Interesting,' she said. 'One resulted in death for the holder of the house keys, and the other resulted in sex, followed by death for the holder of the house keys. It is a tough choice.' She held his look, and then, with a dry smile added, 'Do you have a preference?'

'Funny,' said Jericho. 'I have a preference for not creeping around in the dark, that's all. Hopefully no one will die.'

'I will come with you,' said Badstuber.

'I don't think that's a good idea. We have a view of these people as having some kind of omnipotence. That they see and hear and know everything that's going on. That they have eyes on every street corner. But we don't know for sure. Perhaps they've yet to learn that you and I are working together. On the off-chance they haven't, let's not hand them the information on a plate.'

'That is fair,' she said. 'I will be stationed nearby to aid in rapid escape, should it be required.'

He thought about it for a moment, then finally took a mouthful of salad after leaving it untouched for a long while.

'Hopefully that won't be needed either, as that'd also give us away. However, I'm getting too old for all this running around, so I'll take you up on it.'

'There is a café on the corner of the opposite block,' said Badstuber. 'I will sit there and wait. You will go to Brooklyn after lunch?'

Jericho nodded.

'Next item on the list,' he said, and he took another mouthful of food.

26

He rang the bell of the brownstone, four blocks back from the East River, then lifted his eyes to the very obvious camera above the door.

The door opened. A woman in her forties, something about her that spoke of the women at the houses in the Netherlands and in London, like the keepers of the keys were all cut from the same cloth.

She already looked unhappy to see him.

'I'm looking for the relative of Elizabeth Barnes?' said Jericho, playing it straight.

The woman held his look for a few moments, and then said, 'Dead, is she?'

'I have news,' said Jericho. 'You're Ms Barnes's next of kin?'

She smiled ruefully, the laugh almost crossing her lips, then she stepped back, opening the door a little further.

'Come in,' she said.

Jericho hesitated a moment, then accepted this was why he was here, and chalices just had to be drunk from, regardless of the risks.

She led him into the sitting room at the front of the house. An open fireplace, a low flame burning. Wooden floor, covered by three rugs. Two two-seat sofas, a television. In the corner, a cupboard that spoke of a drinks cabinet. On the wall above the fireplace a mirror, and to its left, a large painting of a seventeenth-century sea battle.

There was no music playing. No sounds of any sort from inside the house. There was traffic on the street, but the windows were thick, and the sounds from outside were barely audible.

'Take a seat,' she said, indicating one of the sofas, as she sat on the other.

Jericho glanced at the painting again, trying to tick off the usual signs, but it hardly mattered. He already knew he was in the house of the Pavilion. Amanda had done her job well. These weren't breadcrumbs, these were neon signposts the height of the Pillars of Kings on the River Anduin.

'You're Anita Bergkamp?' asked Jericho.

'Yes,' she said.

'I'm sorry, I have some bad news,' said Jericho, making one last stab at playing the game. As it was, it was to be the final one.

'I know,' said Bergkamp.

'You know Ms Barnes is dead?'

'Yes, detective.'

She reached down the side of the sofa and produced a gun. Another Glock, this time a 23. Then, holding it in her left hand, she reached into the same side and brought out a Banish 45 suppressor and fitted it to the barrel.

'There's no need for a gun,' said Jericho.

'How disappointing,' said Bergkamp. 'You're wearing a wire.'

'No,' said Jericho.

He was lying. Badstuber had insisted he brought the microphone. It'd been a smart enough idea, and here he was, not used to working with someone else, and he'd instantly blown it with the clumsy piece of commentary, like an absolute beginner.

'Take it off, please,' she said, with a bored gesture. 'And to whoever's listening… I imagine you might be in a nearby van, though I'm not sure there are any likely candidates out there, which means you're more likely in Giancarlo's on the corner. Though I note if that's the case, you've at least got enough smarts not to sit in the window. Your operative is about to go dark. If you choose to intervene, the first thing that happens is he dies. The slightest sound, the slightest any old piece of shit, he dies. So you'd better hope there's not a police siren close by any time soon, because I'm going to assume the worst. And he dies. You, wire off, throw it over.'

He thought of the small device Badstuber had given him to

slip into his pocket. No wire, nothing clumsy. Just a tiny microphone he could swallow if he felt the need.

Working alone, having previously worked at a small Somerset police station, Jericho was completely detached from this kind of thing. He had no Q Branch supplying him with the latest tech, and his last ten years had been, as Haynes had observed more than once, about as old school as it was possible to be.

Another small movement of the gun.

'You know our methods well enough, Mr Jericho,' said Bergkamp. 'Kill first, don't ask questions. If you do anything with the device other than toss it gently onto the seat beside me, I'll kill you.' A moment, and then, 'Do it.'

Jericho reached into his coat pocket, lifted out the small microphone, and tossed it onto the seat. It landed in the middle of the cushion.

Bergkamp lifted the microphone, and then held it in front of her as she examined it, so that Jericho remained in her line of vision.

'Interesting,' she said. 'An off the shelf, Fukujama 750E. That's pretty up-to-date. Who are you working with?'

'I'm working alone,' he said.

'Really? And you just go about recording everything you do, on the off-chance someone, somewhere makes a confession?'

He didn't answer.

'So, who do we know uses this? Not the Brits, obviously. Your people are just about catching up with the turn of the century. They'll maybe have these by, let's say, 2050 at best.' She looked at Jericho, then smiled. 'If there is a 2050. The Taiwanese for sure. Perhaps, the Australians. Unlikely to be the French or Germans. Not sure anyone in Europe's got these yet. Maybe the Estonians or the Finns. Maybe the Swiss.'

She stared at him, thinking this through.

'That sounds right. The Swiss. But then, why are you here? There's enough for you to be investigating in Europe, and here you are instead, shuffling your way ineptly around the Big Apple.'

She placed the device on the hard wooden floor, rested her heel on it, and pressed down. A moment, and then the cracking, then she bent over, lifted it, and picked the pieces apart as much as she could.

'That should do it,' she said. 'I hope your colleague's got himself a good cup of coffee.'

'What's the story with you?' asked Jericho. 'You're indistinguishable from the women at the Amsterdam and London houses.'

'Tell me how you got the addresses?' she asked, ignoring the question.

He stared blankly back at her.

This was another thing he'd started asking himself. Amanda had either left these addresses so pretty much anyone could find them – how was she to know what the Dutch police would do with them – or she'd been far more strategic in her planning. She might have known exactly what the Dutch police would do.

Jericho thought of the woman at the computer, detached and seemingly largely disinterested in Jericho, grudgingly handing over information.

'Like I say,' said Bergkamp. 'You know our methods. Shoot first, ask later. I don't care if twenty seconds from now you're dead. And it certainly guarantees me living a little longer than my colleagues in Europe.' A pause, and then a repeated, 'Tell me.'

'I've spent the last seven years tracing the whereabouts of the collected works of William Hart Melville,' said Jericho, the lie coming to him on a whim.

He indicated the painting to the side of the fireplace.

'I found Melville's work through his association with the Pavilion,' said Jericho. 'I realised…' He pursed his lips, as though trying to decide whether she was worth confiding in. 'I realised there was a lot of money in Melville, round about the same point I realised I was wasting my time trying to pin down the Pavilion. I gave up on the latter, and switched to the former.' A pause, and then he added, 'Melville.'

Her eyes narrowed a little. Not much, but enough to let him know he might have been able to take her in.

She studied him for a moment, and then turned and looked at the painting. The picture she'd become so used to looking at stared back at her, much as it had done all these years.

'And yet, strangely, you visited both of these houses and in neither case did you bother taking the painting with you,' she said. 'Seems like a flaw in you cover story.'

'I'm not going to steal paintings from anyone so brazenly, am I?' said Jericho.

'Tell me, detective,' she said, 'I'm all ears.'

He looked like he was fed up talking about it, reluctant to give up his secrets.

'I establish where they are, I scope them, deciding whether or not they're going to be worthwhile taking the time over, and then I return for them when no one's looking.'

'Sounds just like a movie,' she said, her mockery in a slightly crooked smile. 'You could be played by Steven McQueen. Nope, dead. Who would make a good art thief? Matt Damon, maybe? Matt's good.'

Jericho didn't reply.

'But I'm not entirely sure I can believe you, unfortunately. You were in these two properties, and at least in the case of Amsterdam, you had time to remove the painting from its frame, pack it up, and be on your way. Why didn't you?'

'It's a fake,' said Jericho naturally.

She blankly held his stare, then her eyes narrowed further, her lips pursed.

The Glock was unwavering, and unusually Jericho felt a reasonable degree of certainty that she'd fire if any of her conditions were met. He wasn't entirely sure he was getting out of this alive.

'You're better than I thought you'd be,' she said.

'Why did you think anything?' he asked.

She made a small gesture with her face.

'The end game approaches,' she said. 'The stakes rise, everyone's playing a game. And you're one of them. Don't imagine you've got much more importance than anyone else, and you're a lot less important than a whole host of people.' A pause, and then, rising to her game, she said, 'You're a pinprick alongside a whole tonne of other pinpricks. Nevertheless, you made the list. And just maybe you climbed a spot or two in the rankings the last couple days. But regardless of Amsterdam or London, no one sees you as a threat.' She took a moment now, and Jericho was happy to let her talk. At least while she was talking, she wasn't shooting.

'The paintings aren't fakes, but that was nice. Thinking on your feet. Smart. That's not your reputation. That's not what it says in the notes.'

'There are notes?'

'There are always notes.'

'What's my reputation?' he asked.

'A wasted old man, barely an irritant, searching for something he'll never find, chasing shadows. They used to think you were doing it for love, and then at some point Hammersmith realised you were doing it because you didn't have anything else to do. As you have proved. You were listed as having quit the game two and a half months ago, and yet, here you are…'

'This painting's a fake,' said Jericho, with a small gesture. 'Just like the one in Amsterdam. I didn't get time to look at the London one.'

'It's not a fake,' she said.

'The signature,' said Jericho. 'Melville had a very distinctive way of looping the double L. The forger here didn't quite manage it. And the brushstrokes on the far left. That's not Melville. They imitated the style, but couldn't keep it up for the entire,' and he finished the sentence with a sweep of the hand.

She kept her eyes on him, and then, gun held steady, turned to look at the painting. Just a moment, and then she turned back.

'You don't know Melville,' said Jericho.

'I'm not sure you do either, but here's the question? Does it matter?'

'Because of the Pavilion connection, Melvilles don't come on the market often, but when they do – and if the originals have been stolen, you might well find they have – that's a lot of money they're going for. It doesn't matter how much money the Pavilion has stashed under its mattress, no one likes to lose who knows how many paintings with a black market value in excess of tens of millions. Someone's ripping you off.'

'And why do you care?' she asked.

'I don't. I was going to steal it, and now there's no point, because someone else got here first.'

'Too bad for you.'

'Too bad for you,' he said.

'Why?'

'How long have you been in charge here? Your counterpart in London had been there seventeen years. Well, someday someone's going to come along and do an inventory of this place, and boom,' and he indicated the painting, 'ten million dollars of Pavilion property's going to have gone missing on your watch.'

'Ten million dollars, eh?'

'Conservative estimate.'

She was beginning to buy into the lie, thought Jericho.

Despite herself.

She made a gesture towards the painting with the gun, though the barrel was quickly directed back at Jericho.

'Show me,' she said.

'You want me to get up?'

'Sure, you can get up. And you can walk to the picture, and you can show me. And all it means is I'll be standing a little closer to you, and I'll kill you even more quickly if you try something dumb.'

Jericho nodded his agreement, then got to his feet and approached the painting. She watched him warily for a moment or two, and then followed, standing just outside arm's length, so that it would take a double movement in order for him to get to the gun.

'You know what we have here?' asked Jericho, then didn't wait for a reply, and described the painting anyway. 'This is Encounter during the Battle of Kijkduin, from the third Anglo-Dutch war. This is Melville imitating Willem van de Velde, the Younger. So, what you have is someone copying Melville copying van de Velde, and looks like they just got a little lost along the way…'

'Are you just going to talk forever in the hope I get bored and don't shoot you. Because, believe me, I hate being bored. The shooting gets closer with every wasted word.'

'Like I was saying about the loop of the double-L. You're not going to want to look at your phone, but when you get the time, check out Melville's signature. And you'll see here the artist didn't get it quite right. It's like a typo in a manuscript.'

He glanced at her. She saw him take note of the exact positioning of the gun.

'Anything else?' she asked.

He surveyed the painting, then indicated a patch of sea in the left-hand corner.

'Well, again, you're going to have to come up here and take a closer look, but you can see the brushstrokes here are all wrong. It's like… I don't know, I'm not going to say they were rushed, but there's just something not right. Maybe the artist ended up copying van de Velde's brushwork, rather than Melville's.'

'Here's the thing, cowboy,' she said, her tone speaking loudly of boredom, 'thing is, no one's going to care. Like, seriously, this whole thing, all this Melville crap that's going on, no one gives a shit. Merrick doesn't like Melville, and he's all that matters, so,' and she let the sentence go and shrugged.

'Who's Merrick?' asked Jericho, giving her a sideways glance.

He caught the wave of annoyance at herself, and then she made another gesture with the gun.

'Sit down,' she said.

'I don't think so,' said Jericho.

'You don't?' Bergkamp laughed. 'Wow, OK, guess I'll shoot you where you are.'

'It's not like I'm looking to make it easier for you to shoot me,' said Jericho.

She made a rueful face, then jerked the gun again in the direction of the sofa.

'Pretty please with bells on, will you sit down?'

'Fine,' said Jericho.

He took one step in the direction of the sofa, then moved. A swing of the arm, as he dived forward, low to the ground, aiming for her legs. He caught her hand. The gun jerked to the side, but she held on to it. The two rounds she let off thudded harmlessly into the floor, missing Jericho by millimetres. He grabbed her legs, she brought the butt of the gun down brutally to the side of his face. He grunted. The fight, the tension, went out of his arms. Then, her legs free of his grasp, she raised her boot, and kicked him viciously in the same spot she'd just hit him with the gun.

Jericho fell back further, she stepped in the opposite direction, control re-established, gun still in her hand, looking down at him.

'Jesus,' she said, 'every damn time. What is it with fucking men? They see a woman with a gun and they think, well this shouldn't be too hard.'

'They never learn, do they?' said the cold voice.

Bergkamp froze. Jericho looked behind her, then back at the calculation that was running across her face.

'Drop the weapon,' said Badstuber. 'If you do anything else before dropping the weapon, I'll shoot.'

Bergkamp ran through her options. But this was the Pavilion, and she knew the endgame was in play. There was no surrendering at gun point. You took your chances, and you walked away or you didn't.

She raised her hands as she turned, the gun still held in her right hand.

'What did I just say?' said Badstuber.

Bergkamp brought the gun down, and in the same moment, Badstuber, adjusting to the quick descent of her arm, shot her in the hand, and the gun flew out of her fingers. Bergkamp grimaced, but there was no more thinking to be done, and she did as Jericho had done to her, diving towards Badstuber's legs.

Badstuber shot her in the back as she made contact, and then put another bullet into the top of her neck to make sure, as Bergkamp's body slumped dully and dead to the ground.

Jericho was on all fours, looking up at Badstuber, the blood starting to run following the second blow to the side of the face.

'Thanks, but I had it covered,' he said.

'Sure,' said Badstuber. 'Come on, we need to get out.'

'We have a minute or two to check this place.'

'Not unless you want shot at again,' she said. 'We're leaving.'

27

'I cannot find anything,' she said.

She had joined him in the bathroom of her apartment in Two Bridges, and was doing a more thorough job on his head.

'Merrick?' said Jericho.

'There is no player of any significance with that name,' she said. 'Obviously there are people called Merrick, and equally some of them are wealthy, but we will need more. There is no one of that name with any known association with the Pavilion, or any of its members, such as we've ever known them to be.'

'What about in the tech world, in Bitcoin, in renewables, anything...' and the words disappeared as another sharp pain jabbed at the side of his head, then he continued, 'anything related to any of the strands we've been seeing with the Pavilion?'

'Nothing,' said Badstuber. 'You are OK?'

'I took a boot to the head,' said Jericho, another small scowl sweeping across his face. 'Sharp, jabbing head pain to be expected.'

'I should take you for an X-ray.'

'Makes sense,' he said, 'but we can't. We seem to have managed to be incognito here, even though these people are obviously on the lookout for me. So let's just stay where we are.'

She caught his eyes in the mirror, then nodded.

'Now I clean your wound,' she said. 'I will use an antiseptic lotion. It will sting,' she added, at the exact moment she applied the cotton bud soaked in TCP. Jericho, knowing it was coming in any case, managed not to wince at the touch.

'How did you get into the house in Brooklyn?' asked Jericho, and she gave his eyes another quick glance.

'In the back. It was not difficult.'

'The place wasn't alarmed?'

'I disabled the alarm.'

He half smiled at her, and she curiously returned the look.

'You're better at this than me,' he said.

'Yes.'

'You know the name Hammersmith?' he asked.

'Like the area of London, but not the area of London?'

'Exactly that,' said Jericho. 'It's a person she mentioned. I got the impression it's someone who's keeping tabs on people who are keeping tabs on the Pavilion. They have a list, it seems. I wasn't considered high risk,' he added, ruefully.

'That is good. If you were high risk, you're more likely to be dead.' Another small wince from Jericho, as she dried the area of the wound. 'There is also the possibility that you are considered the most important person on their wanted list, but she did not want to give you the satisfaction of the knowledge.'

'Hmm,' said Jericho. 'Let's hope I'm not the most important person on their list, because if I am, that's a damned short list, and no one else is anywhere near them.'

She was studying the wound closely, running her fingers softly down the side of it.

'I will apply three stitches. It will hopefully not leave a scar, though if it does, I do not think it will adversely affect your looks. You need not worry.'

'I've always been greatly concerned with my looks,' said Jericho.

She stopped for a moment, looking at him in the mirror, then she said, 'You are joking.'

'Yes.'

She got to work with the suture, and Jericho closed his eyes, so that she didn't see him watching her at work.

'You've spent a lot of time on the Pavilion since you joined the FIS?' he asked.

Silence for a moment, and he did not push her for an answer, allowing her to concentrate, then she said, 'Some.'

He waited for a little more, and then looked at her when nothing was coming.

'That's it?'

She was focusing on the job.

Eventually she said, 'I will admit it was why I joined. Since then, I have spent a lot of my spare time on the Pavilion, but I have been wary. I did not want to make the waves.'

'You think they might have operatives within the agency?'

'It is impossible to know, but the reach of the organisation, such as we understand it, would suggest that they will have operatives all around the world. I did not want to put a target on my back, any more than there might already be one.'

'Because of Oslo?'

'Yes. If there is someone at the FIS affiliated to the Pavilion, there is no doubt they will be aware of my presence. They will have been waiting for me to make a play.'

'You think they could know you're here now?' he asked. 'You think they could be listening?'

Another moment, Jericho felt a slight tightening of the skin, and then the quiet clink of her laying the needle down on the side of the sink.

'Anything is possible,' she said. 'But I have swept this place for tracking and listening devices, and found nothing. When I purchased the property, I made every effort to ensure its existence and location was unknown to anyone within the organisation. I believe it is secure.'

'The FIS are OK with you having this kind of place?' asked Jericho.

'We are not discouraged.'

'Why New York?'

'New York is as much the centre of the world as anywhere. Previously, London would have made sense, but now the UK is diminished. America is in decline, but for my working lifetime, it will likely remain the sensible place in which to position oneself in a variety of fields.

'Were my children to find themselves in a similar position, I would of course advise Beijing.'

She applied a small bandage, pressing the adhesive gently against his skin, and then started clearing up.

'We are finished,' she said.

Jericho turned his head a little, looking at the bandage, and then got to his feet.

'Thank you,' he said.

'You are welcome.'

'Did you find anything?' he asked.

'In your wound?'

'About the Pavilion.'

'It has been largely fruitless,' she said. 'I have remembered it all, however. One never knows when something from the past will become important.' She paused, then added, 'I will say if that happens. We should eat. Then we must decide if there is further use to remaining in New York, or whether it would make sense for you to lie low here for a short time while you recover.'

'Recover from what?'

'You have been shot, you have received head trauma. There will be cause and effect, and the effect here is that your physical and perhaps mental capacity will be diminished.'

They stared at each other in the bright light of the small bathroom. He wanted to be annoyed at her blunt practicality, but he was at a stage, of course, where he likely couldn't be annoyed at her about anything. In any case, she wasn't wrong.

'I'll be fine,' he said, nevertheless. 'There's something else we need to do in New York, but when that's done, we leave. We need to go to Amsterdam. Then Switzerland.'

'We are in a struggle against perhaps the most pervasively corrupt and dangerous organisation the world has ever known,' said Badstuber. 'It would be good if you were not distracted by head pains, and did not start bleeding from your side wound.'

'There's that,' he said.

Nevertheless, there was no time to recover, and they both knew it.

28

'The art world is a mire of corruption,' said Badstuber.

They were eating dinner, while talking about Jericho's previous visit to New York, taking a look at the Melville painting, and unexpectedly encountering Amanda.

Badstuber had gone to a deli three shop fronts away, and returned with pizza. Not nearly enough, Jericho had thought, but it would do. Probably best not to be stuffed, given the frequency with which life-threatening circumstances kept being thrown his way.

Two slices of pepperoni, two slices of mushroom each. This was dinner.

'It is ripe for it,' she continued. 'The world is used to these stories. The bidding war, the painting that is valued at one million and goes for ten. The painting that sells for twenty million one year, and then two hundred million the next. These are no longer newsworthy. The great artists are now little but a conduit for global corruption. Although, it can be seen that it has diminished in scale since the arrival of crypto.'

She took a bite of pizza, and then said, 'What do you know of Amanda's time here?'

'Only what she told me that day, and I've no way of knowing whether it was true.'

Badstuber had returned with two bottles of carbonated water. Jericho had kept his mouth shut.

'She said the Pavilion was not in any way related to the Whistler,' said Jericho, pausing long enough for Badstuber to say, 'Of course.' 'But working there gave Amanda credibility within the business, and gave her access to all the major auction houses and bidding wars. People trusted her, and she... she had skills.'

Badstuber asked the question with her eyebrows raised, her mouth full of food.

'She could read people, and she could play them. She could be whoever she needed to be in any given situation. We were married all those years, and I never knew when she was acting. I mean,' he said, and he made a small gesture, 'yes, I trusted her in our marriage, I always did. But when we were with other people, and particularly in the beginning when we worked together, her range was amazing. She played the part like... I don't know, Meryl Streep. What we saw in Oslo? It was as though the script called for an action hero, and the director had said, do this, shoot these people, do the next thing, go there, hit your mark, aim the weapon, and she was as good at that as she was at walking into a crowded room and learning five secrets from every person there by the end of the night.'

'She wasn't a spy? Are you sure?'

'One hundred percent certain she worked for the insurance company,' said Jericho. 'I never doubted it. Then she got entangled with the Pavilion, and...' and he finished the sentence with a fly away gesture.

He took a bite of food, his look slipping away across the small room.

'This is an impossible organisation for one person to beat,' said Badstuber. 'Nevertheless, she made inroads, she did damage to them, and now she has left us the clues to allow us to continue her work.'

'Yes.'

'You would like to go to the Whistler Gallery in the morning?' asked Badstuber.

'No,' said Jericho. 'I want to go tonight. You confident you can break in and hack a computer?'

She stared across the table, a pizza crust held lightly in her fingers.

'You are not joking?'

'I want to steal the Melville.'

Badstuber straightened her shoulders.

'There is no other way to get hold of a Melville?'

'We could go back to the brownstone, but I don't want to

get shot at.'

'What makes you think you won't be shot at at the Whistler?'

'They won't know I'm there.'

'That sounds far-fetched.'

'We'll see.'

'Why do you want a Melville?'

'To study an original, to see if it gives up any secrets.'

'Have you previously given thought to breaking into the Whistler?'

'Right down to planning it,' he said.

'But you never carried out the plan.'

'It would have been impossible, acting alone, and given my limited resources. And, let's be honest, limited skillset.'

'Now you are no longer alone.'

'Exactly.'

'I do not have many resources, and I'm unsure of my skillset.'

'I'll lay out the plan, and you can let me know what you think. If you say no, then we're getting on a plane back to the Netherlands. If you think we've got a chance, then Thunderbirds are go.'

She stared blankly across the table.

'Thunderbirds?'

'Yes.'

'Where are they going?'

Jericho smiled.

'I'll tell you the plan,' he said.

29

Jericho arrived at the Whistler Gallery at eight-thirty, just before last entry. He passed through room two-ninety-eight, to make sure the Melville was where he'd understood it to be – it remained in the same spot as the previous time he'd been there – though he paid it no attention.

He spoke to no one, he lingered over none of the art, though he did not hurry anywhere. In all regards, he looked like someone who was walking through the Whistler, purely because that was one of the things one does in New York, rather than for a love of art.

Seven minutes before closing time he visited the bathroom on the third floor, and entered a cubicle. There were three others in the bathroom. He hung up his coat, took off the dark-rimmed glasses he'd been wearing, removed his long coat, hung it on the back of the door, and then exited the cubicle. His blue overalls were now revealed.

He made his way to the toilets on the third floor, opposite the Art of The Americas. Of the ten bathrooms in the facility, these were the only ones not to have been recently renovated, the revamp cancelled in the midst of Covid lockdowns, and yet to be restarted.

Unlike the other bathrooms, where the cubicle doors were cut the traditional six inches off the floor, and flush to the top of the stall, the three cubicles in this bathroom were enclosed. Doors to the floor, sides of the stall to the ceiling.

He entered the cubicle on the far right of five. Head torch

out of his pocket and fitted, then he was up onto the seat. There was no one else in the bathroom at that moment, but he flushed the toilet in any case, and would flush it again as soon as the noise faded away, and then he reached into his pocket, took out the Tanhauser jabsaw, and began cutting through the PVC roofing.

He cut to the back of the ceiling to get to a point where he'd be able to apply his weight to haul himself up, then fingers set, large hole cut, piece of the ceiling pushed up and to the side, and he was up and into the darkness, illuminated by the narrow beam of the torch.

He hauled himself up into place, then lowered the ceiling fitment back down. Anyone paying attention would immediately see what had been done, but hopefully no one was going to be paying too much attention.

Now he was in a narrow shaft that ran vertically through the building, and he was quickly walking along, bent over, removing himself from the scene of entry.

'Hey,' he said quietly.

'You are in?' asked Badstuber, into the small earpiece in his left ear.

'Yes,' said Jericho. 'Making my way east.'

'You will come to a circuit board on your right,' said Badstuber. 'Five yards beyond that, you will have access to move back across towards the centre of the building.'

Jericho smiled to himself. They'd spent an hour going over the plans.

'Are you going to spend the rest of our lives telling me what to do when I already know?' he said.

There was a short pause, and then she replied, 'Only when I consider it necessary.'

He reached the turning, and then moved quickly along, a little more room in this central passageway.

'You've added one to the number of people exiting the building already?' he asked.

'There was a large group of seventeen who used the 82nd Street exit at the same time, and I added one at that point. It will have gone unnoticed. You are effectively no longer in the building.'

'Thank you.'

Before leaving, she had insisted on augmenting the stitches in his side, since he would be manoeuvring himself through awkward spaces and angles. In the still light of day, removed from the adrenaline of action, the stitching had been painful. She'd apologised three times.

He'd been grateful for it as he'd hauled himself up into the ceiling.

He found his way to the stairwell that led down to the floor below, moved silently down the steps, put himself in position near the vent that led to room two-ninety-eight, then settled into position.

He would have some time to wait.

'The eagle has landed,' he said.

A familiar pause, and then Badstuber said, 'You are more flippant now than I remember.'

Jericho didn't reply.

'I like it,' she said, 'though perhaps you could save it for some time when your life is not in peril, and we do not stand on the precipice of global calamity.'

Jericho couldn't help the laugh.

Φ

Nine thirty-seven. The museum cleared of visitors; guards and cleaning staff making rounds.

There had been no talk between Jericho and Badstuber. The less chatter the better, she had observed, something which they both considered applied to almost every situation, though particularly ones such as this.

'You are ready?' came her voice, quietly into his right ear.

'Yes,' said Jericho.

'The alarm will go off in thirty seconds,' she said. 'The last room to be vacated was one-thirty-four, which is far enough away to draw staff well clear of you. I will focus the alarm there.'

'Good,' said Jericho.

'Good luck,' she tossed in unexpectedly.

'Thank you.'

A pause, and then she said, 'Thunderbirds are go.'

The smile flashed briefly across Jericho's face as the alarm went off. From down below, and up above, the sound of rapid footsteps, and then quickly, shutters falling in exhibition rooms, closing them off. Not all at once, but in ones and twos in rapid succession, a rainfall of closing doors, the sound clanking through the building.

Jericho came to the end of the vent, having already checked out the screws, then quickly, electronic screwdriver in hand, loosened the vent cover, placed it behind him, stuck his head out into room two-ninety-eight, red flashing lights from the corridors infiltrating the room through the bars of the security door, then he lowered himself down, and quickly made his way to the painting.

'About to lift the Melville,' he said.

'I will keep the security door locked as long as possible.'

Hands to the side of the frame – the painting roughly a metre and a half wide – he paused a moment, set himself for rapid action, then lifted the frame from the wall, rested it against his body as the alarm in this room suddenly added to the cacophony, then he pulled out his pliers, cut the security cord attaching the frame to the wall, and lowered the frame to the ground.

They'd discussed the quickest way to remove the painting from the frame, Badstuber suggesting he just cut the canvas around the edges. Now that he was here, however, he couldn't bring himself to do it.

'There's time,' he muttered.

Knife in hand, he eased the back of the frame off, and then carefully lifted the canvas out of position.

'Hey!' a shout from behind, footsteps clattering to a halt by the door.

He rolled up the canvas, held it close to his chest, and then turned.

What did he have now?

One man, gun in hand. Other footsteps approaching. Once there were guards on both sides of the room, he was finished.

'Drop it! Drop it!'

Jericho dropped the knife, then held his hands a little to the side, the rolled up painting in his left hand.

'Drop the painting! Down on the floor!'

He flicked his right hand. The Ruger LCP fell into his fingers, and he fired two quick shots above the guard's head.

It was enough. The guard returned fire, but he was moving as he did so, and Jericho was running back towards the vent.

He let off another warning round behind him, intentionally high again, though he wasn't looking, then he came to the wall, momentum full on, one foot halfway up the wall, and he was leaping for the opening. Tossed the painting ahead of him in an uncomfortable movement, but it was enough, and he was up and into the vent as the bullets clattered into the wall around him from both sides.

'Robert?'

'Back in the vent,' he said.

'You have the painting?'

'Roger.'

And now he thrust the painting down his back, inside the overalls, and then he was climbing up the stairs two at a time, and quickly making his way back along towards the toilet.

It was basic, but it was Plan A, and he would find out if it worked when he got there.

Ten yards short of his original makeshift entry point into the shaft, there was a light up ahead, as the door he'd created in the ceiling was pushed aside, and a head and torch appeared directly in front of him.

'Stop!'

Jericho turned, and lowering himself as much as he could, headed quickly back towards the turn into the middle of the building.

'What was Plan B again?' he asked.

He heard the low curse on the other end of the line.

It had always been going to come to this. His plan had never been sophisticated enough to just allow him to walk back out the front of the building.

'Up one floor,' she said. 'Turn left. There is a door to the roof. I will open it from here.'

Jericho was up the stairs, two at a time, then running along to his left.

All around the sound of alarms; from below, shouting and footsteps; and creeping in through the small spaces, the whirl of flashing lights.

Along to the end of the corridor, coming up to the door.

He tried the handle. Nothing.

Triple bolt on the inside, electronically operated. A double mortice lock.

'That lockpick's not going to do you any good,' he muttered.

'I am working on it,' she said into his ear.

'No rush,' he said.

He turned his back to the door, looking along the dark

corridor. Shouting from below, and then the sound of footfall on the stairs.

'I've got less than ten seconds,' he said.

She didn't reply.

Then, 'Now!' she said, more urgency in her voice, and he turned as the door sprung open, then he was through and out into the night, and as he slammed the door shut, he had another look at the face of the woman who'd followed his path up into the maintenance shaft.

In the moment the door closed, her gritted teeth, the raised gun, the shot pinging into the metal door.

30

The roof of the Whistler is a small city in itself. Covering fourteen acres, in countless sections, some of which are two floors lower than others. Concrete sections, and arches, and glass ceilings, and grass, buildings of various sizes, a maze in the dark, as Jericho sprinted across, aiming for the side of the building backing on to Central Park.

Up here, the sounds of the city in the evening, a familiar low rumble, a siren somewhere downtown. Shouts from the street, and then from elsewhere in the roof. Then overhead, a helicopter. Another. And then searchlights sweeping across the park, now zigzagging back and forth across the roof.

He climbed up steps, and ran across a section of corrugated iron, his footfalls clanging loudly in the night. The helicopter approached, and he dived into the side, pressing his back against the wall of another building, beneath an arch which was one of a few in a short row. The beam swept past and he couldn't believe it hadn't spotted him, the end of it barely seeming to miss his feet. And then he was up again, to the far end of the low, flat section, and then he was jumping down, landing awkwardly on his ankle, and running across to the next ladder fixed into the wall.

'Robert?'

'I'm good,' he said.

Breathless.

She knew not to ask anything further.

The second helicopter overhead. The light swept by, and

then as he started to move, swung back, and now he was in the full beam.

'Hands in the air! Put your hands in the air!'

Up onto the next level, he pressed close to the side of a wall, as a bullet, then another, pinged off the roof next to him.

Then he was onto the glass roof of the Classical Wing, hell bent on escape, and trusting fully in its capacity to hold him.

A crack of glass, and he kept on running. Another gun shot, though the helicopter's light was now struggling to find him. Then he was closing in on the edge and running full pelt.

The top half of the wall, the glass half, was at a forty-five degree angle, and this was the plan he'd hoped to avoid. Run full pelt to the end, then slide down the glass on his backside, before flying into the trees at the end, as he'd done in London.

Heart in mouth, and he was over the side, as another trio of bullets splintered the glass around him, and then he was off the end of the building, careering full pelt into the trees, clutching at branches before thudding abruptly against the trunk of the tree, and only the last gasp of a grab at a branch prevented him crashing to the ground in one continuous movement.

The branch broke. Jericho thumped into the ground. He grunted loudly.

All around, helicopters and sirens, shouts from the rooftops, and from within the park, a cacophony of noise, Jericho's ears bursting. His ankle hurt, and his back hurt, and he couldn't lie there, and he winced as he got to his feet, and then he started running through the trees, and he hobbled and nearly fell, and the pain shot through his body, but he knew he couldn't stop, and then he was running out onto Fifth, and he dodged one car, receiving a loud hoot, and then he got the light, and he was across the road, down 85th then turning into Madison, and the street was still busy, and he slowed, and there was some scaffolding up, and he pressed in against a wall, out of the light, and took off the overalls, which were intentionally kept loose at the ankles, and he dumped them into the side, and then he walked back out, painting in hand, tagging onto the back of a group of six Japanese tourists, three of whom were looking at maps, three of whom were looking at the sky.

Jericho did not say anything, but walked behind them, pointing up at the buildings, as though their tour guide.

The Japanese walked on across the next junction. Jericho turned down 86th.

31

He was badly bruised again, but had no new cuts. The stitches in the wounds in his side and in his head had remained intact.

'You will not die,' Badstuber had said when she'd stripped him naked to make sure he was OK.

Another shower, and now they were sitting at the table in the small living space, the Melville painting laid out, taking up the entire table.

Melville had been a shapeshifter of an artist, occupying a variety of different styles, borrowing, lifting, reimagining, either trying his hand at different genres of painting, or being paid to do the same.

The one hanging in the Whistler was another done after the fashion of Pieter Bruegel the elder. A village scene in winter, though not one with a landscape, distant hills, and a large frozen lake. This was a more intimate village scene. Buildings all around, snow on the roofs. A queue of people waiting at the door of the burgemeester. Children playing in the foreground. A couple of frozen ponds, a lone skater in one, though there was hardly room for them to turn. A pig roasting on a spit. A seller of pots. A child skipping. A fool and his money being easily parted.

There were two banners flying on the roof of the town hall. One bore the image of a two-headed eagle, a goat clutched beneath it in its claws; the other, a unicorn and a griffin, head-to-head.

'Have you ever studied a Melville intimately before?' asked Badstuber.

They had already gone over the reverse of the canvas, and found nothing of interest. If there was anything to be found, it would be in the painting. And Jericho had already looked.

'Only online. This is the first time I've had a canvas in my hands, and I don't see anything I haven't seen previously.'

They studied the painting in silence, conversation coming in fits and starts.

'You have access to an art restorer?' asked Badstuber.

'What are you thinking?'

'Often when art is cleaned, details are unearthed, hidden either beneath layers of varnish or dirt, or because the artist painted over something he wanted hidden. Usually it would be because he'd changed his mind, or had made a mistake, but perhaps it would also be a way of leaving a hidden message.'

'A message that could only be revealed by destroying the original artwork?'

'Yes.'

'And which, if it's still intact now, was obviously not revealed at the time of its original painting, and delivery to the Pavilion.'

She nodded, her eyes still wandering over the picture, her fingers, in nitrile gloves, resting gently on the canvas.

'What d'you think this painting is valued at?' asked Jericho.

'You have not checked?'

'No.'

'In the region of three million dollars.'

'You did check?'

'When it was gifted to the museum, that was the reported valuation. Perhaps now, it would be more. Perhaps, given the connection to the Pavilion which the valuers of the time would have been unaware of, it is ten times more. I do not know.'

'So we're taking a painting valued at anywhere between three and thirty million dollars, and removing all the paint, on the off-chance William Melville decided to leave a message for future generations beneath the conventionality of a Bruegel village-scape?'

She studied the painting, and then gave him a slight side-eye.

'Perhaps it is more than thirty million. You are concerned this makes you even more of a thief?'

'I think it probably does,' he said.

133

'We better hope you do not get caught in possession of it,' she said drily. 'Do you think Professor Leighton would be willing to take a look? You would be giving her stolen property, after all.'

'We'll return to Amsterdam via London, and I'll speak to DI Haynes.'

She nodded, she looked at her watch.

'I will make the booking. We will not travel together. You shall go to London first, and then travel on to the Netherlands. I will travel a little behind you, and go straight to Amsterdam. I will meet you there.' And then, 'I do not know why we are returning to Amsterdam.'

'There's someone I need to speak to,' said Jericho, and Badstuber nodded.

'This is good,' she said.

32

Jericho was waiting for Haynes in a Starbucks, landside of Heathrow Terminal 1, reading the news.

He wondered if he'd be all over New York internet by now. It seemed everything was caught on camera these days, and he was expecting the theft of a valuable artwork from under the noses of Whistler security to be big news, in the Big Apple at least. His face caught on security cameras, and random video footage of him sliding down the side of the building, before blundering into the trees.

There was no video, no security camera footage, no news of a theft, no drama. Nothing.

Had they let him take the painting, and then allowed him the illusion of a dramatic escape? There had been quite a few gunshots fired in his direction, and none had hit. Perhaps they'd been firing at him the way he'd fired at them.

But they couldn't have known he was coming. Even though the Pavilion knew he was in New York, stealing the Melville was hardly an obvious next step. And he stole from the Whistler, not the Pavilion. Was there really no relationship between the two?

This is what conspiracy theory does to you, he thought. The labyrinthine paths down which it leads are endless. There's nowhere it can't go, and so your mind becomes increasingly bogged down, there are ghosts and signs on every corner, demons lurking in every shadow, and every event is easily twisted to fit the narrative, so that it no longer seems like you're twisting anymore.

Perhaps, he wondered, it just wasn't news because there was so much awfulness out there in the world. He'd been so wrapped up in his own story, he hadn't noticed that over the previous few days the world had seemingly lurched ever closer to global conflict. The US Navy was approaching the South China Sea, with the Chinese ready to positively respond. And with the US – as well as Russia – becoming ever more wrapped up in Israel-Iran, the conflict spreading across the eastern approaches of Europe, and now to the Arctic Circle, not to mention American difficulties on their own southern border, and nascent rebellion in five Democrat-controlled states, the Chinese sensed distraction and weakness.

The Chinese, it was being suggested, were on the verge of taking all the self-inflicted wounds necessary to crash the economy of the western world. The Chinese economy had been weakening, and western commentators had begun to think they were pushing for war, of whatever scale might be necessary.

With so many conflicts to get the fingers of internet users of the world clicking, did the theft of a single obscure painting from the Whistler amount to a hill of beans?

Possibly not.

'Hey.'

Detective Inspector Haynes smiled as he sat down, placing the coffee beside him. On the side of the cup was written the word Stout.

Jericho nodded, then couldn't help the wry look at the cup.

'What happened there?' he asked.

'The girl couldn't cope with the name Stuart.'

'Perhaps she's passing comment on your weight gain?'

Haynes took a drink, rolling his eyes.

'I think I preferred the old you,' he said. 'Remember the grumpy one, who never used to make any jokes, never mind vaguely offensive ones?'

A moment, then Jericho discarded the throwaway reply that was on the tip of his tongue, and instead said, 'Thanks for coming.'

'No problem. What've you been up to in the last two days? I see you managed to avoid arrest in London. At least, you're here, and when I checked, there was no mention of you being arrested.'

'Went to the house. Slept with the woman who ran the

joint. At first she mistook me for a Pavilion operative, then she wised up. But when she was about to turn me in, head office obviously decided she couldn't be trusted and turned up, all guns blazing, to do something about it. I got away, she died.'

'How'd you get away?'

'Ran across the rooftops, then jumped into a tree.'

Haynes looked at him curiously.

'No, really, how did you get away?'

'I don't know what to tell you. I literally jumped into a tree, grabbing branches as I fell.'

'And when you say all guns blazing?'

'Guns fired inside the property, as I was getting out, and then fired on the rooftops as the woman and I were effecting our getaway.'

'And this was Tuesday night?'

'Very early hours of Wednesday morning.'

Haynes leaned forward, elbow on the table, hand rubbing his chin.

'It went unreported?' asked Jericho.

'Nothing. I've been checking, but there was nothing so dramatic reported early Wednesday morning. No gunfire, and certainly no report of a dead body. Any chance her corpse is still up on the roof?'

'She fell onto… it would've been Grove Lane. Dead as she fell, I think.'

'Damn,' muttered Haynes. 'So they cleared up their own rubbish, and made sure no one was talking about it.'

'And assuming someone somewhere reported at least the gunfire to the police, then that would mean there was someone within your service making sure this isn't news,' said Jericho.

'Damn,' said Haynes, again.

'Which would tie in with what happened in New York.'

Haynes's eyes widened a little, then he asked the question with a *do I really want to know* look.

'Go on,' he said.

'Ilsa came with me. She's taken leave, so working in an unofficial capacity.'

'So she says,' said Haynes, and Jericho made a small gesture to indicate that was possible. 'She's a spy,' Haynes continued. 'They are literally trained and then paid to lie to you.'

'I trust her, but I guess you're right,' said Jericho.

'So, what happened in New York?'

'Went to Amanda's office in the UN. She was working on clean energy for the Third World. Apparently. Then I went to the Pavilion safe house. That turned ugly, then just as I was about to be shot by the latest female protagonist in the drama, Ilsa arrived and killed her. We ran, and this time, no one came after us.

'Then I went to the Whistler Gallery and stole a Melville painting.'

'You stole a painting from the Whistler? Who even are you?'

'I've expanded my skillset, though I couldn't have done it without Ilsa.'

'Did anyone notice?'

'Yes. And there was more gunfire, and again I managed to escape. Fortunately, neither Ilsa nor anyone else was with me as I committed the crime, so no one died.'

'That's a relief,' said Haynes. A moment, and then he realised where the story was going. 'And today, this thing isn't news.'

'No, it's not.'

'Was your escape dramatic?'

'I don't know if you'd call it dramatic.'

'You walked out the front door dressed as a security guard?'

'I ran across the roof. There were people shooting at me from helicopters. I leapt off the roof and slid down the window, fell into the trees, then ran through Central Park, before blending into late-night revellers on Madison and 86th.'

Haynes stared deadpan across the table.

'What would you call dramatic?' he said.

'I don't know. Something Tom Cruise would do.'

'That is exactly what Tom Cruise would do.'

Haynes shook his head, then took another drink. Laid down the cup.

'And you've been looking, and none of this has been reported,' he asked.

'That's correct.'

'Have you checked social media to see if there's anything, you know, random footage taken by someone in the park of the getaway?'

'I looked, Ilsa looked, we found nothing.'

'That's strange,' said Haynes. Then, 'But it's the same with the death in the Netherlands, by the way. Far as the police know, it didn't happen.'

'Hmm,' said Jericho.

'And ditto for those addresses you gave me. Just regular addresses, owned by regular people who appear to check out. But I'll keep rooting around, try to see if I can find out who's covering this stuff up.'

'That'd be good, if you can,' said Jericho. 'I don't think you'll get anywhere though.'

'Why am I here then?'

'I need you to get the painting examined.'

Haynes stared across the table.

'The painting you stole?'

'Yes.'

'What value of painting are we talking about?'

'Somewhere between three and thirty million dollars, though maybe more.'

Haynes's eyes drifted down to the bag at Jericho's feet, then slowly lifted again.

'It's folded into that bag, is it?'

'Very carefully. I didn't want to walk through the airport with an obvious painting tube. Plus I didn't have a painting tube.'

'And having committed the crime of grand larceny, now you want to involve a serving police officer by passing the stolen goods onto him.'

'It's not good, is it?' said Jericho.

'No.'

'I know, I'm sorry. I promise to return the painting after we're finished with it.'

'I'm sure that'll knock thirty years off your sentence. Wait, our sentences.'

'Again, I'm sorry to involve you. And Margot.'

Haynes looked disappointed, and then started nodding his understanding. Of course Jericho was going to want to involve his wife.

'She knows this stuff,' said Haynes, 'but this isn't her area of expertise.'

'I'm afraid there aren't many people we can trust,' said Jericho. 'And she's as near to an art historian as we have.'

'I'm not going to guarantee she says yes,' he said, and then as soon as the words were out of his mouth, he added, 'Of course she'll say yes. She loves this stuff.'

'I'm sorry, Stuart, needs must.'

'I know, I know. So what is it you want her to do? She's checking it for symbolism, et cetera? No, that's not it, is it, you could've examined the picture online. If you have the actual painting you must be wanting to…' and he studied Jericho's face while he thought about it, and then he said, 'She's made me watch no end of those painting restoration shows. God, they're dull. But that's what you're looking for, right? Is there anything hidden beneath the painting?'

'Yes.'

Haynes took another drink, staring around the café as he did so.

'When's your flight?' he asked, absent-mindedly.

'Gate closes in half an hour,' said Jericho. 'I should get going.'

'How exactly is it you're returning the painting to the Whistler, once Margot's taken off the top layer? Like, once she's literally destroyed the painting?'

'Maybe there'll be something even more impressive beneath it,' said Jericho. 'At the moment it's what, an ersatz Bruegel? Maybe beneath it'll be a work of original magnificence.'

'Sure.'

'Anyway,' said Jericho, as he got to his feet, 'can't they do X-rays on the painting to see if there might be something hidden? You don't need to remove the paint if there's obviously nothing there.'

'I don't know,' said Haynes, wearily, 'I always fall asleep during those shows. I have no idea what it is they do.'

Jericho stood by the table, and handed Haynes the bag.

'Thanks, Stuart. There's a number in there. Text when you've got something for me. I'll call back if I can.'

'Boss,' said Haynes.

'And be careful.'

'You too.'

A nod, and Jericho was gone.

33

'Inspector Haynes was enthusiastic?' asked Badstuber.

There were sitting outside a café on the Herengracht in Amsterdam. The heart of the tourist district. Plenty of people around, and crowds into which they could disappear if they had to run.

Badstuber had arranged to meet Birgit Prosser, the young woman at the police station who had originally given Jericho Isabella Bishop's next of kin list. Badstuber had not told Prosser Jericho would be there.

'Stuart wasn't too excited to get Professor Leighton involved,' said Jericho, 'but he understands.'

He was staring away across the canal, fingers tapping on the side of the beer glass. They were both drinking Amstel, a bowl of sweet potato fries between them, which they were slowly working their way through. Tourists like any other, as far as anyone walking by would think. Except, it was cold, and there weren't so many people sitting outside cafés.

'You are nervous?' she said.

'Agitated, that's all. Every step of the way, at every damn turn of the corner, it feels like we're missing something.' He made a small gesture into nothingness. 'I stole the picture. No reason why they would've been expecting it. But the fact that I was even allowed to do it, the complete silence since the event, it speaks of something suspicious, and I've no idea what that is.'

'Maybe it is exactly what it looks like,' said Badstuber. 'You stole a painting, much more easily than the Whistler

Gallery would like anyone to think you can steal a painting. They are embarrassed. They do not want the news broadcast. If it were, tonight every thief tries to steal from the Whistler.'

'I've considered that and already dismissed it,' said Jericho. 'No one *anywhere* is talking about it. There were helicopters above the building, there were officers firing at a fleeing suspect. It was New York at ten p.m. on a Thursday.'

To this, Badstuber had no counter.

'It's amazing,' said Jericho, taking a couple of fries and popping them into his mouth, 'how virtually everything is caught on film now. Whenever there's a plane crash, give it half an hour, and boom, there it is on the internet, filmed on some random person's phone. Unfolding events on a city street are one thing, people have the time to get interested, to get their phones in place. But planes crashing on landing or take off? Why is anyone filming it in the first place? And yet, there's always someone filming *something*. And there was me, a damned Poundshop action hero, leaping off a building under gunfire, and no one saw a thing.'

'Perhaps you are right. However, this does not tell us anything new. We know these people are omnipresent. We know the extent of their reach is extraordinary.'

'But I'm allowed to be anxious about that sometimes, though, right?' he said.

Badstuber nodded.

'Yes,' she said.

They held the look, one of those that said they understood each other and that there was a lot left unsaid, then he followed her gaze, as she saw Birgit Prosser approaching on the other side of the canal.

When Prosser spotted them outside the café, she stopped and stared at them for a moment. Taking Jericho's presence into consideration. They waited to see which way she would turn, Jericho wondering if it would be the right thing to chase after her if she walked away, and then she bowed her head and continued her approach.

They watched her across the bridge, and then she was by their table, and she pulled out a seat, sat down, and lifted a couple of fries.

'Thanks,' she said.

Then she pulled the tie out of her hair, shook her head, ran her fingers through her hair, then looked between the two of them.

'You're in the wars,' she said to Jericho.

He hadn't been thinking about the small bandage on the side of his head, the other scratches and bruises on his face.

'Hard to get a drink in this city sometimes,' he said.

'Nice,' she said, with a smile. 'I see you didn't get one for me.'

The waiter appeared. Male, mid-thirties, a black and blue striped waistcoat a little tight at the buttons, pigtail, facial hair that had been allowed to grow out of what must have been a carefully crafted goatee a week previously.

'Ja?'

'Droge witte wijn, alstublieft,' said Prosser.

The waiter glanced at the other drinks, established no one needed a replacement, nodded and turned away.

'You are bold,' said Prosser to Jericho. 'I like that.'

'Thanks for coming,' he said.

'That is OK. I'm not sure I would have chosen this place, but we are here now.'

'Where would you have rather met?' asked Badstuber, the one who had arranged the rendezvous.

'Amanda and I would meet at the beach. North of Noordwijk. Far out in the open, when you can see people coming.'

'Easily picked off from the dunes,' said Badstuber.

'She had someone who monitored the dunes.'

'You worked with Amanda?' asked Jericho.

'Yes.'

'This is why I received the call when she was found dead?' asked Badstuber, and Prosser nodded.

'Tell us about Amanda,' said Jericho.

Prosser studied him, glanced back at Badstuber, seemed to make the judgement that Jericho was the one she really needed to be talking to, then took another few fries, and sat back a little as the waiter appeared with her drink.

'Bedankt.'

He nodded, this time he asked the question with raised eyebrows of the table, Badstuber answered with a head shake, and he was gone.

'I don't know half of what Amanda did,' said Prosser. She spoke English easily, much more like a native than the formal, sometimes stilted delivery of Badstuber. 'Much less than half.

She was a whirlwind, and she was a keeper of secrets. We trusted her, that was all.'

'We?' asked Jericho.

Prosser took a drink, and sort of shrugged as she lowered the glass.

'I know only that there was a *we*. That is all. I have no idea who, or how many. I never had contact with anyone else. I had three names, and my instruction was to pass on the information I passed on to you should any of those three names show up asking for it.'

'I was one of those names?'

'Obviously.'

'Who were the other two?'

She stared at him deadpan, she shifted the look to Badstuber, she looked away along the street that ran adjacent to the canal.

An ordinary Amsterdam scene. Cars and canal boats parked, bicycles dodging tourists, the hubbub of the city, in the distance, an approaching tourist barge, the words of the guide through the loudspeaker, carrying along the water.

Prosser spent her life looking over her shoulder, aware that she was highly unlikely to recognise her imminent death when she saw it.

'How did you come to work with Amanda?' asked Jericho.

'Not relevant,' said Prosser, turning back.

'What did you do for her?'

'I was her eyes inside the Dutch police service. I collected information, I passed it on, that was all.'

'You worked there first, or you worked for Amanda, and then joined the police?'

'Not relevant.'

'How secure was your cover?'

'I worked for the police. I did not need cover.'

'What kind of information did you supply?'

'Anything she asked for, anything I thought might be relevant to the activities of the organisation known as the Pavilion.'

'And this list of names and addresses you gave me?'

'She had given me this information. It began as a list of three names, and had grown to five, obviously, by the time I passed it to you.'

'The next of kin addresses appear to be Pavilion safe

houses,' said Jericho.

A moment while she processed this, long enough for him to know that this was news to her.

'You have been to these addresses?' she asked.

'Three of them. All safe houses, all hostile to my arrival.'

'Had you been expected?'

'I don't think so. You know how many safe houses the Pavilion keep?'

'I did not know they kept any, though it makes sense. I haven't thought about it before.'

'The two other names Amanda gave you, have these people come to see you since she died?' he asked, deciding it was worth a try.

She stared at him, and again gave Badstuber a quick glance.

'I'm not sure about you,' she said, making a small gesture towards Badstuber. 'You're too quiet. And you're FIS. I'm not sure I can trust you, though I feel I must because Amanda obviously trusted you.'

'That is sensible,' said Badstuber drily. 'I thought to suggest leaving you two alone, but then we know the inspector would simply pass on to me the details of the conversation, so it seems unnecessary. Nevertheless, if you'd prefer me to go, I can do that.'

'No, it's fine. I'm leaving soon.'

She turned back to Jericho, having made her decision.

'They're both dead,' she said bluntly. 'One car accident, one seemingly accidental death during a mugging.'

'These happened in Amsterdam?'

'Elsewhere. When Amanda died I checked on the location of the three people she'd mentioned. One of them had died the day before, the other then died the following day. And you're still here.'

'There have been attempts,' said Jericho. Then, 'What did you expect coming here to meet agent Badstuber?'

'I expected nothing. I was curious. I came, and now we see where we are.'

'Did Amanda also suggest that you continue to work for us should we ask it of you?' asked Jericho.

'She said that was up to me.'

'And?'

'I do not know. I have not enjoyed it. And… truth be told, the Netherlands is a backwater in this fight. Amanda had work to do through the ICC, but I do not have access there.'

'You know what she was doing at the ICC?' asked Badstuber.

'Yes.'

Badstuber stared blankly at her.

'Her work was related to countries in a specific area of the African continent. South Sudan, Chad, Democratic Central Africa, Central African Republic, Niger.'

'The same places where she was working on solar power projects,' said Jericho.

Prosser narrowed her eyes, and then gave the now familiar small shrug.

'I don't know about that.'

'What is it about these countries?' asked Jericho.

'I don't know,' said Prosser. 'Logically, however, they have untapped resources, a great power source with so much heat and sunshine, relatively few people for the size of area, little infrastructure, a great vacuum in political power, and are ripe for exploitation.'

'You think we'll find the heart of the Pavilion in the heart of Africa?'

'I have no idea. When I said what I just said, I was speculating. Don't take it as anything other than that. Are we done?'

'No,' said Jericho, simply. 'I heard talk that there's a lot of infighting.'

A moment, then Prosser said, 'Yes.'

'You know the cause of the infighting?'

She took another drink, a longer one this time, as she prepared to leave. Jericho had a feeling that Prosser was just about to be shot in the head, but he shook it off. Not everyone got shot in the head.

'For a long time Amanda presumed it was because of the failure of succession. You know how the head of the Pavilion was selected?'

Jericho shook his head. He read disappointment in Prosser's face.

'It is akin to the Chinese Communist party. Since the early years in London, a leader has been elected to stand for ten years. After ten years, they must step down, and be replaced by someone elected by the, for want of a better expression, executive board. But we are, as you will know, in the new age of the dictator, and exactly the same thing happened to the Pavilion as happened to the Chinese Communist party. The leader did not change. That one man has obtained a kind of absolute control that was not supposed to be held by the head of the Pavilion. These are the days in which we live.'

'Who's the guy?' asked Jericho.

Again the look, and once again silence, followed by a lifting of the glass, this time almost finishing off the drink.

'Merrick,' said Badstuber.

It wasn't a question.

'Yes,' said Prosser, accepting that they already knew.

'Who is Merrick?' asked Jericho. 'We know the name, we don't know the man.'

'No one knows the man,' said Prosser. 'Stanley Merrick, that's all there is. Do with it what you will.'

'He's invisible?'

'If you find any details of Stanley Merrick, it's the wrong Stanley Merrick. There is always the possibility that there is no Stanley Merrick. But insomuch as there is nothing factual attached to this name, the name doesn't matter anyway. There is a someone at the head of the Pavilion, and they have been there for a lot longer than ten years.'

'Outstaying their welcome,' said Jericho, and then he shook his head. 'No, that's not it. You said Amanda just *thought* that was why there was infighting.'

'Yes. Whatever internal dispute flared as a result of Merrick's continued occupation of the throne, he managed to quash. One presumes people died. He solidified his power.'

'And now?'

She lifted her glass, drained it, held it to her lips as though savouring the last drop, and then placed it back on the table.

'Something is coming, and Amanda was scared by it. That wasn't normal.'

'There was no indication what that might have been?' asked Badstuber.

Prosser did at least look like she was giving this some thought, though she came out of it with a head shake.

'I don't know. It was just… you've seen the news? You've seen it all. Doesn't it feel sometimes like we're watching the collapse of civilisation? And you think, how did this happen? We're a relatively intelligent species, how could we be so damned stupid? And maybe, just maybe, someone somewhere's pulling the strings. And Amanda was convinced that was the Pavilion, and specifically she was convinced it was Stanley Merrick. And she was sure he was working towards…,' and she thought about it, staring off into space to try to conjure the word, and then when she found it, she looked back at them, leaning into the table, pinching the thumb and forefinger of her right hand together, and said, 'an end. A full stop.'

'The Pavilion has built this extraordinary network, this incredible many-headed beast of power, just to blow it all up?' said Jericho.

Again she stared blankly across the table, and then she slowly shrugged.

'I don't know,' she said. 'And neither did Amanda.'

She lifted her glass, drained the dregs again, then set it back on the table as she got to her feet.

'Good luck, I guess.'

And she was gone.

34

Haynes had said to him once, 'You can't sit in a place like this having a serious conversation about work, without invoking Connery in *The Untouchables*. 'He pulls a knife,' 'n all that.'

At the time, they'd been sitting in the nave of Wells Cathedral, looking up at the magnificent fourteenth-century scissor arch.

'Invoke away,' he'd replied, though Haynes had just laughed, and had not gone down the road of saying they needed to put some of the Madison drug gang family in the morgue.

Ever since, every time Jericho found himself in a place of worship – including these days, once a week at the cathedral for evensong – he thought of Haynes, and his Sean Connery line.

Then there'd been the American, three summers previously. A random name he'd come across, one of those rabbit holes he'd disappeared down. Jericho had been on the verge of getting on a plane to New York – it was what he'd spent so much of the last ten years doing – only to learn the American was in the north of Scotland playing golf. Staying at Skibo Castle, near Dornoch. The man's PA had pronounced it Dor-nock.

When Jericho had arrived in the far north-east, having flown to Inverness and driven the hour further north, the American had been on the golf course in nearby Brora. The men finally found each other the following morning, in Dornoch Cathedral, the thirteenth-century church in the heart of the small town.

Jericho was sitting in a pew, looking along the length of the nave to the chancel and the altar, the magnificent stained glass windows behind. The American had been late, giving Jericho time to sit and think. He had become, by this point, very accustomed to sitting and thinking.

The American arrived at a brisk pace, looked around, identified Jericho by no other means than that this was obviously the man he was looking for, then came and sat beside him.

'Tell me,' he said abruptly, by way of hello.

'I'm here to ask, not tell,' said Jericho, and the American laughed. Then he leant forward on the back of the pew in front, and looked at the altar.

Jericho had thought of Haynes, and Sean Connery.

'I know what you're going to ask,' said the American, 'and honestly, I don't know who you are, or why you bother. Things just are as they are, my friend. And you'll get along a whole lot better if you accept this one simple thing. *You know nothing*. That's it. You don't know it, and you can't possibly know it. Because the people who matter, the people who are actually making the rules...' He shook his head, he turned to Jericho, then made a gesture in the direction of the altar. 'You know Musk got married right there? You know that?'

Jericho shook his head. That hadn't been mentioned in the official history of the building.

'Married an actress right there in two-thousand-ten. Talulah Riley. Lasted two years, for what it's worth, though they married again for a year a while later. Least they tried.'

He paused, but he wasn't finished talking. He was on transmit, which was fine. Police officers – even retired ones – like it when interviewees are on transmit.

'You think the people making the rules,' he continued, 'you think it's those kind of guys? You think it's Musk and Zuck? You think it's Bezos and Bill damned Gates? Seriously? You think *those guys* are the richest men on earth? Spare me.'

'Some investment banker from the upper east side?' said Jericho glibly.

He had no idea whether the upper east side of Manhattan was one of the wealthy areas.

The American laughed.

'Funny,' he said. 'And *those* guys, the investment bankers, everyone knows them. They love that shit, just as much as the Zucks and the Musks. And sure, those guys are rich, but they're not... *rich*. Capiche?'

'You really just said capiche?' said Jericho.

'Ha!'

'Who are they then?'

Jericho's enthusiasm for the conversation had already been lost.

Every time, every damned time, he allowed himself a little hope. Why the hell not? But this guy wasn't going to tell him anything. He was going to give Jericho ten minutes of his time – if he was lucky – and he was going to pontificate, and throw out a few one-liners he might think had been written by Billy Wilder or William Goldman, and then he was going to go back to the golf course.

He was already dressed for it, after all.

'Nobody knows,' said the American. 'That's their secret. No one knows, because those guys, the rich guys, they don't want you to know. They have money, they have power, they have... I don't know, all kinds of shit. Secret armies, security services, spies, protection, you name it.' He tapped his fingers firmly on the back of the pew. 'When the world falls, and the world *will* fall, it won't be because of Trump or whichever idiot rules America, it won't be Xi or Putin, it won't be the Taliban or Iran or Israel, it won't be the conflagration between India and Pakistan. It'll be because of the invisible. The cabal that lurks in the shadows, hidden away, seen by neither man nor beast.'

Jericho grabbed the American's arm in an unusual fit of annoyance.

'I know,' he said, face in an unexpected snarl.

The American looked concerned for a moment, then smiled as Jericho relaxed his grip.

'Well, look at you,' he said. 'Got your juices flowing at any rate. You play golf?'

'No.'

'Too bad. You should give it a try. Keeps you plenty relaxed. Seems you need it.'

'You were saying about the men in the shadows.'

'I was, wasn't I?'

They stared at each other, Jericho annoyed and close to just walking away, aware he was getting nothing from this man, the American seemingly enjoying every second.

'We are in the late stages of collapse,' said the American. 'You see it all around. The downfall. If this was World War Two, the Russian tanks have already crossed the border into

Germany, and they're closing fast on Berlin, my friend.' Then he turned and squeezed Jericho's hand, much to Jericho's annoyance, and said, 'Relax. Try your hand at a few holes of golf. You never know, it might just give you some meaning in these autumn years.'

And with another laugh, he was gone.

35

They had checked into the Imladris Hotel in Lausanne, under the names Dr Helga and Mr Alan Bayreuth. A room with a view of the lake, the light of the half-moon picking out the snow on the Chablais Alps across the water, to the east of Geneva.

They'd spent the hour and a half since their arrival preparing for the following day. Badstuber creating a fake identity with which Jericho would be able to gain access to the headquarters of The International Ecological Mining Alliance – the NGO where Amanda had worked – while Jericho spent his time reading up on the organisation.

As he'd read, and dug deeper into the names of people involved, and the people who had recently died, he'd felt a familiar chill creep across his skin.

This was who the Pavilion was. This is what they wrought. These were the kinds of things that happened to people who became involved with them. Perhaps, in fact, many of the people who'd briefly passed through this organisation, and suffered as a result, were unaware of the Pavilion's involvement.

They'd eaten sandwiches as they'd worked, sitting across from each other at the small, two-seat table by the balcony. Under some other circumstance they might have worked with the curtains open, the window ajar, with the view of the moonlight cast across the water. But when you investigated the Pavilion, you did not sit, backlit, at an open window at night.

There had been very little conversation between them. Computers open, heads down, focussed on their individual tasks.

At some stage Jericho had said, 'I'm done when you're done,' and Badstuber had nodded in reply, and said, 'Twenty minutes.' Followed shortly by, 'Thirty minutes.'

Half an hour later she closed her laptop, as Jericho was reading about the death of Omar Bangura, a government minister from Democratic Central Africa.

Jericho had long since had enough, hopelessness and anger coursing through him in equal measure, and he closed his laptop as soon as Badstuber had done the same, and they stared at each other across the table.

'All set?' he asked.

'Yes. You are a representative of the NGO, the International Mining Federation. Using the same name with which we have checked into the hotel. There is a meeting tomorrow morning at ten a.m. The Mining Federation were invited, and elected not to send representation. I have sent communications back and forth, and now that has been altered, and you will speak for them at the meeting.'

'What's the meeting?'

'Closure of the International Ecological Mining Alliance.'

'I never saw anything about that. The entire operation is being wrapped up?'

'That's the proposal.'

'Unusual for people to vote themselves off a gravy train.'

'It appears their funding has dried up.'

'I saw that their funding has been coming largely from anonymous sources, and we know what that means in this context.'

'Yes. If we are to presume the Pavilion, the Pavilion have now pulled the plug. There's always the possibility other countries step up to cover the deficit, but that seems unlikely.'

'And this is what the meeting is about?'

'Yes.'

'What am I saying?'

'I've prepared a brief for you which you will now find in your inbox. I suggest you read it in the morning, so that it is fresh. I am tired, and you also look tired.'

'Yes,' he said.

'You have learned much about the history of the IEMA?'

'There have been a lot of unexplained deaths. Not a single murder, nor an assassination. All these deaths are typical of the Pavilion. Sometimes, as we know from experience, they send out an assassin. And sometimes people just die, because that's what happens. I have names here, but... dammit, I need the break. I've had enough of this... *crap*.'

'Mining, clean energy, corruption at the heart of government, war crimes, all centred around central Africa,' said Badstuber. 'I think perhaps we are going to have to travel there.'

'I expect so,' said Jericho. 'At the moment, I really don't want to think about it.'

'Yes,' said Badstuber.

She got to her feet.

'It is too early to sleep, I will wake in the night and my mind will overwork, and I will still be tired in the morning.'

'Yes,' said Jericho.

'I will have a shower. I would like it if you could order a bottle of wine from room service. And perhaps some olives. We will drink the wine, and then we will make love.' A pause, and then, with her brow slightly furrowed, she added, 'If that is OK.'

'Should be,' said Jericho. 'I thought –'

'I have changed my mind,' she said. 'I begin to think possibly one, or both of us, will die before this thing is finished. I would not like to die without us making love, so I think we should do it tonight. If that is OK?' she repeated.

'I've been thinking the same thing,' said Jericho, 'though I'm not sure I was ever going to say it.'

'Then it is good I did.'

She walked to the bathroom, unbuttoning her white blouse as she went, then she turned at the door.

'There is an Alsace Gewürztraminer on the wine menu,' she said, she waited for Jericho's nod of acknowledgement, and then she went into the bathroom, and shortly afterwards Jericho heard the shower running.

Ф

Later they sat at the window in the wee small hours of the morning, the lights off, watching the moon go down behind the mountains. And when it was gone, and its silvery light was no longer cast across the lake, they fell into bed, and he held her in his arms, and thought how nice it would be to not have to wake up the following day and face this great weight that sat on them like stone.

36

There were not the same elaborate security measures at the HQ of the International Ecological Mining Alliance as there had been at the UN in New York.

A neat nineteenth-century building, which the IEMA shared with the headquarters of the International Softball Confederation. A large, open area in the middle of the building, with each HQ having their own reception.

Jericho approached, today wearing a large pair of glasses that looked like they might have been attached to his face since the nineteen-seventies.

'Guten tag,' he said.

'Guten Morgen. Sie sind wegen der Konferenz hier?'

Jericho took a moment, then nodded, and said, 'Ja,' as he took out his ID, showing him to be a representative of the International Mining Foundation.

'Herr Bayreuth,' said the woman, nodding, and then she typed quickly, her fingers a brief blur across the keyboard. Jericho had a familiar moment of concern, waiting to see if Badstuber had successfully planted his name into the system, and then the woman smiled and nodded as she looked up.

'My apologies, Mr Bayreuth, welcome to Lausanne,' and Jericho waved away her smile, as though he'd been perfectly comfortable conducting the conversation in German. 'If you could just stand a little to your right, I can get a photograph for your pass.'

Jericho took a pace to his right. Behind him the door

opened, and a woman and two men entered, talking in French. Jericho tried for a moment to keep up, but they were too quick, and not for the first time, he lamented his complete linguistic inability. Badstuber had said she was happy to take on this particular assignment, and once again, he'd insisted she didn't do anything that could openly jeopardise her career.

Neither of them had stopped, as yet, to consider what that might look like when this was all over. Strangely, however, for the first time since he'd left the police service and devoted his life to this insanity, he had a feeling that it would soon all be over, one way or another.

The receptionist turned her back as she printed off Jericho's pass, while the three arrivals stood behind Jericho, waiting their turn, the conversation continuing in an animated manner.

'Mr Bayreuth,' said the receptionist, as she turned back, and she passed the lanyard with the pass over the counter. 'If you could keep that on at all times, there's no need for you to be escorted around the building. The elevator is to your left. If you'd like to go to the third floor, you'll find the other delegates are gathering over coffee.'

'Danke,' said Jericho, with a small bow, as he placed the lanyard around his neck.

'Gern geschehen,' she said with a smile, and Jericho turned away and walked to the elevator.

Φ

There would be a panel of five at the front of the room, with seating for a couple of hundred facing the panel in rows of twelve. To the right of the room, large windows – which must have been increased in size since the original building was erected – looked out over Lake Geneva in all its glory. A pale morning sun, the lake a near-perfect flat calm, the snow on the mountains in the distance beautifully framing the scene.

I could look at that all day, Jericho had thought, as he stood having coffee before the conference kicked off.

He chose not to engage anyone, and stood anonymously in amongst the delegates, trying to pick out conversations, which proved a largely fruitless enterprise. In amongst the great babel of voices there might have been something of interest, but all he picked up in English was talk of the Champions League, the forthcoming Holborn and St Pancras by-election, and the best way to travel to Lausanne from London these days if you weren't in a rush.

The meeting began with a long, largely apocalyptic speech from the chair, on the drastic state of the IEMA's funding.

This, thought Jericho, is not a man who will ever be invited onto the after-dinner circuit. Dry and functional, when he resorted to talking about figures he sounded like he was reading it straight from an Excel spreadsheet, with all the warmth that suggested.

Interesting, Jericho had thought, that the majority of delegates looked as though they were from Africa, or at least were of African descent, while all five panellists on the small platform were white.

'Money has been frittered,' said the chair, but with so little enthusiasm, no one in the crowd could possibly have taken it as an admonition. 'Our donors requested a full audit of the last eight years, during which time they have contributed in excess of three hundred, fifty-million dollars to the working capital of the alliance.'

He paused to look around the room.

'The capabilities of the alliance in this period, in soft power terms, have been negligible. In short, the alliance has failed.'

The words had a certain cold brutality, thought Jericho, and yet were being delivered with a lack of conviction that rendered them banal, and he wondered if every meeting began like this. A row from your sponsors. Next, the list of fools from whom we hope to get our next three hundred and fifty million.

The chair spoke for more than half an hour. In that time, Jericho did not gain any particular insight into what it was the IEMA actually did.

37

A break for coffee after ninety minutes. Everyone filed out into a large reception room. There was also an elaborate collection of pastries.

Jericho once again stood aimlessly, making no attempt to engage anyone in conversation, preferring instead to look out over the lake.

He'd had enough of the meeting, and had no intention of returning to the hall, where there was some talk of splitting off into break-out groups. Only once in the latter years of his police career had Jericho had to split off into a break-out group, and it had not gone well.

'You wonder how many people would attend these things if they were held in Stoke-on-Trent or in the derelict factory backwoods of Romania, rather than Lausanne,' said a voice next to him.

Jericho turned. The woman who had entered the building in conversation with the two men, was standing beside him, cup of coffee in hand.

Everything about her was immaculate. Her hair, her clothes, her make-up, the perfect size of the watch on her wrist. Every pose she took could've been from a Watches Of Switzerland advert in Cosmopolitan.

'Switzerland has to exist for a reason,' said Jericho.

'This isn't enough?' she asked, making a gesture to the lake.

'Without Lausanne and Geneva and Zurich and everything

they attract, it might as well be Slovenia. This,' said Jericho, indicating the multinational world in which they stood, 'is what separates Switzerland, not the Alps.'

'I shan't argue with such a well-put argument. I'm not sure I've seen you here before,' she added, with an abrupt swivel.

'Second day on the job,' said Jericho. 'I just joined the Mining Federation, and they said, might as well hit the ground running. So here I am.'

'Quite the introduction,' she said.

'And you?'

'Oh, I'm a veteran. My mother used to come to these kinds of meetings when she was pregnant. I've literally been attending international junkets like this since I was an embryo.'

He laughed, and wondered how often she told the joke. Nevertheless, there was something about her that said she never told jokes.

He glanced at her ID, resting on the curve of her breasts, lifting his eyes as she noticed him looking.

'Suitably vague,' she said, in reference to her ID which billed her as Joanne Buchman, unattached delegate.

'You finagled an invite for the free pastries?' said Jericho.

She smiled, just as the small bell rang behind them, and immediately the level of chatter and movement increased a notch, as the room began to shift slowly back through to the conference room next door.

'After you,' she said.

'I have to use the bathroom,' said Jericho. 'I'll see you in there.'

She smiled, something in her look that he couldn't fathom, although he did not trust her for a minute, and then he turned away, placed his coffee cup on a table, and walked to the men's toilet, where he inserted himself in a cubicle and waited.

Φ

When he emerged three minutes later, there were staff clearing away the detritus of second breakfast, or however that short break had been designated, as preparations for the buffet lunch were begun. None of them were interested in Jericho.

He stepped out of the room the way he had first entered it, and then walked quickly along the corridor, checking names on doors as he went.

At the far end, Hugo Augustin, the chair of the meeting, who had made the sheep in sheep's clothing opening address. The door was, as expected, locked, and he had the pick in hand. Little more than fifteen seconds and he was inside, closing the door and locking it behind him.

He stood for a moment taking in the room, which ticked every box he would have expected of it. A huge desk at the back of the room, large picture windows overlooking the lake. Two armchairs by one of the windows, with a small table in between. Bookshelves that looked like they could have been in a National Trust property. A drinks cabinet. A large photograph of the chairman meeting Donald Trump. Another large photograph of the chairman meeting António Guterres. A classical painting of a European Cathedral, and since the chairman was French, Jericho was going to assume that so was the cathedral in the painting. He knew enough, at least, to know it wasn't Notre Dame. To the side of the desk, a free-standing globe. Behind the desk, a large map, landlocked within itself, brown and green, and he had to step closer to see that it was central Africa. A line along the bottom, from Yaoundé in the west, as far east as Juba, including Bangui and N'Pala in that stretch, to an area of desert, far north of N'Djamena, running through Niger, Chad, Democratic Central Africa, CAR and Sudan.

There was nothing on the map to indicate whereabouts in this great stretch of land might be of particular interested to the IEMA.

He glanced at the desk, but first walked to the window and took a look down, and then across the lake.

The building was almost flush to the lake edge, a stunning piece of architecture in itself. Everything about this is expensive and beautiful, he thought. No wonder people never wanted to get off the gravy train. Why solve the problems of the world, when their perpetuation allowed you to come and work in Lausanne?

Perhaps Joanne Buchman had been right: they would make more progress if people were forced to attend economic forums in some deserted industrial estate in central Albania surrounded by concrete tank traps rather than the glacial still of Lake Geneva on a perfect spring morning.

'Enough,' he muttered, and he forced himself away from the view, aware that he could be easily distracted, like a guard dog with a piece of raw steak, and quite happily still be standing here in perfect silence when the chairman returned at the end of the next session.

He sat in the chair at the desk, pulled on a pair of nitrile gloves, and tried the drawers down the right hand side. All locked.

Lockpick quickly back in hand, he opened the top drawer with the ease of having the key.

A drawer full of stationery, with a magazine and a slender, unmarked brown file lying on top.

The magazine was something named *Teenage Bunnies*, with a picture of a young girl, who barely looked like a teenager, on the cover. Jericho felt revolted enough by the second-hand slime of being in its vicinity – it was a long time since he'd had to deal with that kind of thing on a regular basis – and he ignored it, as he checked beneath to see if there was anything interesting amongst the stationery. There wasn't.

He left the magazine in the drawer, and laid the folder on the desk.

Inside, short reports on five men. He recognised the names. Mbah, Bukoyo, Hakizimana, Kassoma, Bangura. Leaders of the militia who'd staged the coup in Democratic Central Africa. Rumoured to be under investigation by the ICC. And while the political situation in DCA remained uneasy, the consensus was that these men remained at the heart of power.

Of course, as he'd learned the night before, Bangura was now dead.

The five reports were not potted biographies. In each case, it was a list of the ways in which the men were compromised. Crimes committed, skeletons in the closet, family members who could be abused, or threatened, as required.

Jericho quickly photographed pages, then closed the file and slipped it back into the drawer, beneath the magazine.

Was the magazine a calculated guess, he wondered. That was the thing that most people would be distracted by, rather than look at the folder? He shuddered at the thought, and accepted that more than likely, it was just what chairman Augustin enjoyed looking at. This is who he was.

Jericho rose from the chair, and studied the map behind again.

That made sense. There it was, Democratic Central Africa, in the middle of the snake pit of unrest. Part desert, part forest, part mountains, part dried-up river beds. Massive unexplored mineral wealth, barely functioning government, conflict between the Christian and Muslim populations, ancient, warring tribes thrown together by the detritus of colonialism. Nothing that happened there was ever news, and certainly not now, when war and unrest swept the globe.

DCA could fester in its own sewer and no one cared, bar the multinational governmental bodies, whose funding relied on sticking their impotent snouts into such areas.

He sat back at the desk, and opened the larger lower drawer. Designed to hold upright files, the fittings were not in place, and the drawer was much more sparsely filled.

A bottle of Glenmorangie, 12 years old. Nearly empty. Jericho glanced at the drinks cabinet. There was also a bottle of Glenmorangie there. Back to the drawer. A Panini World Cup sticker book, from 2006, propped behind the bottle of whisky. Jericho lifted the book, and leafed through it. Pristine, all the stickers in place. He didn't know what to make of that, so he thought nothing of it, and placed it back.

Lying flat on the floor of the drawer, a thin pile of magazines and folders. He lifted the pile and placed it on the desk.

A copy of a six-month old Economist magazine, a Playboy from two years previously, and two slim folders. One marked Tax Year 23/24, the other marked Operation Dwarrowdelf.

OK, thought Jericho, that sounds just about insane enough to be of interest here.

A sound at the door. A key in the lock, then the door opened. Joanne Buchman entered, regarded Jericho coolly and without drama, and closed the door behind her.

They stared at each other. Buchman, unruffled and almost casual, Jericho caught with his fingers in the jar, sitting at the chairman's desk, the contents of the lower drawer now placed there in a neat pile waiting to be examined.

Silence.

She held the pose for a few moments, and then walked forward, glanced at the drawer, then at the small pile of papers on the desk. She stood beside Jericho, close enough that he could smell the fragrance she wore, which he hadn't been able to do in the larger room filled with people and food and coffee. He caught a note of orange.

'So, you've learned the chairman likes whisky and naked women,' said Buchman. 'Interesting. That must narrow him down into roughly ninety-eight percent of the male population.'

'There's child pornography in the top drawer,' said Jericho, looking up at her, his voice deadpan.

She grimaced.

'Oh, that's disappointing. So what does that bring the percentage down to?'

He didn't answer, and she raised her eyebrows.

'No, I'm serious,' she said. 'You're a former police officer, you must have some idea. What percentage of you men like child porn?' A pause, and then, 'No? Nothing. Oh, well.'

Then she leaned across, and separated out the small pile of papers.

'Hmm, the Economist from six months ago. Now, that must be interesting. Why this particular one? If there were a host of editions, it would be mundane, but just this one. Must be something relevant to your investigation, don't you think? You don't need to take the time to read that here, though, you can log the edition in that giant detective's brain of yours.

'Then there's the naked women, yadda-yadda-yadda, although perhaps there's something specific in this one. Why this, from two years ago? You think it's been sitting in his drawer all this time?'

She lifted the magazine, then quickly flicked through the pages, not really paying any attention. Then she opened the magazine at a double-page spread, made an appreciative face, then turned the magazine round and laid it on the desk.

'What d'you think?' she asked.

Jericho played along long enough to glance at the picture, then looked back at her.

'Nothing? Again? I don't know, Robert, seems to me there's something of your Swiss girlfriend in this woman, don't you think? Similar hair, that attractive cool look, the same perky little boobs. Oh, wait, perky, is that a good word for boobs? And maybe Ilsa's boobs aren't so perky anymore. Nice to see you're age-appropriate with your liaisons, at least. You always have been.'

She smiled.

'Oh, the girl in Vietnam. Bit of a misjudgement there, I think, though at least she was legal, so there was that. Bit of a low point for you, Hanoi, wasn't it? You were lost.'

She looked back at the nude, glanced at him again to see if he was going to join her in her admiration, then made a face to accept it was time to move on.

'OK, so what else have we got here, then?' she said, pushing the magazine to the side, but not closing it.

She was cutting Jericho open, bit by bit. Letting him know she had dominion. In a few short sentences, telling him she knew the intimate details of his life.

Here he was dashing from dramatic scene to dramatic scene, hopping across continents, agonising over details, constructing plans, attempting to forge a believable narrative, and these people knew where he was, and who he was, every damned step of the way. And always had done.

'Tax year, twenty-three, twenty-four. OK, boring on the face of it, but just the kind of thing a police officer loves. Who knows what secrets might be unearthed in a tax return? So, that's a keeper. And this last one…'

She turned it round, and read the small print at the bottom of the otherwise blank folder.

'Operation Dwarrowdelf. Ooh, that sounds intriguing, what d'you think?'

He stared at her coldly, but he couldn't deny it. Regardless of what look he managed to arrange his face into, she had diminished him. There was only one cool person in this room, and it wasn't him. Everything about these few minutes told him he should give up. Time to walk away, and retire to the life of nothingness he'd just begun to try to lead back in Somerset, when Badstuber had come calling out of the blue.

'You know the name Dwarrowdelf?' she asked, eyebrows raised, still playing the one-sided game. Jericho did not answer. He felt small, the old feelings of self-loathing sweeping back through him, like an old, bitter, unwanted friend.

This was the Jericho he recognised so well, the self with whom he'd existed for decades. Somehow it had been lost along the way, these past ten years of more or less frivolous, wasted searching. But it hadn't taken much.

'It's from *Lord of the Rings*. What d'you make of that?'

He said nothing.

'Really? Nothing? You're not interested in *Lord of the Rings*?'

When he'd stood at the window a few minutes earlier, he'd seen it as an escape route. A full-pelt run at the glass, hands up to protect his face – now he'd found someone worth protecting it for – and he would crash into the water, avoiding the hail of bullets all around him, swim to the right of the building, a quick dash to the main road, where Badstuber would be waiting in the anonymous, hired Hyundai. And he would have escaped from another difficult situation, soaking wet, another minor cut or two, but none the worse for it otherwise. And like every step of the way, another little piece of the puzzle would have fallen into place.

And now, out of nowhere, he'd been weakened, reduced to nothingness. A dead weight sitting heavily on his shoulders.

'I like it,' she said. 'Some might say otherwise, that the way to go is to invoke classical literature. Dwarrowdelf, if you don't know, was another name for the mines of Moria. Khazad-dûm, by yet another name. So, what do we have in the classics? Odysseus and the cave of Polyphemus, that'd be one. They could've invoked that, and perhaps this operation would have sounded more sophisticated. Operation Polyphemus. That has a ring to it, doesn't it? And yet, the *Odyssey* is just something someone wrote, just as *Lord of the Rings* is something someone wrote. And I dare say, of all the junk literature that has been written in the last century, the tale of Frodo will survive thousands of years, as has the tale of Odysseus.' She smiled. He didn't know if she was amused by the subject, or by his air of defeat.

He silently held the stare, long enough for her to raise her eyebrows.

'Nothing?' she said eventually.

'What was the question?' he asked, dully.

'This mythical operation that's so grand, so incredible, it demands a secret folder in a locked drawer in the office of the chairman of the International Ecological Mining Alliance... What d'you think might be going on here?'

'So, grand,' said Jericho, 'so incredible, it gets put in the same drawer as a bottle of illicit booze and a porn mag.'

She laughed.

'There we are, there's a bit of the spark we've come to expect.'

Jericho did not feel encouraged to use up any more of his spark.

She held his gaze a little longer, then shrugged.

'You're probably right,' she said. 'Nothing to get excited about. After all, we're standing in a building where mining is in the title.' She laughed lightly. 'So, they have some secret operation named after a fake mine? Big deal. And you know what, maybe it's not even a secret. It's not written on the folder in scary red letters like you'd get in a film. Just a plain old, boring brown folder. No secret, no anything.'

The amusement remained on her face as she watched him, waiting for some movement. *She knows, though,* thought Jericho. *She knows she's broken me.*

Hadn't taken much.

'Might as well have it,' she said, and she made a small gesture. 'On you go.'

Jericho didn't move.

'No? I mean, you take anything you like, though I'm not sure there's going to be much more of interest there for you. Between you and me, now you've discovered the chairman's little secret,' and she gestured towards the top drawer with her eyebrows, 'he's a bit of a creepy guy.' She shivered. 'I don't like him. We don't like him. The chairman's... what is it you say? His goose is cooked, that's it. His goose is cooked. He's been useful, but time is not on his side.'

Jericho lifted the folder marked Operation Dwarrowdelf, took a moment, and opened it.

It was empty.

He stared at the void for a moment, then lifted his contemptuous eyes.

'Oh,' said Buchman. 'I forgot about that. Looks like someone saw you coming.'

She fired his contemptuous look back at him, and then turned away and walked to the window, looking down on the lake, her contempt and disregard for him more than enough to allow her to turn her back.

She stood for a moment, gazing out on the lake, and then turned back with a small sigh.

'I expect you stood here a short while ago and contemplated your exit. A dramatic leap through the window, a jump into the freezing water, your love waiting for you in her Hyundai just along the road.'

Another knife into his head, with every stab the life, the hope, the fight draining out of him.

There was no knife, of course, just as there were no bullets, no explosions, no car chases, no anything. Just words, crushing everything he'd built up in the past few days, all the hope that Amanda's death, and the legacy she'd left behind, had given him.

'You can go,' she said, coldly. 'You can leap out of the window if you like, although if that's how you choose to leave the building, I think everyone would prefer you to leap from an open window, rather than smash the whole thing apart. No need for the drama. You're free to walk down the hall, take the elevator, and leave by the front door.' A pause, and then she added, 'Don't forget to drop off your pass at reception.' Another pause, but she wasn't finished inserting the knife in minute, agonising thrusts. 'Agent Badstuber certainly knows what she's doing, but she left a few too many breadcrumbs for our people, I'm afraid. Far as I know, it fooled the IEMA, so there's that. Not a complete bust. Let her know. You can give her a report card. Let's call it a B+. Maybe just a B.'

Jericho held her gaze for a little longer, looked down at the empty file and the tax file and the pornography and the Economist and the open drawer with the whisky and the Panini World Cup 2006 sticker book, all the ashes of a wasted effort collected in one pointless, immaculate and very expensive desk.

'It's for the Chairman's granddaughter,' she said. 'The sticker book. The girl loves football. She loves Zizou, the tortured villain of the piece from the final. Such a tragic tale. Oh, don't worry, we'll make sure she gets the book, even though the chairman's never going to see his granddaughter again. We're not absolute bastards. She can enjoy it for a short while.'

She sighed again, shaking her head, walking away from the window.

'I'm talking too much, boring even myself. You should go. Now.'

She nodded towards the door.

Jericho waited a moment, and hated himself even for that, a pathetic few seconds, as though trying to reclaim the narrative, like he had any control whatsoever over how this was playing out, and then he got up, took off the gloves, thrust them into his pocket, and left the room.

38

Jericho opened the car door and got inside.

Badstuber turned, curious, having watched his approach in the rear-view mirror.

He didn't look at her, though he didn't have to for her to recognise the change in him. She knew this Jericho from ten years previously.

'I'll buy you a ridiculously expensive lunch at the hotel,' he said, after a few moments of silence.

The hotel was only a hundred and fifty yards away, the car had been there entirely on the basis he was liable to have left the building in a rush.

She had questions, obviously, but Badstuber could read a room. She started the car, and drove the short distance to the hotel.

Φ

They were eating outside. The setting was perfect, but it was a little too cool for most people, and they'd been able to get a table in the sun down by the water. The air was still, and they were fine in their coats.

'We would eat outside in fifteen degrees colder than this up in the mountains,' Badstuber had observed to the waitress, who had acknowledged the common sense, and retreated with the blankets she'd brought to the table.

They were drinking a bottle of Leflaive Puligny Montrachet, and mineral water that was stupidly expensive in itself. Jericho was starting with cold veal in tuna sauce, Badstuber with octopus carpaccio.

They had not talked. With a flick of a damnable switch, Jericho had been cast back to his past. He hadn't given much consideration to the man he'd been, but if he had, he wouldn't have thought he was still in there, surreptitiously buried beneath layers of new-found bravado. His life had changed, his priorities had evolved, he had left the police force and the paperwork and the politics behind, and he'd thought this was who he was now.

And just like that, one conversation, and he'd been proved wrong. The old Jericho, the dark and brooding beast of ill humour, had been there all along, waiting for the bravado to be swept away.

Small waves lapped against the edge of the piazza, across the lake there was the sound of the Evian ferry, heading towards Lausanne. From one of the other tables, a man who was a little too loud on his phone, talking about the lack of snow in St Moritz.

'Tell me,' she said, deciding it was time to force the conversation.

He took another bite of veal, swallowed, took a drink of wine, set down the glass, then looked across the silver-blue lake.

'They know. They know everything. They knew I'd be there, they knew you'd hacked the system. They know what we've done, they know we've started a relationship, they know, I'm guessing, every damn thing I've done in the past ten years. They even know what I did in Hanoi, and that was six years ago, and I'd almost forgotten about it myself.'

'What did you do in Hanoi?'

'It involved sex, but that wasn't really the point.'

'They took the smallest detail, and let you know they knew even that.'

'Yes.'

He finally looked at her.

'They're playing with us. They're playing with me, and I've stupidly brought you along for the ride.'

'It was me who –'

'Here I am, living my Boys Own adventure, getting into scrapes, James damned Bond multiplied by whatever the hell Tom Hanks is called in those movies, and they've been playing with me. Those times... you know, those times when I've been running away, and there's gunfire all around, and I weave and duck and dodge, and I think, phew, got out of that one. That doesn't happen in real life. In real life, bullets hit people. This, though? They've been letting me go. The idiot who shot me in the side probably got put on traffic detail for a month as punishment. *You weren't supposed to hit him!*

'They've watched us every step of the way, and we're no closer to them.'

'Yes, we are.'

He held her gaze.

'I genuinely don't think so,' he said. 'If we know something, they want us to know it, or they don't care if we know it. Where does that get us? I've been their sport, and I'm sorry I dragged you along with me.'

'I came for you,' she said. 'We have been in this together.' A pause, and then, 'We are still in this.'

'No.'

He gave her another hopeless look, and then turned away and looked back across the lake.

A perfect spot to finally admit defeat, he thought.

Finally? He'd admitted defeat so many times in the past, and he had absolutely, definitively admitted defeat at the end of the previous year. This had been nothing more than one of those pointless comebacks that a faded sportsman makes years after his glory days, or the crooner who seeks one last standing ovation when his voice is long since cracked and broken.

'And what will you do if I go to the Lausanne safe house after lunch?' asked Badstuber. 'What will you do if I go to the safe house in Rome, if I break into the Vatican? What will you do if I go to central Africa, and ply my trade around Juba and N'Pala and N'Djamena?

He hadn't turned to look at her while she'd been speaking, then finally he forced himself to turn away from the lake, to look her in the eye. Her face had a familiar look. The bravest, most defiant look he could imagine, her eyes speaking volumes.

He swallowed.

If anyone had asked him, if they'd given him a notepad and asked him to write it down, he couldn't have begun to conjure up the words for how she'd just made him feel.

'I'd come with you,' he said.

'Good.'

She held the look for another moment, and then her fa

relaxed a little, and she took another drink.

'This is a very nice wine,' she said. 'You should not have paid so much for one bottle, but I appreciate it. Nevertheless, we should not have more than one glass each. There is work to do.'

'Not in Lausanne,' he said, resuming eating.

'We need to go to the safe house.'

'There's no need, no point. What have we actually learned from these other houses? Every step of the way we pick up a little piece of information, but ultimately, we already knew that the Pavilion marked their territory using the art of William Melville, and all I've really learned from these places is that they're Pavilion safe houses.

'The only thing we can learn from going to the one in Lausanne is the same thing that has us going there in the first place. And maybe I'm right about them not really trying to kill me, but if I'm not, then all going to one of these places means is we're putting our lives at risk for nothing. It doesn't make sense. It did. Now, it doesn't.'

She was nodding by the time he'd finished.

'Very good,' she said. 'That is a well-constructed argument, and I accept your conclusion. We go straight to central Africa in that case?'

He smiled, though the conversation had not been entirely able to remove the feelings that had overwhelmed him while he'd spoken to Buchman. The old Jericho, so quick to return, would not be so easily vanquished.

'There was a file in there,' said Jericho. 'A detailed list of five men at the heart of the coup in Democratic Central Africa. I've read rumours that they're under investigation by the ICC.'

'But you presume the Pavilion intended for you to see this. You are unaware if it is a wild goose chase, or if they are happy leave you tentative breadcrumbs, vague connections along the te, to continue this game they play with you.'

He nodded, he took another drink. He stared at his food, hen decided that his appetite hadn't been ruined quite to prevent him enjoying it.

'rious that they would present me with another clue, the same time crushing me in their velvet grip, and out on the sidewalk,' he said. 'But it's all part of the 't leads to N'Pala. Well, perhaps not the capital, it where in that damned country. But that's where it

'We shall go there,' she said automatically, with the same matter-of-fact tone she'd used when she'd told him the previous night they would make love.

'You have people there?' he asked.

She looked at him as though that had been a strange question, then said, 'We cover N'Pala from Abuja,' and he smiled in response.

He finished off his appetiser, took another sip of wine, and then pushed his plate away an inch or two.

'There was one other crumb,' he said, as Badstuber finished off her food. 'There was an empty file marked Operation Dwarrowdelf. You know that name?'

She shook her head.

'It's taken from *Lord of the Rings*, but even within that world, the name itself is rather obscure. It may mean nothing, but it's a reference to a glorious, enormous mine, big enough for a city of dwarves, with a great, cavernous hall.' There was something in his voice when he said the word dwarves, as if embarrassed to be so seriously talking about it, and the slightest smile came to Badstuber's lips as she recognised his discomfort. 'Even Buchman said it, you know, big deal. We're in the offices of a mining federation, and they use a mining term to talk about an operation they're working on. Why wouldn't they? But it's something, that's all. Operation Dwarrowdelf. A name to toss around, see if it gets us anywhere.'

'It tells us something beyond the simple act of it being a mining operation,' she said.

A waitress arrived, and paused before collecting the plates.

'Everything was all right for you?' she asked.

'Perfect, thanks,' said Jericho.

'Yes,' said Badstuber.

And the waitress gave the merest of bows, stacked the plates, then walked efficiently away.

'Go on,' said Jericho.

'It is frivolous. A junior member of an organisation is unlikely to give something important such a throwaway name in case it met with disapproval. To me it says that the person in charge named this project, and that person is not a serious person, regardless of how much power they might have.'

'Hmm,' said Jericho, 'I'm not sure. I think maybe you're viewing that through your lens of common sense. Nevertheless, the nomenclature aside, we have, at the very least, Democratic

Central Africa, and we have mining, and it's somewhere to start, though to be honest, it's hard to imagine that the Pavilion is making such a big play in African minerals, regardless of how much unexploited wealth there might be there.'

'We shall travel there and find out,' she said.

'You're desperate to get back on a plane,' said Jericho, and they managed to share a smile for the first time since she'd picked him up.

'You propose something else?' she asked.

The waitress arrived, and placed a plate in front of each of them, containing a tiny bowl.

'A melon sorbet, madame, monsieur,' and she smiled, and turned away again.

They stared at the palate cleanser, then Jericho automatically lifted the spoon and took a bite.

'I'd like to hear from Stuart first.'

He took another bite, while he formulated his thoughts, and she recognised he was putting something else together, and left him to it.

'I won't deny I feel defeated,' he said. 'They seem so… *omnipresent*. However, there's always the possibility…' and he took another mouthful of sorbet so that it was already almost finished, sucked the ice off his tongue, then continued, 'there's the possibility that somewhere along the way we've done something they weren't expecting, or we've found out something they would actually have preferred us not to find. Then Buchman shows up, and she acts all casual and dismissive, and lets me know just how much she knows, and it makes me feel like it's been a waste of time. And you know, I'm largely convinced that it has all been a waste of time. But maybe, in there somewhere, there's something they'd rather we didn't know.'

'So, why not just kill you?'

'I don't know. They expect me to keep going, and they have other plans for me, perhaps. Or, maybe someone within the Pavilion is happy for the game to continue. And, if we're going to continue to play it, then we might as well tick the boxes as we go along. I want to hear what Stuart has to say, and then I want to go to the Vatican.'

'You do not want to go to the safe house in Lausanne, but you will go to the one in Rome?'

'No, not the safe house, the Vatican.'

She took a bite of sorbet, then delicately licked some of it from her lips, the sun glinting off the edge of her tongue.

'You wish to go to the Vatican itself?'

'It seems like a little bit of an outlier, doesn't it?'

'Perhaps.'

'Perhaps?'

'Perhaps there is a cardinal from Democratic Central Africa.'

Jericho nodded, something in his eyes, a little of the fight returning, and he took out his phone, and quickly searched.

'Well, there we are,' said Jericho, and he turned the phone so that Badstuber could see the name and picture.

Cardinal Ndakara, Archbishop emeritus of N'Pala.

'Interesting,' said Badstuber, 'though I am still unsure how it fits the narrative.'

'I know,' said Jericho. 'Nothing about the Pavilion so far has involved religion. Only one way to find out.'

'OK, we shall travel to Rome. However, it seems unlikely that Cardinal Ndakara will actually be present at the Vatican, waiting to host us.'

Jericho smiled, finishing off the small sorbet.

'You'll literally have the guards on your side,' said Jericho.

She ruefully returned the smile.

'Of course, the Swiss Guard will do anything the FIS instruct them to.'

'You must have people embedded though, right?'

'I do not know,' she said. 'I will make a call.'

'Thank you.'

'You should call DI Haynes,' said Badstuber.

'Yes,' said Jericho. Then he got to his feet, and walked away from the table as he took out his phone, dialling the number as he stood looking out over the lake.

One ring.

'Boss,' said Haynes. 'Where are you in the world?'

'I might at some other time have thought it best not to tell you, but the people we're pursuing already seem to be aware. We're in Lausanne, sitting by the lake, eating lunch.'

'Hell of a mission you're on there,' said Haynes. 'You're still with DI Badstuber, then?'

'Yes.'

'How's that going?' asked Haynes, with just enough of a smile in his voice for Jericho to know exactly what he meant.

'We seem to be getting by,' he said. 'Although, to be honest, I'm not sure how much progress we're making. How are you?'

'All good, all good. You'll be calling about the painting, and I don't have anything for you yet. Margot took it to work today, and she's already been in touch. She has something to tell me, so as soon as I get it, I'll give you a shout. You still going to be in Lausanne later today?'

Jericho thought it through. They could fly to Rome, but he really wanted the drive across the Alps, just for the sake of it. What would that be? Ten hours perhaps. Maybe it would stretch to eleven or twelve, depending on the traffic.

They'd only had one glass of wine each, so really, they were fine to leave here after lunch, arriving in Rome in the early hours. Have a hotel booked for their arrival, get a few hours' sleep, and kick off again in the morning.

His eyes drifted across the lake, to the sound of the gentle lapping of the water against the base of the piazza.

'Dammit,' he muttered to himself.

'Sir?'

'Just thinking things through,' said Jericho. 'We might be here, doesn't matter. Just call when you get an update.'

'Will do. I'll probably nip out for an hour so I can go round there, see what she's picked up. And if there's anything, I'll call.'

'Thanks, Stuart.'

'Boss,' he said.

They hung up. Jericho took a moment, and then turned back to the table.

'There is news?' asked Badstuber.

'Not yet,' said Jericho, 'though Professor Leighton seems to have found *something*. Stuart'll call when he's been over there later.'

'You are on edge,' she said.

He looked away, head shaking as he went.

'I'm not sure if I am. It's just… I had given up half an hour ago, and now here we are, still going, still looking for clues, still blindly ignoring what's in front of us. That we cannot beat these people.'

'Perhaps you were right before.'

'How d'you mean?'

'When you posited the notion that they are not as in control as they make out. They take what they do know and create a narrative. They gaslight you into thinking they have dominion.'

'Maybe,' said Jericho.

The idea that he could be gaslit, even though it was him who'd suggested it in the first place, depressed him even more, if that was possible.

The waitress arrived, and placed their plates of lightly fried fish in front of them, asking the question of whether they required anything else, with a lift of her eyebrows.

'Thank you,' said Jericho, Badstuber answering with a small head shake.

And then the waitress lifted the wine bottle from its bucket of ice, and poured more into the two glasses.

Jericho and Badstuber looked at each other as she did so, and they understood. That was the decision made for them, and they'd let it happen.

Perhaps civilisation itself was in peril, and there certainly was a lot of talk about something approaching, as though the near two-hundred-year existence of the Pavilion was about to come to an apocalyptic end – apocalyptic for everyone else, if not the Pavilion – but here they were, possibly two of the only people on earth aware of the extent of the Damoclean sword that hung over the world, and yet they would cling to this idyll of perfection just a little bit longer.

One more afternoon, one more evening, before the adventure, and the trauma drew them further on.

And with the acceptance of that, and the acknowledgement that they'd both allowed it to happen, they lifted their glasses, clinked quietly in the afternoon sun, and set about eating lunch.

They finished the bottle of wine, they drank coffee, they sat and looked out over the lake. Then at some point in the afternoon, they began to find it cold, and returned to the bedroom.

39

The following morning they ate breakfast at seven-fifteen a.m. and left Lausanne at just after eight. Jericho drove the first leg, with an agreement Badstuber would take over somewhere this side of Milan.

Jericho might have felt guilty taking an afternoon and evening off from the battle, but he drove now with an enthusiasm and a belief that he hadn't felt since Badstuber had first turned up at his door. He'd needed the break. He'd needed the rest, the food, the wine, the physical contact, and he'd damned well needed the good night's sleep he'd got at the end of it all.

Haynes had called at what had been, frankly, an inopportune time, but Jericho had felt compelled to take the call in any case.

Haynes, as ever, could read him well, and the first part of the conversation had consisted of Haynes saying he could call back, and Jericho irritably insisting he should just get on with it.

'This seems like a throwback,' Haynes had said, when he'd finally got around to it.

'A throwback to what?'

'We spent so much time on those Tarot cards back in the day, right? And particularly that second time, when they were killing off the team who'd climbed Kanchenjunga, we were getting those damned things turning up every fifteen minutes. Then you got one when you were in hospital at the end of all that, and since then... well, last time I asked, you hadn't received a thing. Anything in the last few days?'

'Nothing,' said Jericho. 'It's like a game they had, and now they're bored with it. What've you found? Neither you nor the professor have received one, have you?'

'No, it's not that. It's just… there's a card been painted into the Melville. It's the only anomaly that shows up in the X-ray. And interestingly, once you know it's there because of the X-ray, you can kind of see it woven into the painting without needing the X-ray. Hell of an optical illusion, but obviously it was done for someone's benefit, and whoever that someone was, they must have known what to look for. It's not like they would've come across it in someone's house and thought, I'll just need to run this painting of yours through the X-ray machine, if I could borrow it for a few hours.'

'I'm embarrassed to admit I don't know when X-rays were invented,' said Jericho, though as he said it he wasn't sure why he should be embarrassed.

'Invented accidentally by Wilhelm Röntgen in Bavaria in 1895,' said Haynes, 'I checked. So whatever the secret was, and maybe it was something all members of the Pavilion would've known, they had some other method by which they worked out the card. Perhaps its placement is the same in every other Melville. That's next on our list, though obviously in those cases we'll be working off images we've had to download. No other Melville originals to hand. I'll send you updates if we find anything.'

'Which card?' Jericho thought to ask, just as he was about to thank Haynes for his work.

'On the Melville you took from the Whistler? The Fool.'

'So, the same one I was given ten years ago.'

'Yes.'

Not a great compliment, he supposed, but then, better probably than the Hanged Man or Death, both of which had been used as death threats or perhaps death announcements in the case of the latter. Exactly what the Fool had been a threat of, he wasn't sure.

They'd spent a lot of time with the previous two cards, examining what they could mean in the context of the Tarot and the situation in which they were being used. Then in Oslo, Develin, who seemed to be heading up the Pavilion's operation there, had told Professor Leighton that, despite all the evidence to the contrary, they weren't Tarot cards.

It was no bad thing Develin had died shortly afterwards, but nevertheless, it meant they'd never got any more of an explanation. They had three cards, The Hanged Man, Death and The Fool, everything about them said they came from the Tarot, except the word from the horse's mouth.

Later in the evening, Haynes got in touch with another slew of images. In the same place in every Melville painting they'd looked at, woven into the picture, an outline of a card. Either similar to a card from the Tarot, or else something that resembled Tarot pastiche. Some cards were repeated, indicating that not every painting had its own individual card embedded within it.

It was fascinating, and another insight into how the Pavilion carried out its clandestine business, particularly back in the early days, when communication would have been slower, but like so much they'd learned in the past few days, ultimately it did not get them any nearer the heart of darkness.

Φ

The drive through the Alps on a cold, clear day was as beautiful as Jericho remembered. He would come back here, he thought, when this madness was over. That was a small dream he allowed himself, albeit in some other clear-thinking part of his brain he already believed he was unlikely to get out alive.

Death he could live with, he thought to himself, with a grim smile. But he had to make sure the same fate didn't befall Badstuber. Her kids might have been getting older, but she was still far too young for them to lose her.

Badstuber read the news on her phone as they passed over and through the mountains, reading parts out to Jericho as she went, taking her time to go through all the regions of the earth.

War was everywhere, and with every passing day it seemed the time when all the wars merged into one giant, global, all-consuming conflict grew closer.

'You know the *Hitchhiker's Guide To The Galaxy*?' he asked at one point.

He glanced at her, the familiar furrowed brow in her serious face.

'I know the name, I think, but I do not know the context.'

'I shan't explain,' he said. It felt strange even talking about it. The radio show, which he'd grown up listening to, seemed to be from another life. The one he'd had before the police. The one he'd had before his daily life had become immersed in crime gangs, and rape, and domestic violence and assault and murder, and every day had been a bludgeoning of his soul, and he'd been forever unable to leave the job behind at the office, and it had consumed him. 'But there was an idea in it, the Total Perspective Vortex, about how huge everything in the universe is, and how it reduces individual humans to nothingness.' He paused, she waited for him to continue. 'It can be like that listening to the news, and the awfulness of the world. There's so much... shit.'

'You would like me to stop?' she said.

'No, we need to know.'

She watched him, his eyes steady on the road ahead, and she knew there was something else coming, and so did not immediately read the next item from the panoply of abomination unfolding across the earth.

'You were right what you said the other day. Each generation sees an imminent hellscape just around the corner. And why not? Great civilisations have risen and fallen throughout history. But now we live in a global society, where countries are connected in a way they never have been, so why should the collapse, when it comes, not be global?

'The internet has let loose the dogs of war, and hell has followed. The weaponry that will kill us all is now in the hands of simplistic fools, not the brutal, hard-nosed statesmen of old. The men who had lived through global war, and known the pain of it. These idiots now are playing video games with civilisation, augmented by weapons of untold destructive power.'

He sounded like there was still a thing or two to be said, but he finally stopped himself, shaking his head, and then glanced at her.

She was smiling at him, and she nodded.

'I will stop reading the news,' she said.

'Sorry, I don't know where that came from.'

'Nevertheless,' she said, 'when your children are losing sleep because of a bullying teacher, you are more concerned with their mental well-being, than whether or not they are about to be vaporised along with the rest of humanity.'

Badstuber had spent half an hour on the phone with her youngest daughter that morning, and was due to have a phone call with the headmistress of the school in a short while. It was the intrusion of a kind of real life that Jericho had never known, and while she'd spoken to her daughter, he'd spent every second thinking he ought to have fled that morning without her, and gone straight to N'Pala.

'You don't need to stop reading the news,' he said. 'I need to know, and I'd prefer to get the potted version from you, rather than have to listen to it or read a news report.'

Another quick glance between them, she checked the time, and then she brought the news up once again on her phone.

Intensified Russian attacks on Kyiv and Lviv, coupled with the collapse of Ukrainian lines in the Donbas. Three massive explosions at oil refineries inside Russia. Catastrophic oil spillage in the Black Sea from collateral damage to a tanker operating under the flag of Palau. Russian troops reportedly massing on the western border, from northern Finland all the way to southern Latvia, and within Belarus, on its borders with Lithuania and Poland.

Large scale troop movements in the South China Sea. Taiwan mobilising. Philippine and Chinese warships exchanging fire. The US Navy on the verge of joining the fray.

US troops starting to gather at the Mexican border, with rumours of an imminent invasion. Meanwhile, the massive expansion of US military bases in Greenland continued. The Silent Invasion it was being called, though it was being called that on the fifteenth item in the news, everywhere except Denmark. There were so many other seemingly more important events taking place, and besides, everyone now took it for granted that America's appropriation of Greenland was a given.

America had almost completed the takeover of the Panama canal, although fighting had unexpectedly broken out with a rebel group that some said were backed by Cuba. As a result, America was said to be talking about taking Cuba.

There had been a first exchange of fire between heavily armed police forces in Los Angeles, loyal to the governor of California, and the National Guard. Civil war was being screamed from the rooftops.

Israel and Iran now bombing each other on a daily basis, with Qatar, Jordan and Lebanon already dragged into the fray, and Russia firmly stating they were ready to come to Iran's aid if Israel did not back down.

Massive Saudi-led bombing in Yemen, with several thousand reported casualties.

Iran mobilising on the border with Iraq. India and Pakistan mobilising in Kashmir, with rumours there were now more than half a million troops in the area about to be thrown into conflict.

Collapse of governments in Sudan, South Sudan and Chad.

She paused finally, exhaustingly, after another ten minutes. She looked at the time, which she automatically did by looking at her wristwatch, even though she had her phone in her hand.

'There are many more unpleasant domestic stories, but I think there is no need to add them to this list for our purposes, albeit some of them may be relevant.'

'Nothing about Democratic Central Africa?' asked Jericho.

'Not since we last checked. The news agencies have yet to be allowed back in. The country is currently a black hole, but no one seems very interested.'

Silence returned to the car. Ahead of them, the flatlands, the mountains now sadly in the rear-view mirror.

Maybe that's it, thought Jericho, the last time we see the Alps. Down to Rome, then if we get out of there alive, a flight to Abuja, followed by the hazardous trip into DCA, and then who knew what awaited them?

He wanted to say that he should have left her in Switzerland, but the words remained unspoken.

40

They'd slept well, they'd woken to a grey day in Rome, and had eaten breakfast in the hotel restaurant. Coffee and orange juice and croissant and fruit.

Overnight, the US Pacific fleet had sailed into position to defend Taiwan. The Chinese had responded angrily. The North Koreans, even though no one was including them in anything – and Taiwan was well over a thousand kilometres away – were threatening the west coast of America with nuclear attack, and Seoul with all-out conventional warfare, if the Americans did not leave the area by midnight the following day. The US president, when cornered on Air Force One on the subject of North Korea had said, 'If I hear one more word out of that fat fucking guy, there won't be a North Korea. I've had enough. Had enough, believe me.'

Once you've said fuck once as a president, and no one cares, you start using it all the time.

Jericho and Badstuber had contemplated taking a slow approach in the first instance. This would have seen them sign up for the Vatican tour. Do the rounds, try to establish if there was anything in the great panoply of classical art that spoke of the Pavilion. But the idea seemed so far-fetched. And even if there had been, even there'd been a piece of art – modern by the standard of everything else on display – with a card beneath it stating it had been provided by the Pavilion, what exactly were they going to do with that? Jericho was not going to be able to pull off the absurd manoeuvre he'd pulled at the Whistler in

New York a second time. And the longer this continued, the more convinced he'd become that he'd pulled that off only because they'd allowed him to.

And so they'd decided to take as direct an approach as they possibly could. Badstuber spoke to her boss to make sure she was cleared to do what she wanted to do, calls were made, and a meeting was set up with Alois Hirschbühl, head of the Swiss Guard at the Vatican. Mid-fifties, a shock of grey hair, a pair of rimless Gucci spectacles with red temple tips.

They had arrived at nine-twenty-five, they had been ushered smoothly through security, and now they were sitting in a small office, with a window looking down on a courtyard that would perfectly catch the shade in summer, a large stone pine at its centre, but which now looked cold and empty.

Hirschbühl, who Badstuber speculated had once been a member of her security service, had spent a few questions establishing Badstuber's credentials, and had turned to Jericho.

'You look as though you have been in some combat, and I note you walk with a profound limp. That is recent?'

'Yes,' said Jericho.

'And you are here in an unofficial capacity?'

'Former detective chief inspector,' said Jericho. Despite living this life for ten years, he'd never grown comfortable with having to justify himself, and why he was asking so many damn questions. That was why he'd used so many fake identities. Now, however, it seemed the Pavilion knew every little thing he did. What was the point in the lie?

'My last case as a detective was open-ended, and I've spent the time since continuing to investigate it.'

Hirschbühl glanced at Badstuber, then turned back.

'You are here in an unofficial capacity?' he repeated.

'Yes.'

'You are effectively a private detective.'

Jericho didn't answer. He didn't feel like a private detective, and it wasn't like he took on cases, but really, he couldn't argue.

So he didn't.

Hirschbühl let out a long sigh, as though this whole thing was beneath him, then he turned back to Badstuber.

'We are where we are,' he said. 'How can I help you?'

They had agreed beforehand that Jericho would lead the questioning, and he wondered if Badstuber would change the play on the hoof, given how dismissive Hirschbühl was of Jericho's presence, but then he wasn't surprised that she continued to conduct the investigation exactly as they'd agreed.

'Chief Inspector,' she said to Jericho.

Hirschbühl's eyes switched to Jericho, the look of contempt undiminished.

'We're investigating the activities of a group known as the Pavilion,' said Jericho.

He held Hirschbühl's gaze, looking for the reaction in the eyes. Hirschbühl pushed his glasses a little further up his nose, though there was something affected in it. The glasses had nowhere to go.

'What is this, the Pavilion?'

'An organisation with access to power all around the globe. They have money, they have connections, they make things happen.'

That was all he had? Sometimes he hated himself.

But then, the truth of it, everything they'd learned, sounded preposterous. How did you distil that into two sentences?

'A secret society?' said Hirschbühl, though at least he displayed no signs of amusement with the question.

'That does not do them justice. They kill, they control.'

'Do they?'

'You will remember an incident in Oslo ten years ago,' said Jericho. 'Over twenty people killed in a shoot-out.'

Hirschbühl stared at him unblinkingly, then finally nodded.

'Yes,' he said.

'Agent Badstuber and I were there. It was the work of the Pavilion. It is only one such event out of many in the past ten years as their activities have increased.'

Hirschbühl's blank expression continued to demand more of him. Jericho recognised the interview technique as one he would have frequently employed in his time on the force.

'You think they are at play in the Vatican?'

'We don't know. But we had a fellow operative working on –'

'By fellow, you mean FIS, or another lone wolf like yourself?'

Glorious contempt, thought Jericho. He would rarely have sounded so disdainful himself.

'The latter,' he said. 'She was killed by the Pavilion in the Netherlands last week. She left something of herself behind for us, including four false passports. One of them had been issued by the Vatican in the name of Isabella Blackwell.'

'I don't think so,' said Hirschbühl.

Jericho reached inside his coat pocket, took out the copy of Amanda's Vatican passport, and passed it across the desk.

Hirschbühl couldn't keep the grimace from his face, then he lifted the paper and looked at the photograph. He studied it for a moment, glanced up at the two of them, as though he was in passport control, then turned to the computer and typed in the details.

Silence.

Behind Hirschbühl, an image of Jesus on the wall. *Salvatore mundi*, dressed in blue, the fingers held in the sign of benediction. In the corner, a Japanese peace lily with a single white flower, on top of a filing cabinet. Somewhere far beyond, the angry sound of a motorbike.

'You know the name?' asked Jericho. 'If she has the passport, she must have been employed here.'

The glance Hirschbühl threw across the desk was more contemptuous than any he'd previously given.

'The Vatican employs more than four thousand, eight hundred people,' he said, then he left a small gap during which he imagined he withered Jericho with his gaze, and added, 'I do not know them all.'

He turned back to the computer, and made a small gesture towards the screen.

'This woman is not dead,' he said.

'We viewed her corpse last week,' said Badstuber. 'I can assure you, Chief Hirschbühl, she is dead.'

'This has not been reported to us,' said Hirschbühl. 'I will need to speak to some people.'

'Where did she work?' asked Jericho.

He looked like he was contemplating not answering, then he said, 'The apostolic library. I will need –'

'When was the last time she was here?' asked Badstuber.

He contemplated her, but seemed a little more forgiving of her having asked a question, then said, 'Two weeks ago.'

Badstuber and Jericho shared a quick glance. That would have been not long before she'd been killed. Which meant that whatever she learned here, was possibly the thing that had pushed the Pavilion over the edge, and made them decide it was time to end Amanda's search for good.

'And you can see who she met then?'

'Yes, of course.'

His eyes ran over the computer, the brow furrowed. He shook his head, the brow creased a little more, he pursed his lips.

'Ms Blackwell only came here the one time, and yet she had full access to every part of the building.'

Then he started to say something, and immediately stopped himself, something he followed with a suspicious glance at Jericho. Then back to the monitor, a quick head shake, after which he decisively hit the lock screen button, and got to his feet.

'I need to speak to someone. I can't ask you to come with me. You will stay here.'

He stared at them, long enough that they realised he was waiting for their agreement, then they both nodded, and Jericho said, 'Yes.'

And he was gone.

Door closed, Jericho glanced over his shoulder at it, left it a few moments then got to his feet, opened the door, checked the corridor, then closed the door again.

'You were paying attention when he logged in?' he asked.

Badstuber got to her feet, walked round the computer, stared at the keyboard for a moment, then brought up the log-in page.

'You mean, did I manage to follow his rapidly typed password while sitting opposite from him at a desk?' she asked.

'Yes,' said Jericho, thinking as she said it that that sounded fairly unlikely.

'No. I am going to try the two passwords from the USB stick which you stated were likely to have been created by Amanda.'

She typed one of them while she spoke. It didn't work.

She quickly typed the second one, and this time the screen flashed into life.

'You will stand at the door and wait for the footsteps,' she said.

'The corridor's short,' said Jericho. 'He'll be in the room before you can extricate yourself.'

She glanced at the door again and nodded.

'Yes,' she said. 'We will need to be quick.'

She brought up details of Amanda's brief time at the Vatican. She had been there two days ahead of what the coroner in Noordwijk had estimated as her time of death, and that had been her only visit. She had searched the library for any books that detailed the activities of the Pavilion, and had found nothing. She had asked for a meeting with Cardinal Ndakara, to be arranged the following week in N'Pala, and this had been granted. She'd arranged this during a meeting with an official in the Second Section of the Secretariat of State.

'We need the name,' said Jericho, and Badstuber nodded, opened up a new page, and began to manoeuvre through the website, until she found the list of staff in each department.

There were forty-seven officials in the section, but only one listed as dealing with central Africa. Georgina Barbieri.

'We're going to need to speak to her,' said Jericho, and Badstuber nodded, then clicked on to her file.

She was thirty-six, her long dark hair immaculately elegant in the photograph. An MA in Art History from the Courtauld in London. Junior diplomat with the Holy See, having worked there for just over a year.

'Georgina Barbieri,' said Jericho, something in his voice.

'You know her?' asked Badstuber.

'Same woman who so easily dismantled me and my life's work in the chairman's office in Lausanne.'

Badstuber glanced back at the screen.

'Joanne Buchman,' she said.

'Yes.'

Phone in hand, Jericho took a photograph of the screen, then another, close-up, of the woman's picture.

Out of nowhere, the sound of footsteps, no more than a few seconds away.

Badstuber logged out of Amanda's account, returning the screen to where it had been previously. Then she grabbed Jericho as he was about to retreat from the desk, lifted her skirt to her waist, sat on the desk, and pulled Jericho on top of her, as she fell back, their lips finding each other as the door opened. Hirschbühl stopped, wide-eyed, exasperated.

They broke apart, Badstuber with an affected gasp, and a, 'Jesus,' breathlessly expelled from her lips.

Jericho pulled back, looking desperately embarrassed. Acting wasn't in his skill set. He was genuinely embarrassed.

'Sorry, sorry,' said Badstuber, straightening up, leaving her skirt at her waist for a moment, while her fingers fiddled with the buttons of her blouse, as though they'd needed sorting out.

'What are you doing?'

'I'm so sorry,' said Badstuber. 'It's Rome, it's been so romantic. We keep getting carried away.' She used her hand as a fan, and then remembered to pull down her skirt.

Badstuber sat back down, giving herself a mild rebuke, muttering, 'I'm so embarrassed,' to herself. Jericho sat down beside her, looking not much less perturbed by events than Hirschbühl. He still wasn't acting.

Hirschbühl sat in his seat, took a moment to consider if the seat felt warmer than it should have done, then opened the computer. It remained on the same page on which he'd left it.

He read over it again, and then turned back to them.

'I am sorry, but I'm afraid I'm going to have to ask you to leave. There's more going on here than I currently understand, and I'm not letting this go any further for now. If you want to leave me contact details, I can be in touch.'

'Would it be possible for us to take some time looking at the archive?' asked Jericho, clinging to their time there, thinking that some opportunity or other would present itself.

'You can certainly make an appointment to do that, but I believe all our spots are taken for today,' said Hirschbühl.

He looked between the two of them, and then said, 'And so, you must go.' He dramatically locked the screen, as though channelling all the relief in the world that he was able to get rid of them, then he got to his feet and ushered them towards the door.

'Thank you for coming,' he said.

Φ

They were shown to a door that led out onto a small side street, adjacent to St Peter's Square. A curt nod from the Swiss guardsman, and then the door was abruptly closed.

The day was warmer now, slightly humid, the sun still locked away behind thick cloud.

They turned and started walking up the short alleyway, to the opening onto the square.

'You've come a long way,' said Jericho after a short while.

'How do you mean?' asked Badstuber.

'The first day we spent together ten years ago, remember? Sitting in the car. You told me you were never going to sleep with me, and I hadn't to bother wasting my time trying.'

He couldn't stop himself glancing at her, though he managed to keep the amusement from his face.

'Now you're jumping me on a desk.'

'It made sense,' she said, determinedly not rising to the joke. 'Some people are discomfited by sex, and that was always likely to be the case in that scenario. And in any case, we are lovers now.'

They walked on.

'Nevertheless,' she continued, 'you are right. I am sorry I said that stupid thing. But I believe I previously apologised.'

Jericho smiled wryly to himself.

'Did you note the home address of Georgina Barbieri?' said Badstuber.

'I did. Different name, but coincidentally the same address as the next of kin of Isabella Blackwell.'

'Yes,' said Badstuber. 'We will go there now.'

'Yes,' said Jericho, then he couldn't help, 'probably best if you don't force me into bed, though,' and she turned with a furrowed brow, and then couldn't help smiling ruefully at the look on his face.

41

They had stopped for coffee, to allow Badstuber to contact her head office, and run a check on Georgina Barbieri. They had been unable to discover much of her existence, other than that two weeks previously, the day after she'd met with Amanda, she'd travelled to Amsterdam.

There was a line to be drawn there, and it didn't necessarily run straight, but there was a good chance that in that opulent office in Lausanne, Jericho had met the woman who'd killed Amanda.

The first ten years Amanda had been missing, Jericho had assumed she was dead. This, then, was who he'd been looking for. Her killer. And even though they were sure she'd been murdered now, they'd given virtually no thought to who'd actually carried out the deed. The Pavilion was so vast, the people they could call on to commit such a crime so great in number, Jericho had barely given any thought to who it might have been. And now, when he hadn't particularly been looking for it, here they were, and the killer may well have fallen into their lap.

A beautiful apartment building off the Via Angelo Schiavio. Four stories, the building, and those either side of it, immaculately presented. Neat balconies, many with greenery growing, barely a leaf out of place. Marbling around the doorway, automatic doors to be opened on being buzzed in, or on the waving of a fob. There was no lock to be picked.

'I'm going to have to leave you to it,' said Jericho.

'Yes,' said Badstuber, acknowledging that it would be much easier for her to piggyback in alone on someone else opening the door, than in Jericho's company.

'In fact, I should wait out here, watch for her coming home, and call.'

'Yes,' said Badstuber, 'that makes sense. And you will notice the slip road to the underground garage,' she said, indicating to the left of the building, quickly followed by, 'I am sorry, I am telling you how to do your job. You should walk away from me, allow me to choose my moment – it may be some time, as this is not a big building – and then you can position yourself as you see fit.'

'Roger that,' said Jericho, and he turned away with a nod, and headed back down to wait for a short while on the Via Meazza, where the number of pedestrians was greater, and he quickly disappeared into the throng.

He checked the route map on his phone to make sure that this was the way Barbieri would approach her apartment, and it transpired there really was no other way, then he slipped the phone back into his pocket.

Seven minutes later it pinged.

I am in.

He sent the thumbs up, he walked to the corner of the road, he checked the time, he bought a copy of *Il Messaggero*, then he sat in a table outside a small café on the corner of Meazza and Schiavio, ordered a macchiato, and settled in for the wait, hoping that Badstuber would have searched the entire flat, and would be back out before Barbieri returned home.

A few minutes later, he'd finished the coffee and was wondering whether or not it was the done thing to have a second one, or if this would instantly be greeted by the waiter's attention-grabbing scorn, when there was a seat pulled quietly out at a table behind him. He did not turn, and therefore did not see the face of the woman who was now sitting behind him. She leaned into Jericho, stuck the barrel of a Glock into his back, and said, 'You do persevere, Robert. I thought perhaps I'd managed to persuade you it was time to trundle back to the Shire, and your Avercamp jigsaw. But no, here you are, bothering security at the Vatican. I don't like that.'

He started to turn, and she jabbed the gun a little more firmly into his side.

'We're going to go up to the apartment now, you and me.

You make any move, you indulge in even the slightest bit of bravado, you and your girlfriend are dead. *Capiche?*'

Jericho started to turn again, and this time the gun was jabbed in firmly enough that he winced.

'People have different books,' said Barbieri. 'But in my book, turning round like that when you've been told not to, that counts as bravado. Do it again and I'll shoot you right here in the street, and if you think I wouldn't, I'll send you the link to the stories of the three times I've done it before in this city and no one's batted an eyelid.'

The gun was withdrawn from his back, Jericho left to presume it was still aimed from very close range.

He took a moment, but accepted that really there was nothing at this stage to be gained from prevarication, then he folded the newspaper and left it on the table, pushed the empty coffee cup away from himself, and slowly got to his feet.

'Keep walking,' said the voice behind him. 'And don't make me do to you what I did to your wife.'

42

Badstuber was in the principal bedroom, going through the bedside drawers, not finding anything she wouldn't expect to find. It had been the same in the other rooms, and she was getting frustrated.

She was not demonstrative, but inside, she felt the same turbulence as anyone else. This morning, she was worried about her daughter. Worried about all three of them, in fact, for different reasons, and she was beginning to wonder if she would ever see them again.

How much thought had she given this path before deciding to take it? When she'd been brought on board in Amsterdam, she could have reported it quickly back to the centre, and there would've been someone in the FIS happy to take it off her hands. She would never have known if that person had been part of the Pavilion.

She'd been bound to this drama since she'd met Jericho, and what had it really meant to her life? Most of the people on the planet were managing just fine, dealing with their own crap, and not having to worry about something that might be an existential threat to mankind's existence, or might just be a sad little group of rich men playing at being supervillains.

She let out a long sigh as she closed the bottom drawer. Then she had a thought, and pulled the top drawer all the way out of the unit, and felt around the top and sides of the inside, before deciding that this was nothing more than a regular IKEA bedside cabinet, as unlikely to give up secrets as anything else in the house.

Sure, there was a Melville painting in the hallway, though as yet she hadn't stood and looked at it long enough to see if there was one of the cards fashioned into the pictorial narrative. But what if there was? What of its presence here in the apartment? It was, like so many of the things they were uncovering, confirmation of what they already knew.

She straightened up, giving up on looking for a secret bedside table compartment, the top drawer still on the floor at her feet, when there was a sound behind her, and she turned.

'Hey,' she said, her voice betraying a little of her surprise, 'how'd you get in?'

Jericho walked silently into the room, and then Barbieri appeared, gun drawn, behind him.

'Same side of the bed,' said Barbieri to Jericho, and he did as he was told, gave Badstuber an apologetic glance, and then turned to face the door.

'I need to know if either of you is armed,' said Barbieri.

They stared blankly at her.

'Only one way for me to be sure. Get undressed.' She waved the gun at Jericho. 'You first. You can keep your underwear on, I'm not a barbarian.'

Jericho didn't immediately move, and she gave him a withering look, but did not gesture any further with the gun.

'Get undressed and lie on the bed,' she said. 'If you don't, I'll kill you. Then I'll kill her. Then I'll find her children, and it's not like I don't know where they are,' and she glanced at Badstuber and added, 'Heidi is currently in third period, English language with Ms Shelby. Or didn't you know, because you've grown too detached?'

Badstuber stared coldly back. Jericho was possibly even more annoyed on her behalf than she was.

'Come on,' said Barbieri, turning her focus back to Jericho.

He took off his jacket, and dropped it to the floor.

'Nice and slow,' she said.

She watched him, unmoving. Jericho had already calculated the distance, the reaction time needed, their chances if he and Badstuber communicated to make a move at the same time.

'I'm guessing you're Hammersmith,' said Jericho.

She gave him a slight eyebrow, and then nodded.

'I dare say you've spoken to enough people in the past few years to have heard of me,' she said.

'Is that your actual name?' he asked.

'It is how people know me.'

She was being completely professional, which was exactly as he'd expect. Standing away from the end of the bed, while the two of them were side-by-side. Jericho and Badstuber would each have a couple of moves to make before they could even attempt to swipe the gun from her hand. It was never going to work, and they would likely be dead.

Their only chance would be if she didn't actually want them dead, and in some way pulled her shots by aiming at the legs, or the shoulder. Nevertheless, she had an air about her that said she would have total command of any situation, regardless, and if she wanted to maim them, then torture and taunt them, she would. And if she wanted to kill them outright with one shot, that would happen also.

'I can see your mind working,' she said. 'Both of you. The genius detectives at work, on how to get out of a tricky situation. So let me help you out. You can't. For reason that I cannot fathom, Mr Merrick wants you kept alive. You amuse him, but you've long been an irrelevance. You're the king's jester, but I expect you know that already. You seem smart. Long ago you'll have worked out the point of the card. The Fool.' She smiled. 'Mr Merrick calls it Pavilion old money. You might have noticed we've moved on from that frivolity after a hundred and eighty years.'

'The cards fashioned into the old Melville paintings,' said Jericho, as he sat on the edge of the bed to remove his shoes, socks, and trousers. 'The Fool would let someone know they weren't viewed as a threat? They could relax, and know they'd been crushed.'

'Those paintings? Not so much. They weren't letting the recipient of the painting know anything. Those fools wouldn't have known any better. They were letting Pavilion operatives at large in the world know that this nobleman or that industrialist was of no threat. Or that they needed to be warned off, or eliminated, or whatever.'

'So each individual card was an instruction or a threat?'

'Correct, for what it's worth. It was a silly game these men played for all that time, until Mr Merrick put a stop to it. Threats and death and tribute and gold and riches, all doled out via the hand of the hard-working William Hart Melville.' She laughed. 'There was, of course, no William Hart Melville. Just a name attached to a long series of paintings. Comical really, you two discussing the value of the painting you stole from the Whistler. Upwards of thirty million dollars?' A pause, and then, 'I think not. Now lie on the bed, head on the pillow, hands behind your head, fingers linked. Do it.'

Jericho did as he was instructed, and now couldn't help the feeling of vulnerability, naked bar a pair of tight-fitting boxer shorts, stretched out in a position from which it would be impossible to move quickly.

'You've been in the wars,' said Hammersmith. 'Cuts and bruises, stitches on your face, stitches on your side. That'll have been from where that idiot maimed you in London. Oh, and look at that, but if it isn't a couple of bite marks in your chest. Well, well, well.' She smiled darkly as she looked at Badstuber. 'And there was me thinking you were sharing a room in Lausanne to save money.' And then quickly, the false amusement leaving her voice, she said, 'Your turn,' the gun turning on Badstuber.

Badstuber didn't hesitate. She had no more idea of how to get out of this than Jericho, but it wasn't going to happen at this moment. This, whatever this was, had to play out. It had to go where it was going, it had to find them lying side by side on the bed almost naked, before anything else could happen.

Jacket slipped off and laid on the floor, and then she unbuttoned her blouse, removed it and placed it on the jacket, and then slipped off her shoes, her skirt, until she was standing in slender white underwear.

In the quiet of the room she heard Hammersmith swallow, felt her eyes upon her. Without further bidding, Badstuber removed her underwear quickly, placed both items on the small pile, lay on the bed, then stretched her arms behind her head and linked her fingers.

She looked at Hammersmith, and recognised the look she was getting in return.

'Well,' said Hammersmith. She swallowed again. 'Look at you. How bold.'

With her captives now prone, hands behind their heads, Hammersmith allowed herself to step a little closer.

'Perfect white skin,' she said, her eyes running all over Badstuber's naked body. 'No blemishes, no stretch marks, no cuts, no bruises. And look at that… no bites. Doesn't look like you're getting your boyfriend here too excited, does it? Aren't you a little hurt?'

A pause. Badstuber stared coolly back. Maybe there was something in her look that suggested she was enjoying the appraisal.

'What age are you?'

Nothing.

'Seriously, what age are you?'

'Fifty-three.'

'Fifty-three. You look sensational.'

She turned her eyes back to Jericho, giving him another dismissive look.

'You really over-snagged, didn't you? Has it occurred to you that your girlfriend is using you? Look at her. Look at that perfect body. Whatever it was I said about her tits back in Lausanne, completely wrong. She looks amazing. You? Not so amazing. You think maybe she saw an in, she thought that she, Ilsa Badstuber of the FIS, could be the one to crack the Pavilion code that's eluded so many over the years, and so she turned up on your doorstep one dark and stormy night and asked you to join her on an adventure. But look at you. You have been used. Shot at, hurled off buildings, crashing through trees, kicked and punched, chased through the streets of Amsterdam. You've been in the wars. And meanwhile, look at Ilsa. Ilsa is…' She made the chef's kiss gesture. 'While poor DCI Jericho runs around like a fool, everybody's fool, doing as he's told.'

Hammersmith put her hand to her face in a gesture that somehow managed to be not at all affected, running her fingers softly over her lips and chin, and then down over her neck.

'There could be space for you, you know,' she said to Badstuber.

'What does that mean?' said Jericho, interrupting the flow. 'Space?'

'The Pavilion always has space for people of quality,' said Hammersmith, ignoring Jericho. 'You could work for us, your children would be safe. Their father would be safe too, they wouldn't lose him. They wouldn't have to rely on a sub-standard replacement, brought off the substitutes' bench.'

'You couldn't trust me,' said Badstuber.

'Of course we could. This is how it works. You come into our employ. You are well renumerated. But more than that, as we've already discussed, we know where your children are. There is no removing the threat against them, but there is ensuring the threat is never carried out. And over time – and I can confirm that this happens to *everyone* who joins us – you come to realise that the Pavilion, this scorned organisation that this fool and his wife have spent so long trying to bring down, is the purist, most honest organisation on all the earth. Ultimately, under the direction of Mr Merrick, the Pavilion will save the planet.'

She kept her eyes on Badstuber, then let them drift down and then back up her body.

'The thing is, Ilsa, it's not you who's the fool. Just as Amanda Raintree was no fool. Former Detective Chief Inspector Jericho here, lying impotently in his big boy pants, he's the fool. He's blundered around in the shadows getting nowhere for over ten years. And then Ms Raintree leaves him a plethora of clues, and you come to his doorstep to lead him back into the frame, and boom, here he is, the great adventurer, flying around the world to save civilisation.' She paused, she cast Jericho a contemptuous glance, then looked back at Badstuber.

'You know what I'm saying, Ilsa?'

'Yes.'

'Explain it to me.'

'I would not be sent The Fool. I would receive some card with two heads. A choice. One way or the other. In fact, short of you having such a card on you, this is you letting me know my choices, because being cast aside on the streets of Rome is not one of them.'

'Join us or die,' said Hammersmith, and she smiled as she said it. 'I like it when things are succinct. I expect you do too.'

She held Badstuber's gaze for a while, then once again ran her eyes over her body.

'Tick-tock, tick-tock,' she said. 'And before you think the logical thing to do here is play along by saying you'll give us a chance, then making a move when you think I've been lulled into a false sense of security, look around you. Behind the mirror, in the corner of the television set, either side of the bed. Microphones and cameras. I switch them off when I'm here on my own, of course, but they've been activated since you entered. For example, I know you liked the vibrator. It's called a G-spot ripple rampant rabbit. A bit silly, but oh boy, it's fun. I won't lie. I would *love* to see you using that.'

'What happens to the DCI?' asked Badstuber.

'The DCI has a decision to make. I will confess I'm in disagreement with Mr Merrick. He enjoys this charade, as I've said. He likes his court jester. Me, though, I don't. I don't like court jesters. They're too dangerous. I'd just shoot them in the face. So, this is where we are with the DCI…' And now she turned to talk to Jericho, having been speaking like he wasn't in the room. 'Unfortunately for you, I have dominion. Mr Merrick employs me obviously, but I have the remit to do as I see fit with potential threats. I've been this close to putting a bullet in your head on many occasions, and maybe now I'm the closest I've ever been. But I'd rather not have the argument with Mr Merrick if I didn't have to. So, how about this? I let you go, and you return to your hobbit hole, and your jigsaws, and your walks in the thrilling Mendip hills, and don't leave your hole again. Return to the life which a week ago you thought was forever. That's all. Go back to the shadow, and we're done. If I ever come across you again, and I promise not to come looking for you in Wells, but if we meet again, you're dead. I realise this means curtains for this nascent love affair of yours, chief inspector, but seriously, you must realise it's doomed before it begins. Let her go. If you need someone else, I'm sure you'll find a suitable woman while doing sit-ups at the leisure centre.'

Suddenly, without warning, Badstuber lifted her hands, and sat up on the edge of the bed, a quick and graceful single movement. Hammersmith took a step back, a flinch across her face, gun raised another inch or two, poised.

But, of course, she did not fire.

'I am going to get dressed,' said Badstuber, 'then we will talk over coffee. If I am going to work for you, I need to know what it is I will be doing.'

She held her look for a moment, and then indicated the small pile of clothes.

'Yes?' she said.

Hammersmith smiled, and made a small go-ahead gesture with the gun.

'I like you,' she said, then she turned the gun on Jericho. 'You, I don't care about. You can't get dressed. I like you like that. Naked, bruised and vulnerable. But I need eyes on. When we go through, you go ahead. And remember, we are being watched. You cannot get out of this house alive. Doors are locked, windows are locked. You have witnessed the mechanisms we have in place in our safe houses.'

'I got out of the London house,' said Jericho.

'That's because the idiot who was there showed you the

escape route. I am the only one who knows the escape route. I will not help you escape.'

'Maybe the same thing that happened to her, will happen to you.'

'I do not think so. I have no intention of sleeping with you, and besides, it was me who ordered her death.'

Badstuber was dressed, and now Hammersmith stood back, ushering them through to the sitting room ahead of her, unable to stop herself saying, 'Nothing stupid. I don't like stupid.'

43

'What are we waiting for?' asked Jericho.

He felt vaguely ill at ease, based entirely on his state of undress.

He didn't look awful like this, sitting straight-backed in a comfortable chair, torso stretched, his fingers entwined at the back of his head. He didn't have the belly of many a sixty-one-year-old man. Those four times a week gym classes he took had been working for him the past few months. But still, he remained British and of a generation where this level of undress in company made him feel uncomfortable, regardless of the situation.

She had had him make two coffees – revelling in his being reduced to making drinks for the women – and now they were sitting around the small table, Badstuber on a sofa, Jericho in a single armchair, Hammersmith in a dining chair, staring deadpan across the table.

And Jericho was quite sure he knew why she was waiting. She wanted something to happen. He had no idea why he was of any interest to Stanley Merrick, but it appeared he was at the centre of a disagreement between these two people. Hammersmith was quite happy to put a bullet in him, but they were obviously being filmed as they sat here, and if she just shot him without reason, it would not play well with her boss. She needed one of them to make a move, and both Jericho and Badstuber had so far complied with instructions.

'Where are you from?' he asked, when it was clear she

obviously wasn't going to answer the previous question.

'Nowhere,' she said.

'Are you being vague, or did you move around when you were growing up?'

'What do you think, detective?'

Jericho held her cold stare across the table.

'Your father worked for some international company. Maybe a bank, maybe mining or oil. He was posted around the world. Singapore and Hong Kong, Cape Town, New York, London, Madrid. You never settled. Then at some stage he sent you to boarding school in the UK. Cheltenham Ladies', or Badminton maybe. No, wait, not the UK, Switzerland. You did the Baccalaureate in Switzerland, Beau Soleil perhaps, then on to the Sorbonne or Oxbridge. Maybe Yale, maybe Georgetown.' A pause, and then, 'And now you do this.'

'Bravo, inspector, a solid, what, two out of ten perhaps.'

She leant forward, lifted her coffee, took a drink, and then set the cup back down. Her eyes were on Jericho most of the time, though the gun was trained on Badstuber. There were only a few feet between the two of them, and it would be the work of a fraction of a second to take them both out.

'Dad was a sergeant in REME. We travelled. Germany, Cyprus, Salisbury Plain, back to Germany. Sent to boarding school when I was twelve, and it was the Alexandra and Albert rather than Badminton. Then a degree in international relations at Southampton. And yet, look at that, I'm here now.'

Her tongue edged out, removing an imagined speck of froth from her top lip. A beat, and another.

'Why the Vatican?' asked Jericho. 'Hasn't your job been monitoring global threats to the Pavilion?'

Hammersmith smiled, then she glanced at Badstuber to include her in the conversation.

'The very idea that a woman could do two things at once,' she said. 'Who'd have thought it possible?'

'Glib,' said Jericho. 'Monitoring global threat seems like a pretty big deal. A low-key diplomatic post at the Vatican, not so much. Why are you here?'

He had to wind her up, he thought. He had to do *something*. The Pavilion, at every step of the way, had the advantage, and this was just another of those situations. He had to create an opportunity, and hope that Badstuber could take advantage of it, even if it meant that he himself took the first bullet. He just had to give Badstuber time to make sure the bullet aimed at her missed.

'Here's what I think,' said Jericho, and Hammersmith couldn't help the smile.

'Women never tire of hearing men explaining things,' she said.

'It suits you to have some inside channel on the diplomatic world. Could be anywhere, but there's something about the Holy See. On one hand, diplomatically invisible, on the other, they carry a weight that far exceeds their actual influence, just because of who they are historically. And then there's the matter of Cardinal Ndakara of N'Pala. This has allowed you to play him, and promise him the world, and he has done your bidding. You could likely have done that anyway, but the cardinal must have an important part to play and your position within the Vatican, regardless of how lowly it might appear on paper, has allowed you to keep closer tabs on him.'

He paused. Hammersmith's face was expressionless, but he was sure there was something in those unmoving, unblinking eyes. It wasn't annoyance, and it wasn't any level of discomfort or fear that he was close to the mark.

He was hitting the nail on the head, and she was seeing an opportunity.

'So, whatever's going on in N'Pala, or somewhere in Democratic Central Africa, you need the cardinal. The country is split ethnically down the middle. Christian and Muslim, they've been fighting, and killing more or less permanently since the French pulled out in sixty-three.

'It used to be news, but not anymore. Now it's… nothing. No one cares. There are so many other conflicts, so many other areas of apocalyptically awful news, so many wars, so much existential angst about *everything*, what is one more shitstorm in a tiny country in central Africa, stuck in between the CAR and Chad and Niger and Cameroon, and most people couldn't find it on a map if they tried?'

There was a small smile beginning to come to her lips, a dangerous light in her eyes.

'We have mining and we have solar power,' said Jericho. 'DCA has unlimited, untapped resources. The desert is empty and waiting to be covered in solar panels, and there are mines that endless civil war have prevented from being exploited. What is it there that's so special, given there are gold and minerals all across the planet?'

The smile remained. This time Jericho waited for an answer, though he didn't expect to get one.

'Keep talking,' she said, 'you're doing very well. Maybe you'll even manage to work it out.'

'You have free reign there,' said Jericho. 'That's what the coup was about. That's what the cardinal's about. He's helped you mobilise that community. There are no international journalists there, the internet has been jammed for two years. You're doing something in plain sight, and yet no one can see it.'

'Very good.'

She lifted her eyebrows, the quiet look of triumph on her face. A glance at Badstuber, who hadn't moved. Shoulders straight, face expressionless, her eyes locked on Hammersmith.

Jericho fell into silence.

'Interesting,' said Hammersmith. 'You've talked yourself into a bullet in the head. A perfect illustration of someone who knows too much. On camera, on microphone. You cannot be allowed to walk out of here, which means… you will be leaving in a box.' A pause, and then she added, 'Tragic, really. Such a waste of a life.'

'Looks like Thunderbirds are go,' said Jericho.

Hammersmith smiled, and then couldn't help the mocking laugh.

'Really? Is that some sort of call to arms. You have a microchip –'

Jericho blinked three times. On the fourth beat, he suddenly catapulted himself to the side. At the same time, Hammersmith fired the Glock, just as Badstuber brought her hand sweeping down, catching the cup of coffee on the side, and firing it at Hammersmith. The cup flew, its trajectory shifting with the weight of liquid flying from it.

Hammersmith got to her feet, right hand – her gun hand – automatically swiping the cup out of the way. Badstuber, her momentum carrying her forward, had one foot on the coffee table, and then she leapt at Hammersmith.

The gun swung round, and Badstuber caught it with a perfectly timed swing just as it went off, the bullet thudding harmlessly into the wall. And she was on top of Hammersmith, pushing her back into the chair. Grabbed her right arm, as Hammersmith shifted the gun. Faces strained, the barrel of the gun almost at Badstuber's head. Another shot let off, deafening in Badstuber's ear, the round exploding into the ceiling. Badstuber's hand at Hammersmith's throat. Hammersmith let go of the hand at her throat, swung a vicious punch, catching Badstuber's jaw. She reeled. A slight give in her grip on Hammersmith's right wrist, another two shots fired, more blasts into the ceiling, Badstuber's head buzzing. Tight grip on the throat, Hammersmith letting go another punch, then once again her hand to Badstuber's wrist, to loosen the throat grip. A headbutt one way, the position not right for a good contact, and then returned the other, this time Badstuber catching Hammersmith on the bridge of her nose. The crunch of bone, then blood. Gritted teeth, instant retaliation, another ineffectual hit, catching Badstuber's nose roughly, but in such a way that blood flew. At the same time, brought her knee up best she could, catching Badstuber's lower back. Another two shots, this time Badstuber feeling it in her hair, then, gritted teeth, spittle on Hammersmith's face, Badstuber squeezed her fingers around her windpipe. Thumb and forefinger pinching, Hammersmith gasping for breath. Face straining, muscles and tendons in her face and neck taut, three more shots, one after the other, Badstuber feeling the graze on her head, and then the click of the empty barrel. The game changer. She let go of Hammersmith's wrist, and now both hands at her neck.

Vicious squeeze, face in a desperate snarl of effort. Hammersmith unleashed, flailing with everything, punches raining down on the side of Badstuber's head. Then a switch, and her nails pressed into Badstuber's eyes, and that was enough. Badstuber jerking her head back at the last gasp, the slight shift in momentum Hammersmith needed, and she managed to jerk her head forward, just enough drive to catch Badstuber's chin, a headbutt uppercut, and her head juddered backwards. Hammersmith's hand up and through the gap between Badstuber's arms, separating them and freeing them from her throat. Then she was pushing Badstuber off her in the same sweeping movement, and it tossed Badstuber backwards. She fell harshly and violently and unprepared, her back hitting the edge of the coffee table. The coffee table pushed back, the top shattered. Badstuber slumped, winded, to the floor, in amongst shards of glass, and suddenly the position was reversed. Hammersmith on top of her, hands to her throat, and no hesitation. Thumbs pressed into her windpipe, hard and brutal, her face twisted, teeth bared, oblivious to the punches Badstuber started throwing at her head. Badstuber's mouth in an open, silent howl. Desperate for breath. Eyes wide and watering.

Jericho, from nowhere standing behind, brought a heavy ornament – a Benin bronze bust – down onto the back of Hammersmith's head, with all the force he could muster. A wide swing to the side and through, rather than up and down, so that he didn't inadvertently catch Badstuber.

Hammersmith fell instantly to the side beneath the ugly crunch of bone. Blood and matter flew, her hair mangled in red and grey.

Badstuber breathless. Hammersmith thrown off, tossed onto her back, blood quickly pooling behind her head.

Jericho stood over them for a second. He and Badstuber stared helplessly at each other. His chest was stained with his own blood. His legs gave way with his final effort, and he fell to the floor.

Badstuber pushed herself up, eyes wide, instantly cutting her hands on shards of glass.

And then the walls fell.

Just as had happened at the London house, the shutters dropped. Doors and windows, no alarm, barely a sound. With no lights turned on, they were instantly thrown into darkness, as the steel shields descended over the windows.

She found Jericho in the dark, her hands clutching his head.

Silence, bar the still desperate sound of Badstuber recovering her breath. And then, in the darkness, a new sound.

The quiet hiss of gas.

Badstuber lifted her head, her eyes wide, breath still laboured. She frantically thought of what she could do to combat the gas. Her brain an ugly whirl of desperate uncertainty, her hands now covered in Jericho's blood.

Her last thought, from nowhere in the carnage, as the fog swept across her brain, was of her daughters, and if they'd be safe now that she was dead.

And she folded to the side, almost softly to the floor, falling away from Jericho, her arms above her head.

And there the two of them lay.

44

He woke with a yawn, at the first light of dawn.

Something new in the air. An unfamiliar heat. Dust. A taste of the unfamiliar.

Jericho could not move, and he made no effort to. He closed his eyes. He might have drifted off. Just a moment, a flickering of sleep, and then his eyes opened again.

He squeezed them tight, lifted his hands to rub them. His hands wouldn't move. His eyes opened a little more. Directly in front of him, the headrest of a seat, and the back of a head.

He tried to think of where he was, but it was too early in the waking up process to think about anything much. He just had to take in the information.

He turned his head, and looked out of the window.

Sand and dust. Arid landscape, a pale, yellow light, stretching away to low mountains in the distance.

The word Africa lodged in his head, and then Sahara came from nowhere, but for now that was as far as he got. That didn't make sense, they'd just been in Paris.

Paris? That wasn't right. Not Paris. Somewhere else that spoke of European history, and European classicism, and European decline.

Rome. They'd been in Rome.

He thought of Badstuber. He looked to his right. She was there, strapped into the seat next to him. They were in a small minibus, a narrow aisle between the seats. Badstuber was sleeping, her lips closed, her breathing easy. Bruises on her chin.

A narrow bandage down this side of her face. He noticed her hands and feet were strapped in, then he looked down and saw that he was similarly bound.

That was why he wasn't able to lift his hands.

Better than paralyzed, he thought, the first cogent, rueful thought since he'd woken.

He tried turning his head, to see if there was anyone behind him, and felt the shooting pain through his chest. He looked down. Beneath the blue shirt he didn't recognise, he could see the edge of the bandage, strapped around his chest.

She'd shot him, that was what had happened. Not in the chest, in the back, and the bullet had passed straight through.

He couldn't remember her name, and he glanced around the mini-bus, as best he could, to see if she was also here. Then he remembered the blow he'd struck to her head, how he'd felt the bone give way on impact. She must be dead, he thought, though he still couldn't remember her name.

His mouth was dry. He licked his lips, and tried to swallow.

'Where are we?' he asked.

The man in front did not move. There was no sound from behind. He could not see the driver.

No one answered.

Φ

Later, he had no idea how long as he'd drifted off to sleep again, they were both awake, as the bus slowed to drive through a small town.

He'd asked Badstuber how she was. Before she could answer, a voice behind said, 'One more word and there will be severe pain.'

She had nodded, and tried to smile. He had returned the look.

An occasional glance aside, they had not communicated.

Now the minibus slowed even more, and they looked to see what the hold-up might be.

Jericho swallowed, a feeling of horror crawling up his spine. He glanced at Badstuber, who'd already closed her eyes. She opened them again, just as he looked away from her, back out over the scene of slaughter.

Low buildings, none of them higher than two-storey, most of them only one. Aerials on rooftops, and small satellite dishes.

Water butts. Palm trees, and other plants Jericho didn't recognise moving in the light breeze.

There were corpses everywhere, the images being ticked off in Jericho's head, as though a running news commentary. Lone bodies, bloodied, left where they fell. A figure shot in the back of the head, arms spread wide. A child struck down, chest riddled with bullets, flies buzzing around her eyes. A decapitated head on a stake. Another, then three in quick succession. Then three women hung from the same doorway, their legs severed above the knees, the stumps only inches from the ground. Bodies in small piles, heaped one on top of the other, and even in the horror, Jericho admonished himself for the tautology of the internal commentary.

The mini-bus slowed to a crawl, obviously swerving around victims in the road. A slow-moving judder as the driver was forced to drive over a corpse. Again, shortly afterwards, and then again.

A burned-out building, charred bodies on the ground before it, gunned down as they fled, then caught by the flames.

They passed a small group of soldiers, standing at the side of the road. Guns held casually on shoulders, two of them smoking. One of the smokers looked barely ten years-old, thought Jericho, though what did he know of any child? They watched the minibus go silently by. They were not smiling or laughing, they were not celebrating their easy win. Dead eyes in dead faces, they passed out of sight.

At last the smell found them. Burning flesh. Rancid, choking, gagging.

Someone in the bus said, 'Jesus.'

It was the on other side of the minibus. A funeral pyre, piled high with corpses, warm smoke in the morning sun. The same person said, 'Fuck me.' Someone else said, 'Pick it up, will you?'

The driver didn't reply. He was the one having to drive his bus over the bones of the dead.

It would be two more minutes before he was able to leave the village behind. Jericho did not take his eyes off the scene. He wanted to see it all. He wanted to be able to write down what he saw. He wanted, in that moment, to be able to find everyone responsible. And he knew that at the top of that list, would be Stanley Merrick, and whoever was left of the five soldiers who'd led the coup, and more than likely, Cardinal Ndakara of N'Pala.

This was a Muslim village, and Christian soldiers, armed to the teeth by the Pavilion, had slaughtered everyone who lived there.

They were coming to it now, he knew. You didn't do something like this unless you wanted to keep something nearby a pretty big, damned secret.

He swallowed, the stench of the dead still in his nostrils. Another glance at Badstuber, who was staring away across the desert, across a huge array of solar panels, panels beyond counting, stretching to the horizon.

Jericho shifted position in his seat as best he could, so he could try to see where they were heading.

After leaving the village, the road had swung round, and was now heading straight for the mountains. There were no obvious structures in place on the mountainside, then the commentary running in Jericho's head reminded him of another box that was being ticked as they continued inexorably onwards.

Mining.

There wasn't going to be any obvious structure. When they came to the rock face that seemed to descend to the desert floor out of nowhere, there was going to be a passageway into the mountains, or there was going to be a doorway.

And just like that, after years of fruitless searching, Jericho was about to be delivered to Pavilion headquarters by the people he'd been chasing all this time.

He grimaced, and then his face set hard. You should've killed me in Rome when you had the chance, he thought. When you had me gassed, unconscious and bleeding on the floor.

The minibus approached the side of the mountain, seemingly heading straight for it, and only when it was a hundred yards away did it start to slow. And then, from nowhere, a long, dark, narrow slit appeared ahead of them, and then the doors slid away from each other, the slit grew into a large entrance, and the darkness became a long road running deep inside the mountain, illuminated by dull yellow lights interspersed along the ceiling.

At last Badstuber, who had been lost in a trance of horror since they'd passed through the village, turned to look at Jericho, and they shared a grim, silent look in the minibus.

The endgame had begun.

45

They were in a gilded cage. A comfortable room, buried deep in the mountain. A double bed, a dining table, two chairs, a small coffee table. The room had no central focus, no windows, no fireplace, but there was a solid unit with a large fish tank on top, permanently lit in blue light.

There was a single painting on each of the walls. A Pissaro, a Gainsborough, a Hopper, a Seurat. They did not work as a set of four, but each individual painting was a nice piece. They decided, on the basis of very little art knowledge, that they were modern copies.

To the left of the Pissaro, the door to the bathroom. A shower, a toilet, a sink, lots of space, large, light grey tiling.

The capabilities of their prison had been pointed out to them on their arrival. Multiple cameras and microphones. A vent system which could be deployed to deliver lethal gas, in exactly the same way as the non-lethal gas had been delivered in Rome. Any attempt to deactivate the cameras would lead to the activation of the gas. There was no escape, and there were no small items left in the room from which they could attempt to fashion a weapon in the dark. And there was, of course, no dark in any case.

They would be held there until further notice. They would receive food at uneven intervals, so that they'd be unable to establish a routine. When food was due to be delivered, a buzzer would sound, and they would have to stand at the rear wall. The food would be delivered on a tray at the door. The person delivering the tray would be accompanied by an armed guard. Any untoward movement would result in death.

If they attempted to communicate with the people delivering food – and so far it had been a different person every time – there would be no food for the next forty-eight hours.

And those were the rules.

'I've seen this movie before,' said Jericho, once they'd been freshly installed.

Badstuber was flat. Expressionless, and unwilling to talk too much, but beneath it Jericho could still sense the determination burning inside her.

'And we know how it ends,' she said.

Φ

Time passed. They had no idea how long. The lights in the room remained at the same level. Sleep came and went. There was nothing to do. No reading material, no contact with the world, no television.

Conversation was possible, but they knew everything they said was being listened to.

They also had no idea how much time had passed between the incident in Rome, and their arrival in DCA. Jericho had collapsed from the force of the bullet wound, and had lost blood. While he was unconscious, the wound had been sewn up. Perhaps he'd been given blood, he wasn't sure. There was still pain, and now as the hours passed into days, and he was no longer being given painkillers, the discomfort was increasing. The other multiple bruises and scrapes and injuries were slowly healing. The same for Badstuber, the small bandage on her face now removed.

Jericho woke once to find her sitting on the floor, back against the wall, staring across the room, tears on her cheeks. Her face was blank, eyes dead, no emotion. Just silent tears.

He knew why. He said nothing, as there was nothing to be said. He could not make it any better. He sat down and laid his hand beside her, and eventually she put her hand in his, and slowly their fingers began to interact, and finally she laid her head on his shoulder, though it was some time before the tears ran dry.

They took to watching the fish.

At some point – the third day, or the fourth, they had no

idea – they started talking. Anything to alleviate the boredom. Jericho asked Badstuber about her childhood. They started talking, and then they did not stop.

They slept in the same bed, but there was no intimacy. Not while their lives were on hold, not while every move they made was being watched.

This was a strange period they knew would not last forever. There was always the possibility, however, that some disaster befell their captors, and they would be abandoned and forgotten.

This was something that prayed on Jericho's mind, and he could not shake the idea that they might die here and never get out.

46

There was a small envelope pushed beneath the door. Jericho lay on his side, having just woken, wondering if it was the sound of the envelope being delivered that had woken him, or whether it had been there for some time.

Badstuber was sleeping beside him. Their sleep cycles had remained in synch, and that was all that spoke of the rhythm of the days.

He remembered as he sat up in bed that, once closed, the door was a sealed unit. Nothing could be pushed beneath it.

He got out of bed, Badstuber stirring beside him, and opened the small envelope.

A short note, printed on card.

Mr Merrick will meet you now. Get ready to be collected.

He turned the card over, he read it again. There would've been no point in them including a time, after all.

'We have been summoned?' asked Badstuber.

Jericho nodded.

'Presumably they'll come when we're ready,' he said.

They stared at each other, and he recognised her look of determination.

'I am ready,' said Badstuber.

'I mean, up and dressed,' said Jericho.

'Yes,' said Badstuber, a slight furrow in her brow.

Φ

They came to a cave of wonders.

Jericho was a misanthrope. Perhaps, if this ever ended and neither he nor Badstuber were dead, then he might allow himself some hope. But his time in the police service had scarred him. He saw no joy, he expected little of the world, or of the future. He never looked upon anything with wonder, he was rarely surprised, he was never delighted, he had certainly never been in awe of anything.

And that changed the second they walked out onto the balcony.

They had been led down a series of wide corridors. Lightly carpeted at first – the domestic quarters, he assumed – leading to starker corridors, where the doors, similarly, were designated with both letters and non-sequential numbers. If you wanted to know where to find somewhere, you would have to memorise the floorplan.

The walls of the domestic corridors were lined with artwork from all the ages. The walls of the corridors leading to the business end of the operation, whatever the business actually was, were decorated with framed chemical symbols and physical equations. Science as art. Many of them looked like old original documents, the pieces of paper on which the scientists themselves had written formulae, and made notes.

Through a random, unmarked door, they were led into a large, elaborate dining room. Magnificent art on the walls, huge paintings reminiscent of Roderick MacKenzie's *Delhi Durbar*. Three dining tables, eight chairs around each. To the far end, beside the floor-to-ceiling windows, there was a smaller table, with two chairs.

The lighting was low and warm, the temperature in the room, as it had been throughout the facility, perfectly even.

Outside the window, there was a wide balcony, a man sitting in one of the chairs overlooking the huge cave before him. To the right of him, a waterfall was plummeting from above, down into the void.

The room was completely silent, as though someone had turned off the volume of the waterfall.

They approached the window, led by a security guard dressed in dark grey, another behind them. The guard in front waved a hand, and the window began to slide to the side. As soon as it did, the cacophonous sound of the waterfall rushed into the room.

The guard ahead walked out onto the balcony, and stood to the side. With a nod, he ushered Jericho and Badstuber out, the other guard followed behind him, and then he took up position at the other end of the balcony, as they walked to the railing that ran along the balcony's edge, staring down into the abyss.

Jericho felt his knees go weak with the sheer scale of the drop, and he automatically grabbed hold of the railing.

They were in a vast cave deep inside the mountain, or perhaps, deep beneath the mountain. They were on a point three-quarters of the way down the side of a cliff face. To their right, the waterfall, thousands of gallons of water tumbling down a precipitous drop. Directly beneath them, a huge lake, illuminated at its edges by blue light.

The ceiling of the cave was lit by elaborate lighting. Jagged rock formations descended, far down in some places, barely in others.

As they stared around the cave, they could see this was not the only balcony. There were others positioned throughout, and on the other side of the lake, there was a small area of developed ground beside the water, with a series of small buildings. To the right, a large area of grass, foliage beyond.

Beneath them to the far left, a long area of beach, although even from here it could be seen that the lake sloped quickly away from the edge of the shore. There was no sandy bottom anywhere in this lake, its depth unfathomable.

There was a small rattling of a chain, and finally, snapped from their reverie, they turned to the man who'd been waiting for them.

'I have to chain myself to the chair here. I have the key,' he added, with a laugh, though he was having to raise his voice to be heard above the waterfall. 'I'm not a prisoner in my own, you know, cave system. But look at that.' And he rose and leaned on the balcony, his leg chained at the ankle to the base of the fixed chair behind him.

He shuddered, a spark running through him, and then he straightened, and pulled back a little.

'There's something about a drop like that,' he said. 'It makes you want to…' and he made a gesture of going over the balcony. 'You know. It's like the gravity literally pulls you over. I went to Pulpit Rock in Norway. You ever been? No railing, no safety, nothing. Good for them. You go near the edge if you like, but it's on you not to die. It's on you to fight the primal urge to *jump*. I couldn't get anywhere near it, because I knew what would happen.

'But this, I love. I love it, and I'm safe, and when I unchain myself, I have my back turned and I walk straight through there, and that's all there is. Come have lunch.'

He turned away from the cave, bent over, unlocked the chain around his ankle, and then walked quickly from the balcony, and back into the large dining room. Jericho and Badstuber followed, the guards behind, then the glass doors closed.

Silence.

Three places had been set at the small table, a third chair added, and Stanley Merrick gestured for them to take a seat.

It was Merrick who Jericho had met in Dornoch Cathedral three years previously. The American. Merrick who had talked so dismissively of the wealth of Musk and Bezos and Gates. Merrick the golfer, and who was now sitting here, quite possibly the most dangerous man in the world.

'It's nice to see you again, detective,' he said to Jericho, and then he nodded at Badstuber. 'And agent Badstuber, a pleasure.'

They gave him nothing in return, but he was hardly expecting it.

A tall man with greying hair, slender, fit. Wearing a short-sleeved polo shirt, as though just about to go out on the golf course. He gestured in the direction of the balcony.

'I wondered if you'd be able to survive the drop into the water. Coupla hundred feet. People have done it from around this height, though not in here. I had a few of the locals try it out for me. None of them especially willingly, I'll admit. How many was it?'

He looked away, vaguely across the room.

'Twenty-nine,' one of the guards said.

'Twenty-nine,' said Merrick. 'One man, we thought he might make it, but really, he was in a bad way.' Then he made a small gun gesture, and added, 'We did the right thing.'

A movement to Jericho's left, and a man approached, pushing a small cart. Three plates of food, a basket of bread, a bottle of water, and a bottle of white wine.

'It's early, but let's drink,' said Merrick.

Three glasses of wine and three of water were poured, the

plates were placed before them. Crayfish and rocket salad. The waiter retreated.

Merrick lifted his glass without attempting to make a toast.

'I shan't insult you,' he said. 'I know you'd rather not be here. And look, I'm sorry about your wife, detective. She was really, really good, but you know, I couldn't trust leaving her out there. And, I'm afraid, the fact we brought *you* here but felt we had to kill *her*, says exactly what you think it does. Now, I know you've been getting served some decent food, but this, really, this is another level. You may hate me for bringing you here, but you should eat. And I know what you're thinking. You're thinking, this is pretty much a prawn cocktail, like it's nineteen-seventy-five for crying out loud, but you've got to try this.'

He laughed, then started eating. They didn't join him.

'Look,' he said, the wine glass coming and going from his lips, 'you might be pissed off, but ultimately, down here you live, up there you die, so you know, maybe you'll thank me.'

'My children,' said Badstuber, not looking at him, voice strained.

'Yeah. I don't have children myself,' he said. 'I find it hard to… I don't have empathy, I admit. I can't imagine what having children is actually like. The feeling that the life of this thing is more important than your own life. Makes no sense to me. Sorry. I just don't care about your kids.'

He took a mouthful of food, then made a small gesture with his fork. He never looked her in the eye. 'Of course, you two killed my head of security. I liked her. I don't appreciate that.'

'What d'you mean, up there you die?' asked Jericho, moving the conversation along before Badstuber could react.

And, having joined the conversation, he decided he may as well play along. At some point he was going to have to try to do something, but until then, he had to fit in. He glanced at Badstuber, he tried to say what he was thinking in a look, but all he had was the hope they were on the same wavelength.

He lifted his knife and fork, and started eating. Badstuber lowered her eyes, took a deep breath, and joined them. Playing the game.

Merrick didn't answer. He was enjoying his food, and proceeded to eat it as though he were eating alone.

They ate in silence, until Merrick shook his head, and said, 'Babette, play Mozart.'

Babette, who Jericho took to be the AI in the room, said,

'Now playing Mozart,' and *Rondo Alla Turca* started playing. Merrick scowled, and said, 'Come on, Babette, seriously? We're having a nice meal here. I'm looking for some of that string quartet whatever.'

'Very well, Mr Merrick.'

A moment, and then Mozart's String Quartet no.1 in G started playing.

Merrick lifted his chin and listened, then nodded.

'That's nice, I like that,' he said. 'No idea what it is, but I like it. You like Mozart?'

The question was directed at the table. Jericho said, 'I like Oscar Peterson and Hoagy Carmichael,' and Merrick laughed and said, 'Ha. I knew that, but it ain't mutually exclusive.'

Conversation was secondary to the food, and he let it go while he finished off the small plate. Then he lifted a piece of bread, and ran it round the plate, mopping up. He ate the bread, he took another drink of wine, he dabbed at the corners of his mouth with a napkin.

Jericho ate the lunch, watching Merrick, looking around the room, taking in as much as possible. Something about the second guard that reminded him of an actor. Owen Wilson maybe. That was bad. He'd likely take the guard less seriously, but he was no less likely to discharge his weapon, just because he looked a little like Owen Wilson.

'I know what you're thinking,' said Merrick when he was done, and had sat back a little, looking at Jericho.

'Could I stab you in the eye with this knife before your men shoot me?' suggested Jericho.

Merrick had not been expecting that as an answer, his brow furrowed, and then he laughed loudly.

'Very good,' he said. 'No, that's not what you're thinking. And, by the way, no you couldn't, so you can try if you like, but you're signing your death warrant. No, as you said back in your room there to your friend, you've seen this movie before. Evil genius, massive bunker, the hero gets brought in so that the evil genius, desperate for the respect of the hero, can explain himself, and then the hero saves the day, evil genius gets killed, all his henchmen get killed, good guy wins, millions of lives saved, so on and so forth. Right?' He made a claxon noise, an ugly sound that likely didn't quite come out as he'd intended. He waved it away. 'There's nothing for you to do here. You kill me, blow this place up, get away… fine. War is inevitable up there. We're only a coupla days away from event horizon. I have connections, and even I couldn't stop it. You two? No connections.'

'What d'you mean, war is inevitable?' asked Badstuber.

'Come on, agent Badstuber. You've been watching the news. The world is in freefall. And yes, the Pavilion, such as it still exists, has played its part. We've pulled some strings, but really, this was happening anyway.

'Now that we're here, on the precipice, which will be the first domino to fall? The war in Kashmir, the South China Sea, North Korea, Iran, Ukraine, the Arctic Circle? So many to choose from. And if you think they're all of our making, you're way wrong. Couple of those we haven't even leant a helping hand. This shit's just real, my friends. This is why, you know, you can pull some shit or other. You can pull some moves, here. Take on my guys, kill 'em both – there's zero chance you could do that, by the way – break out of here, find our ops room – not much chance you do that either – bring everything down.' He shrugged. 'Go ahead, see where it gets you. This ain't, I don't know, *You Only Live Twice*. This ain't some kind of Lex Luthor shit. You kill everyone down here, then go up top and somehow contact every government leader? What are you saying? Hey stop arguing, seriously this is all the fault of a secret organisation started in the 1840s by a British soldier who found the secret of eternal life in the Himalayas!'

He looked at them both, finally managing to engage Badstuber's eyes.

'Sounds crazy, doesn't it? Sounds about on the same level as that nut Alex Jones, or all those Covid deniers, or the world is ruled by lizards brigade. Go on, fill your boots with bullshit. No one's listening to you. Up there, everyone needs to calm the fuck down, and no one's calming the fuck down. Darkness has been unleashed, the genie is out the bottle, Pandora has opened her box. The Pavilion... we did little more than give a helping hand.'

'What did you mean, *the Pavilion such as it still exists*?' asked Jericho.

Merrick put his elbows on the table, lifted a piece of bread, and then started tearing off small pieces, putting them in his mouth.

'I never got to thank your wife, by the way,' he said. 'If it hadn't been for her... You know the story of William Featherstone, right? Found the secret of eternal life. And, seriously, it's not eternal, that's just for the books. It's extended life. Long life…'

'Is he still alive?' asked Jericho.

'He was. I killed him.'

'Book of Lazarus didn't do him much good, then.'

'The Book of Lazarus. Ha. Nothing any dumb book can do about decapitation, my friend.' More bread, more wine, a glance at the amount of food still on Badstuber's plate. 'Featherstone was a rogue, but he was smart back then. He started the Pavilion, he put structures in place. Those fellas ran a tight ship. And then he got tired of the politics and the games, and he decided to hand over the reins.' He tapped the side of his head. 'Like I say, he was smart. He institutes a policy of a ten-year rolling leadership. There's like an executive board structure, over the course of the ten years one or two people rise up, the principal – and that's me now, I'm the principal – he steps down at the end of the ten years, and likely his successor will already have become apparent. If not, there would be discussion, followed by a vote.

'So, some time ago I was lucky enough to rise to the post of principal. Throughout my time, there was a very obvious successor in place.' He kept his eyes on Jericho, nodding along to his own words as he talked. 'Name was Develin. Your wife killed him in Oslo.'

He pressed his lips together, head slightly at an angle, nodding again. He's been watching De Niro, thought Jericho. He's playing a part. Doesn't mean he's not every bit as dangerous as it appears, but it's a game, that's all.

'That left a vacuum. And you know, nature abhors a vacuum. Hey, you know who said that?'

He stared between them, seemingly having asked the question seriously.

'Aristotle,' said Badstuber, the word crossing her lips as though she hated herself for engaging.

'Exactamundo. And on that occasion, I was only too happy to fill it. I admit it, I played them all. Man, they all fell for it. All of that, you know, I'll just do another coupla years until we get the right person in place crap. There was never going to be a right person.

'Hey, look, the eighteen-forties had their place, but all that crap from back then, that was old, man, you know. The cards that were like Tarot cards but weren't Tarot cards. Come on. That's Sherlock Holmes level bullshit. And sure, that shit was happening on my watch, but I'd had enough of that. All that crap in the Melville paintings you've spent so much time running around after? All bullshit.

'Look, eat up, darlin', plenty of food still to come.'

Badstuber took a moment, then placed her knife and fork neatly across the centre of the plate, and pushed it a little away from herself. Merrick gave a small glance in the direction of the two guards, and shortly afterwards the door opened, and the waiter reappeared to clear the plates away, Jericho too leaving food unfinished.

They sat in the silence of Mozart, while the plates were removed, then Merrick leant back into the conversation, lifting another piece of bread as he did so.

'So this is Dwarrowdelf, then?' said Jericho, before Merrick could speak, but he wasn't perturbed at being interrupted.

He smiled, he made a sweeping gesture towards the cave.

''Bout seven, eight years ago,' he said, and really, he was fulfilling his remit as evil genius, happily telling all his secrets, even as he insisted that he wasn't like all the other evil geniuses, 'I was having a discussion with some folks, and one of them was saying about Putin, you know, they were talking about how likely it was he'd start a war. I don't mean Crimea, and Georgia, and the Ukraine invasion he finally got around to. I mean *the* war. The big fat nuclear war. And this guy was like, he doesn't give a shit, man. No one should imagine the guy's going to have some shitty, like Hitleresque bunker somewhere outside of Moscow. He's going to have a palace of a bunker. He's going to have taken over a cave system, and adapted it, and he's going to have running water, a lakeful of it, and the place'll be opulent, and he'll have his doctors down there, and his dentist and his judo partners, and his hookers, and some guy he can play chess with. The whole shebang, you know what I'm saying. And it made me think. And the first thing I did was use some of my people to find out what kind of bunker that guy's got. And you know, it's a step up from Hitler, but it ain't anywhere anyone's going to want to spend the rest of their life after they've destroyed the earth. And how much life has that pudgy-faced little weasel got left anyway?' He laughed. 'Then I thought, well, who's the richest fucker on earth? That'd be me. And I need to find myself one of those cave systems.'

He made a gesture, indicating the cave outside.

'Eight years work getting here, my friends. An old gold mine. Gold ran out, and at some point in the mine's history, they stumbled into this beauty. If this was under the Alps, they'd've developed the shit out of it. But here we are in Democratic Central Africa, and nothing's developed. So, we moved in, and took over. We've been running this place the last few years. Divide and conquer, as you may have seen on the way through here.'

'That wasn't divide and conquer,' said Jericho, his tone harsh. He hated this guy. 'The pyres were still smoking, the bodies were still covered in flies.'

'Yeah, that's fair. That village was just a little too close, you know. They'd been involved, a lot of them had worked here. But they'd started asking for whatever, and they'd started yammering on about making waves. I don't like that kind of talk. We got our Christian friends to do a little bit of *ethnic cleansing*. Those guys don't know shit. They think they're getting control of the country. I mean, they are, but there ain't going to be much left to control.'

'If you have such dominion,' said Badstuber, 'why bother pushing for all-out war? Why not push for peace? Why not push for saving the rainforest, saving the oceans?'

'Because, I don't have dominion. The planet is fucked, sweetheart, and the number one biggest problem is humanity. Time to get rid of them all. Planet-wide cataclysm, wipe out the majority of life on earth, and then let's see what emerges on the other side.'

'What if nothing emerges on the other side?'

Merrick laughed.

'As your man Goldblum said, life finds a way. And as long as it's not human, it has a shout at, you know, survival. Coupla thousand years from now, no humanity left, and life on earth can have another go. Who's the evil guy now, huh?'

'How many people do you have down here?' asked Jericho.

'Final numbers not in yet. Around three hundred. And before you ask about the gene pool, it's not about the gene pool. Folks will live their lives, those lives will be extended an amount, we'll all get well over our four score years and ten 'n all that, but eventually, humanity…'

He ran his finger across his throat.

'And are we part of that three hundred, or did you just get us down here to grandstand, before killing us?'

Merrick laughed.

The waiter arrived, pushing the trolley. He placed bowls of soy and ginger steamed cod with noodles in front of each of them – Jericho annoyed to find the food smelled amazing – chopsticks laid beside Jericho and Badstuber, but a fork for Merrick, then he topped up Merrick's glass of wine, asked the question of whether anything else was required, Merrick shook his head, and the waiter turned away.

Merrick immediately started twirling noodles around his fork like he was eating spaghetti, and shoved some into his mouth. He did not eat with any elegance.

'Maybe I'll have mastered chopsticks after fifty years down here, but I doubt it.' He laughed. 'But you two go ahead.'

'Are we here to live or die?' asked Jericho.

'Haven't made up my mind. I mean, it's always good to have pushback, you know what I mean? Surrounding yourself with yes men, and to be honest, I have more or less surrounded myself with yes men, is a one-way ticket to megalomania. It'd be good to have you two here, you know. Keep me grounded. Now that you've killed Hammersmith. She kept me grounded.'

He looked at Badstuber.

'Maybe once you tire of the detective here, you and I… you know? I mean, we're going to be down here for like fifty years. Maybe a hundred, or a couple hundred. I mean, seriously. Plenty of time to go round everyone. And once you start on the Lazarus routine, baby, you'll barely have aged a day in that time. But then,' he continued, ignoring her look of distaste, 'maybe I'll just kill you both. Like I say, you killed Hammersmith, and I liked Hammersmith. I mean, I really liked her. You have big shoes to fill.'

'We will kill you too,' said Badstuber, coldly.

'Right, there we are,' said Merrick. 'There we are. I like those kind of balls, you know?'

He broke off a piece of fish.

'Look, if you fellas have any more questions, ask away, but we don't have all day. I just wanted to say hello, proper introductions and all that. But I've got some things to do up top, and then back down here in a couple days and wait for the,' and he made an explosion gesture.

'How can you know?' asked Jericho. 'If you're not controlling these people, how can you *know*? What if no one can bring themselves to be the first one to pull the trigger?'

'Yep, decent question,' said Merrick. 'And you know, I genuinely think there are enough mad fuckers in the world right now that someone'll do it. But just in case, just in case, we have procedures. My people have hacked into the defence system of five of the nuclear powers. We're covered. If it hasn't happened by,' and he paused to look at his watch, then shook his head. 'Doesn't matter. There's just over fifty-two hours, and then kablooie.' Then he laughed. 'Kablooie. Huh, nice.'

'So, all that about it definitely happening regardless,' said Jericho, 'that's just chutzpah. It's not definitely happening unless you choose to kill eight billion people.'

'You've seen the news, detective,' said Merrick. 'I'm barely giving them a nudge. And if it doesn't happen now, it happens later. Or we all die because of the climate, or because of the whatever. This way, we create a new earth. Sure, it'll start off radioactively toxic, but let's see how that plays out.'

He laughed again, and took another large piece of fish.

'Seriously, I'll admit to a little selfishness on my part,' he continued. 'This control that we have over events here, such as it is, it's much more about timing than it is about making it happen. I'm one hundred percent certain it happens, but I don't want to be caught unawares. You know, some asshole pulls the trigger while I'm on the fourteenth at Royal Dornoch? I ain't getting back here in time. Hell, I ain't making it to Inverness airport.'

'And you're primed for fifty-two hours from now?' said Jericho.

'More or less.'

Neither Jericho nor Badstuber were eating. Merrick was chewing quickly, as though he'd suddenly decided he really needed to leave.

'And that's what you're dashing up there to do? A last game of golf?'

Merrick smiled while he ate.

'Hey, look,' he said. 'Down below, ground level, there's a tee built into a deep recess in the wall. The grass patch you saw over there, that's the green. Hey, it's one hole, it ain't much, but you know, it'll scratch an itch. I can hit fifty balls, then walk round, see if I can make the putts. Then when we get back up top sometime in the future, we'll just have to go see the state of these golf courses. It'll be exciting.'

He laughed again.

'Tell me about the Lazarus book,' said Jericho.

'Sure, sure,' he said, waving away the question. 'I'll get a copy delivered to your room, for what it's worth.'

'What does that mean?'

Merrick took another drink, then glanced at the guards, then sat back, pushing the plate away from himself by a centimetre or two.

'Imagine Jesus showed up,' he said. 'I mean, really, actual Jesus, turns out to be the actual son of God, and he shows up. Hey, everybody, it's me, Jesus, he says.' He did the claxon sound. 'The guy's going to have a massive credibility problem. The son of God in today's cynical world? Sure thing, buddy. How's he going to separate himself from Manson and Jim Jones? From all the other nutjobs in the world? Not to mention all the people who'd just say, the son of God? Big fucking whoop, man, you weren't born here, you ain't getting a visa.'

He looked between the two of them, eyebrows raised. This was presumably going somewhere, so Jericho didn't bother asking the question.

'This is where we are with the Lazarus Book. It's health supplements. I mean, it's fucking health supplements, man.' He laughed, like he was trying to get them to laugh with him. 'There's some plant grows in that valley in the Himalayas. Only place it grows. It's sacred, some shit like that. Don't take the plant out of the valley. We know Featherstone was a disrespectful asshole. He steals the plant. He brings the secret back. There are enough people in London who know him, to know there's something other worldly going on. He gets buy-in, he starts the Pavilion. The Pavilion quickly grows in power. He shares the secret a little, but keeps it close.'

'And the secret is a plant?'

'It's a plant.' Merrick giggled again. 'I mean, the Victorians had scientists perfect it, you know. Ways to ingest it, times to take it, other things to eat with it. But you want to hear something funny? I published the Book of Lazarus on Amazon four years ago. Didn't call it the Book of Lazarus, of course. Gave it some generic title, some shit about eating right to live longer, stop ageing, all that crap. I even advertised. Sold a tonne of copies, and then… crickets. No one's talking about it. Because it's long term. Long term. And people don't do long term anymore. They want results now. Today. But this? Results you won't really notice for ten years, with the real benefits coming, I don't know, fifty, a hundred years from now. No one's buying that.'

He shrugged.

'Featherstone's original manuscript was really placed at the top of Kanchenjunga?' asked Jericho, and Merrick laughed, slightly hysterically this time.

'Can you believe it? He could've just burned it, of course, but that was all part of the myth.'

'Why the modern day secrecy, then? Why kill the climbers who got to the summit? Why go after Geyerson and his people?'

'They thought they had something, and it was meaningless. So, the Victorians didn't want the secret getting out, in case everyone followed it and everyone lived forever, and there would be chaos. We didn't want the secret getting out, because everyone would've laughed at us. All that time, carefully constructing alliances through threat and an unseen aura of omnipotence? We'd have been laughed outta the fucking joint. You're immortal because you eat some Nepalese herb? Big fucking deal, man.

'So, we killed everyone, and our reputation for ruthlessness and omnipotence was enhanced. And, of course, Raintree killed Develin, and that opened the door for me. That night in Oslo was the best night of my life, and I wasn't even there.'

'What age are you?' asked Badstuber, and Merrick smiled at her joining the conversation.

'I was born in nineteen-o-four. Changed my identity three times.'

'How many more are there like you in the Pavilion?'

He took another drink of wine.

'This is a little awkward,' he said, then he laughed. The smile didn't leave his face.

'You killed them all?' said Jericho.

'You could say.'

'You killed them all?'

'Sure. If you're going to take control, you have to *take control*. That's the way the cookie crumbles, my friend.'

He downed the glass of wine, laid it back on the table, pushed the chair back and got to his feet.

'You'll need to excuse my rudeness, but I have to go. Look, I haven't made up my mind yet. I think I'll likely kill you both, but we'll see how it goes,' he said, as though discussing whether or not he was likely to buy their used car. 'In the meantime, I'm afraid you're going to have to wait it out, back in your room. If you'd like anything, you know, just ask.'

'I'd like a news feed,' said Jericho.

Merrick stopped, giving this consideration, then he smiled.

'How'd you know I'd give you the real news feed? I could feed you a fake, one that says America's attacked Moscow, or Delhi's been nuked. You wouldn't know.'

'I'd like a real news feed,' said Jericho, refusing to play along, and Merrick laughed.

'Your wish, et cetera, et cetera. Now, if you'll excuse me.'

He bowed marginally to them both, and then turned quickly away, nodding to the guard as he went.

'Let them finish dinner,' he said. 'If they want to look at the balcony again, I don't mind. They try anything dumb, you know what to do.'

The guard nodded.

Merrick left the room.

Jericho glanced at Badstuber, and then took a look out of the window at the cascade of water.

'Might as well chew slowly,' he said, lifting the chopsticks for the first time.

47

They relaxed a little with Merrick gone, though what he'd told them hung heavily over the table. Perhaps they both clutched at human nature. That the big bad thing, the gigantic all-encompassing disaster, wouldn't happen. Merrick was, naturally for someone in his position, full of hubris. But they had this to cling to, thought Jericho: total global destruction would only happen if the Pavilion instigated it, and if that was the case, then it could be stopped.

They took their time over the noodles and fish. They finished the bottle of wine. They took dessert, a delicious, and perfectly executed Paris-Brest, they had a glass of dessert wine, a 2013 Chateau D'Yquem, then they had coffee.

They talked freely, unconcerned about the two guards. They were hardly in a position to make plans, they knew so little about this place, so they chatted about how this madness had unfolded, the eddies and currents of the investigation, and how it tied into what Merrick had been telling them.

Everything Merrick said could've been a lie, it wasn't as though they could trust someone who was game-playing the end of civilisation. Nevertheless, they believed him.

Merrick's dismissal of the Pavilion certainly rang true. The way this had played out felt completely different from before. That had been a game, a brutal one, vicious, deadly, but they'd been playing, nevertheless, leading Jericho down an absurd labyrinth. This time it had felt like Jericho had been doing all the chasing, having to create things when he'd previously been led into them, while what was left of the Pavilion had sat back and enjoyed themselves, watching his futile attempts to slip under the radar.

This organisation, this thing that had lurked in the shadows so long, playing untold parts in the history of the past hundred and eighty years, had become little but Merrick's personal fiefdom. Amanda killing Develin in Oslo had been the turning point, he did not doubt Merrick on that.

She'd obviously been a big player in the hunt for the Pavilion. They had orchestrated the entire business with Durrant and *Britain's Got Justice*, using Jericho to try to draw Amanda out. It hadn't worked, yet it had been a perfect illustration of who the Pavilion had been at the time. They toyed with people, and they still conducted themselves like they were in a nineteenth-century Conan Doyle short story.

The matter that had ended in Oslo, had been them taking out the trash, while still trying to use Jericho to get at Amanda. That part of it had at least worked for them, in that Amanda had been drawn into the fray. Amanda, however had won. She had badly damaged the operation, but she had killed the heir apparent, not the head.

That had been that for Merrick. No more games. No more playing with death. No more taunting and teasing. People were just going to die, while the Pavilion, and Merrick in particular, strengthened his position.

And now, more than eleven years after Jericho had had to endure the awfulness of the absurd television game show, here they were. The end was upon them, though sadly not just the end of the investigation. The end of everything.

'Remember what I told you at dinner in Lausanne,' said Badstuber.

Dessert and dessert wine were done, coffee was done. They could always request a digestif, but at some point they were going to have to move, and they were both thinking the same thing. It was now or never.

If they were sent back to that room, they'd have no idea how long they'd be there for.

'I feel we talked about a lot of things,' he said, a little curious.

A look in her eyes, then she turned away from him. Toyed with her empty coffee cup. Letting him realise that this was no idyll chatter. This was something she couldn't say out loud. This was significant.

'I miss Hanna, that's all,' she said. 'I miss Saturday mornings.'

She looked at him, smiling sadly at the reminiscence. But the message was hidden behind the truth of the smile, and he recognised what she was talking about, and his automatic reaction was to say, no… no. You can't… But all he did was mumble, 'That must be tough,' very quietly, because to say anymore would have required acting, and he knew he couldn't act.

Hanna was Badstuber's eldest daughter. On Saturday mornings, they would go up into the mountains, and swim in a small lake, diving in off the rocks. And as the years had passed, the rocks they dove from had got higher, and higher.

Nothing, thought Jericho, like the precipice out there, but she was telling him that was what she was going to do.

And it absolutely made sense, because the two guards would be anticipating Jericho being the action hero. He, after all, was the one covered in cuts and bruises and gunshot wounds. He was the one who'd killed Hammersmith. He was the one leaping off buildings, jumping into trees, flying around like a great adventurer. If either of them had been going to attempt the leap from the balcony, it was him. That, in fact, was likely why Merrick had said to the guards to let them back out there.

It wasn't a trap, as such. It wasn't a game. Merrick was just curious, that was all. Would Jericho have the guts to make the jump, and what condition would he be in if he survived.

Jericho reached over unexpectedly and took hold of her hand, giving her fingers a light squeeze. They held the look, and then, with the flick of a switch, determination took them. There would be time for whatever this thing was between them when it was all over. And if it was to end badly, then they would know nothing of it.

Their fingers parted, they both effected a look of sadness, a look that spoke of the end of the party. Time to wrap it up, and return to the comfort of their prison.

Jericho lifted his coffee cup and drained the dregs. He lifted the small glass of wine, and drained the dregs. He sighed, he turned to face the room.

The two guards remained in place. Something determinedly implacable about them. Something that said they were untouchable, so do not even try to touch them.

These, thought Jericho, were exactly the type of people Amanda had so summarily dispatched in Oslo. The front of invincibility was little more than that.

'I think we're done,' he said, and he didn't have to act the melancholy in his voice at the end of the meal. It was, potentially, the last time he and Badstuber would ever dine together.

They pushed their chairs back, they got to their feet. The guards, a few yards apart, did not move, waiting for them to walk to the doors.

'Can we?' asked Jericho, taking the lead, and indicating the doors to the balcony. This was what they were expecting, after all.

The guard nearest the balcony nodded, stepped towards the door, and made a gesture for it to open.

The glass slid to the side, the thunder of the waterfall invaded the dining room, and then the door was fully open, and Jericho walked out ahead, the guard indicating for Badstuber to follow.

Out on the balcony, they took a moment to stand in awe at the vastness of the cave, and at the cascade of water, then Jericho approached the edge and looked down. Again his head swirled with vertigo at the plunge of the side of the cave, and then he turned and looked up, and the vertigo was even worse, and he clutched the railing, his legs unsteady, and a low mutter of, 'Jesus,' escaped his lips, though it was lost in the noise.

Badstuber did not go to the edge. She stood back, looking at the lights in the roof of the cave, her eyes wide.

She had taken the time previously to study the drop, and remembered every detail about what was below. As soon as she'd seen it, she'd known it was something she was going to have to do. She'd been tempted there and then, but thought she should first get a better idea of the lay of the land, where they were in this drama.

She had a pretty good idea now.

Jericho looked at the guard closest to him, the one with the greater air of authority.

'This water,' he said, pointing at the waterfall, his voice raised, 'what's its source? Won't it become contaminated from above after the… apocalypse?'

Even mentioning the apocalypse sounded far-fetched, absurd, like talking about a video game.

'It's fed from two sources,' said the guard. He was happy to speak, but his eyes were locked on Jericho, aware he was keeping one of his hands on the railing. Ready, he assumed, to suddenly make the jump. 'One of them will be cut off in advance. The other, the lesser source, comes from a stand-alone aquifer. It will not flow with such force, but it will flow for at least two hundred more years.'

'Damn,' said Jericho, and then he forced himself to look back at the waterfall, and once again lifted his eyes to the roof.

He shuddered, he turned back to the guard.

'And this lake? How deep is it?'

'Maybe it is five hundred metres,' said the guard. 'Maybe it is one metre.'

Jericho smiled, then glanced down.

He closed his eyes, he turned back.

'And it runs off? You have some sort of hydro power here? Those solar panels might not work so well up there if the earth plummets into the nuclear winter everyone used to talk about.'

'The nuclear winter is a myth,' said the guard.

'Right. But you have hydro?'

The guard remained deadpan.

'Because myth or not…'

There was a movement to the side, then Badstuber was behind Jericho, up onto the balcony and jumping off.

'The fuck?' cried Jericho, turning in horror, his eyes wide.

The main guard took one step to the railing to look down, gun instantly drawn. But he would have been instructed not to fire. The other approached quickly, a curious look on his face that turned to unexpected laughter.

Jericho swung his right arm out of nowhere. Caught the main guard in the throat. Grabbed the gun from his hand in the fleeting moment of shock, turned and put two bullets into Owen Wilson's chest as he was in the act of drawing his gun. His body flew back, his head bounced off the floor.

Jericho whirled back round, was met with a blow. The gun flew over the railing. The guard reached for his back-up weapon. Jericho kicked hard in the groin. A swift punch down into his hand. The guard dropped the gun. Jericho brought his foot down onto his knee. His leg buckled, but in the movement, as Jericho opened himself up to swing the haymaker, the guard caught him flush beneath the chin with a wild swing. Jericho staggered back, the guard, pain cast aside, was upon him, pushing him back against the railing, and then pushing him up.

Jericho flailed against him, his balance beginning to shift towards the top of the railing. Ugly grunts from them both. Jericho pushing at the guard's arms, the guard still in the ascendancy. Jericho's back bent over the railing. A final gasp, he threw his weight forward, headbutt aimed at the nose. The guard dodged, Jericho caught him on the cheek. He was forced back, head suddenly dangling backwards, hands now able to do little more than grab the guard's clothing, clinging on.

He looked down. Upside down, staring into the abyss of the blue lake, two hundred feet below. He couldn't see Badstuber.

He closed his eyes. He gripped the guard's clothing. The guard's hands reached at his neck, pushing him down.

Jericho opened his eyes. The vertiginous view scythed through him. Then a movement in the water, across the lake. Had to be Ilsa.

Rage surged through him. Desperation and fear.

He looped his legs around the guard's waist. Detached his right hand, jabbed the guard two-fingered in the eye. At the same time, the guard briefly reeling, Jericho pushed his momentum through his legs, thumbs into the guard's eyes, head brought up into the guard's face as he brought his body swinging upwards, and then Jericho was tumbling forward onto solid ground, a kick to the guard's stomach, pushing him back, and as he was regaining his balance, Jericho reached down, lifted the gun, and fired three times. One to the head, one missing to the left, one to the throat.

The guard fell.

Jericho went to the railing, and looked for Badstuber. The water, the far shore. Nothing.

A bullet pinged off the railing, then another, and Jericho retreated quickly from the balcony, back into the dining room.

Away from anyone's line of sight, he hesitated a moment. No point in going back into the corridor system, he was liable to get stuck, or at the very least, completely lost.

He should run at the railing, take the jump.

Fear thundered into his heart, made his skin crawl.

'Babette, can you tell me how to get down to the lake level?' he asked.

'I am not authorised to provide that information,' said the detached voice.

Jericho looked at the railing, the doors still open, the noise of the waterfall all-encompassing.

They would be here soon.

He turned to the two doors. One to the corridor, the one on the right presumably to the kitchen.

'Babette, open the door to the kitchen,' said Jericho.

'I am not authorised to follow that instruction.'

Jericho kept the glib comment to himself, and approached the door, wondering how effective a hail of bullets would prove.

The Mozart string quartet played on.

Jericho rolled his eyes at himself, then returned to the main guard and detached his keycard. He waved the card over the small monitor, and the door opened.

A short corridor, white walls, a couple of framed prints of food. Three doors led off, none of them open.

He entered the corridor, confident the keycard would continue to work, and that he wouldn't be stranded in the confined space.

The door to the dining room fizzed shut behind him.

There was a door to the right. That wouldn't be it. Merrick was not the kind of man who would think of giving his kitchen staff any kind of a view. A door to the left, another straight ahead. Beside each door, a small panel.

He went instead for the door directly in front. Keycard to the monitor, and the door opened.

There were five people there, none of them armed. The waiter he'd already seen, and four kitchen staff. They'd obviously been scrubbing the place clean.

A look of shock at the gun in Jericho's hand. One of them grabbed an iron frying pan, another an empty Marsala bottle.

Jericho lowered the gun.

'Is there an operations room somewhere?'

They all acted like the question had been directed at someone else.

'Who's the head chef?' asked Jericho, aware of the reluctance.

Nothing, and then an Asian man, small, in his mid-sixties, Chinese guessed Jericho, took a single step forward.

'I am,' he said.

'Is there an operations room?'

'We do not know. No one will know, apart from those who work there, if it exists.'

'There's no schematic of the cave system?'

'No.'

'Tell me everything you know about where you go from here.'

The head chef did not immediately answer. Jericho gave him the few seconds. He didn't want to have to brandish the gun, it would be entirely unconvincing. He may just have shot and killed two security guards, but he had no intention of even threatening a non-combatant in the kitchen. And who knew how many of the people down here, actually wanted to be here.

'There must be stairs,' said Jericho, when the seconds seemed to be stretching, although really they had not stretched far.

'This door,' the chef said, this time without leaving him hanging. 'Doors on right, elevators, door on left, stairs.

'How far down are we?'

'Long way,' said the chef.

Jericho looked around the rest of the kitchen.

'Anyone know how deep beneath the surface we are?'

Blank faces.

He turned away, through the door at the back of the kitchen, which opened as he approached, and as the chef had said, a series of elevator doors on the right, stairs on the left.

Security would be coming, and they would likely be coming in an elevator. He didn't have time to call one, wait for it, then send it off elsewhere as a ruse. And there was the chance that the first one to arrive would contain security.

He turned into the stairwell. Low light came on as soon as he entered. He stepped forward, leaned over the edge in the centre, looked down and then up. The lights had come on for the five or six floors either side of him, meaning that in the middle of the light, in both directions, was an impenetrable darkness.

'Dammit,' he muttered, and then he started jogging down.

If there was a control centre, and presumably there must be a control centre, it was going to be buried as deeply as possible. He could hope it went not much deeper than the bottom of the cavern, but he wouldn't know until he got there.

He opened the gun cartridge, checked the number of rounds he had remaining – six – and then began to jog quickly down the stairs, keeping his footfalls as light as possible in order to hear the arrival of others.

Not thinking about Merrick. Not thinking about Badstuber. Mind in neutral, every muscle tensed, ready for the next fight.

48

Badstuber was in a first aid room, strapping up her left foot. Now that she'd made her escape, and found some space, the pain was shooting through her. The door out to the cavern was closed, but the window didn't offer the same protection from the sound as the room in which they'd just eaten lunch.

She had entered the water feet-first, body tall and straight, hands tight to her side, the prescribed method. It was all she'd had, and it had mostly worked. Apart from her left foot. Her head and neck and back were safe, which was the main thing. Why her right foot was OK, she had no idea.

But the lake was obviously as cavernously deep as the rest of the cave, and the water was bitterly cold. She'd struggled to do as she knew you must in such cold water. Don't gasp for air, don't breathe too quickly, don't panic. Then swimming, fully clothed, with her foot screaming at her in pain, had been difficult.

She'd made it, nevertheless. Deep though it may have been, the lake was not wide. She had looked back to see the fight over the railing, and had watched long enough to hear the ensuing gunshots, the sound distant in amongst the cascade, and now was just having to hope it was Jericho who'd pulled the trigger.

She'd crawled her way to a recreational facility, though there was no one around. She was, nevertheless, waiting for the arrival of security. She'd smashed the glass on the medical cabinet, she'd found the morphine, and injected herself. Then she'd found the splint, and had strapped her foot up as best she could, having to stop herself screaming with the pain.

It had drained her, the jump and the swim and the pain of it all, and she was sitting on the floor, back against the wall, taking a breather, thinking through what she was going to do. The pain was beginning to lessen, as the blessed haze of the pain killer began to slowly envelope her leg.

More than just her leg.

'Might have overdone it,' she said quietly to the room, and giggled slightly at the end of it.

It was hard to choose between options for the way forward, when she didn't know what those options were, but regardless of how either would be achieved, it came down to one of two things. Get out, and get help, or find the nerve centre and bring this place to the ground.

Footsteps.

'Shit.'

She pushed herself up, and went to the medicine cabinet. Grabbed three syringes, found the midazolam-3 which she'd earlier ignored. Filled the syringes.

Footsteps approaching, two voices. A door opened, closed again. Then another, a pause, a shout, then the door closed. A garble of conversation, the words, 'Fuck me,' followed by a guffaw of laughter in the middle of it.

This ship, she thought, is not run as tightly as Merrick must have run his operation above ground. They're safe down here, and Merrick really did see her and Jericho as the fools. These people were viewing this as nothing other than a regular security issue, in a confined facility holding a few hundred people.

She hobbled to the side, pain shooting up her leg with the movement.

When the door opened, she was ready for them. Syringe up and stabbed brutally into the neck of the first one. She grabbed his weapon, and spun his body around, so that he was held in front of her, the gun at his head.

'Drop it,' she said to the other guy.

He looked into the eyes of his fellow guard. An instant calculation made. This wasn't a job worth dying for. He dropped the gun, and kicked it away, at Badstuber's direction.

'There's tape in the cupboard. Bind him, then lie on the floor, hands behind your back.'

The guard she was holding had no fight to give. He wasn't about to collapse just yet, but the midazolam-3 was already kicking in.

'Start taping in five seconds, or he dies,' said Badstuber to hurry the guy up.

She could make an empty threat with the best of them, and within three seconds the man's hands were being bound with surgical tape.

49

Jericho stepped into the large control room, and took a moment to orientate himself.

He hated the cliché of this, the absurdity of it, but here he was, playing dress-up. As a police officer he'd never gone under cover, he'd never tried to be something he wasn't. He wouldn't have been able to do it.

But it had yet to occur to him, as it had already occurred to Badstuber, that security was lax. Merrick had not viewed them as a threat, and so therefore had not tightened it.

He'd met two security guards on the stairwell. He'd fought, briefly, with them both. One he'd ultimately been able to shoot in the head, the other he'd tossed down the centre of the stairs. And now he was dressed in the uniform of the man he'd shot, using his security card to gain access to the rooms at the bottom of the great stairwell.

This was the seventeenth door he'd tried, in his long search of what he believed to be the ground floor, several levels beneath the surface of the lake. The corridor went in a long circle around the deep body of water, some of the doors off the circular corridor leading to further corridors, some leading to large rooms. A sports facility, a games room, a cinema, a swimming pool. Another large cavern, through which Jericho did not take the time to walk, but there was artificial sunlight built into the roof, lots of greenery and flowering plants, a stream running through the middle of a beautiful garden.

This guy really was ready for the apocalypse, he thought.

The ops room was large, but scarcely populated. Monitors on the wall, CCTV from around the facility. Screens with details of how many people were where. Oxygen levels. Heat. Water flow. Energy production, and energy consumption. There was a bank of TV screens running international news from a variety of outlets. Five long rows of computer stations set up, space for fifty people, though as it was, there were only four people present.

At the far end of the room, a row of narrow, wall-mounted cabinets, doors closed.

Jericho filed into the second row, where there was one other woman sitting, four seats away. He sat down, he looked along the row. He nodded at the woman.

He felt ridiculous.

'Hey,' he said.

'Hé,' she replied, 'qu'est-il arrivé à Travis ?'

Jericho had to think about it. Stared to the side, nodded to himself.

'Got the day off or something,' he said, not bothering trying to answer in French. A vague understanding and an ability to communicate, were two entirely different things.

'Huh,' said the woman with an eye roll, and she turned back to her screen.

Jericho stared at the screen in front of him. He was looking at an octo-screen of eight live CCTV feeds. Nothing was happening in any of them.

'You know anything about the thing on twenty-five?' asked the woman.

Jericho turned to his right. At least she'd switched languages.

'Just that there was something,' he said, 'but I don't know what's going on.'

'Jesus,' she muttered. 'It's the same every time Hammersmith's away. She's here, this place is locked down. She's not here, place turns to shit.'

'I heard she died,' said Jericho.

'What?' she said, genuine shock in her voice. 'Hammersmith? Hammersmith is not dead.'

'That's the word. Killed in Rome… I don't know, like a few days ago.'

He was hoping for a lead, a something, some indication of exactly how many days ago that had been. But then, if the woman didn't know anything about it, she wasn't going to be any kind of help.

'Merde,' she muttered.

Jericho gave her a sideways look, could see her agitation. Then she stabbed at an off key, the monitor returned to the home screen, and she got to her feet.

'I do not like this,' she said.

She glanced once more at Jericho, and then walked quickly from the room. She had not, he noticed, bothered asking any of the others sitting quietly at monitors.

Jericho studied the screen, he studied the keyboard. Then he accepted it was pointless studying the keyboard, as it was exactly the same keyboard as any other, and he looked back to the screen.

There were no icons to click on, nothing at which to aim an arrow.

He clicked on an image, and it filled the screen. The Canteen. About ten tables occupied. Nothing much happening. He wanted to click back, but he couldn't see how to do it, so he pressed the same button as he'd just done.

Nothing happened.

The chair next to him was pulled out, and he turned, heart in mouth, hand automatically reaching for the holstered gun at his right hand side.

Badstuber.

'Good afternoon,' she said. 'You are well?'

She was still wincing with the movement, then she took a deep breath and her face relaxed as she settled into the seat. She too was wearing a uniform, though it was obviously too large for her.

'Jesus, it's good to see you,' he said, surprising himself with the forcefulness of his words.

'And you too,' she said.

Her voice sounded lighter than usual.

He looked beneath the desktop.

'You hurt your foot?'

'Shattered. It will be very painful, but I have filled myself with morphine. As a result… I'm a little light-headed. I might not be of much use.'

'You got here,' he said.

'Yes, I suppose I did. You are on top of the game?'

'I don't think I am. I want to get into the computer system,

I'm here, literally on the computer system, and I still don't know what I'm doing.'

'This is not your skillset,' she said.

'No.'

'I see now that making love is your skillset, but that might not be useful at the moment.'

'Uh-oh,' said Jericho, 'you really are light-headed.'

'Yes. I said I was. I will find what you're looking for, but I think you're going to have tell me what that is. I can't think. I decided to get out of here and go for help, and now I'm sitting next to you. You look nice in a uniform.'

'Thank you. We need to shut this place down. Blow it up, if possible.'

'No,' she said. 'We cannot.'

'Why?'

'As far as we know, there are several hundred people down here, and that will take a long time for them to get out. We need to evacuate the place before anything else happens, we cannot be responsible for killing all these people. We don't know how many of them are down here voluntarily. And even if they are, do they know who they're working for?'

Jericho nodded in agreement.

'Good point, for someone not thinking straight.'

'Thank you. Shall I?' she said, indicating his keyboard, even though there was one in front of the seat at which she was sitting, and Jericho gestured for her to get to work, pushing his seat away a little.

'I was wondering,' she said, as she came off the CCTV octo-page, onto a home screen of heat graphs, and power usage levels, and all the information that was showing on the larger screens on the walls of the room. 'The passwords on the USB stick.'

'You think they might be for here?'

'Only one way to find out.'

'How would Amanda have got hold of those?'

'Smart woman, your wife,' said Badstuber, tapping the side of her head.

She looked at the screen, she looked at Jericho. She had a smile on her face, like a drunk who's just managed to work out how to open the mini-bar.

If Jericho was right, then two of the five passwords had been created by Amanda, which meant there were three to try.

She typed quickly, and she got in on her second attempt, another silly smile of triumph coming to her face.

'What shall we do?' she asked.

'As little drama as possible,' said Jericho, trying not to laugh at the absurdity of this. 'If there's an equivalent of a fire alarm, where everyone has to troop outside, we could do that. No panic, no stampede, just get everyone out. They'll all likely think it's a test, but…'

'Will they troop outside, though? Why would your fire alarm send you outside when in a few days outside is going to be a radioactive inferno?'

'How many people know that?' he said. 'This has obviously taken years to create, they'll have needed procedures in place while all this was being done. Maybe those procedures are still in place.'

'I like that,' she said, crisply.

She worked her way through the system, until she found a schematic of the underground structure, then her eyes ran over it, her fingers tracing paths around the facility.

'We can't have everyone trooping up the stairwell, that'll take too long. And people won't go. We need to… here, we need to isolate the emergency to this section here, and direct everyone to the elevators in these four sections.'

'That's a plan,' said Jericho.

'You'll need to do a Tannoy announcement.'

'You should do it. Better accent for it. Efficient.'

'I feel a little… drunk.'

'You're doing fine. And your accent hasn't changed.'

She saluted, then she placed a small bag on the desk beside him. She lowered her voice, to what was not far removed from a comedy, drunk whisper. 'There are several loaded syringes. You need to administer it to the others in the room, because when we set off an alarm, they will want to know why.' Her brow furrowed. 'We will not have good reason.'

'OK,' said Jericho. 'When you find the alarm, let her rip.'

She giggled a little, presumably at the words *let her rip*, and Jericho stopped himself smiling, and then moved along the back row to where there was a man sitting at the far end.

The other two were still in the room in the front row, sitting together, paying no attention. This, thought Jericho, really is a sleepy operation, hardly one on the brink of being the only functional facility left on earth. Apart from all the other megalomaniacs and their bunkers, of course.

The guy glanced at him as he approached. Jericho nodded, loaded syringe held down by his side. And then, as he was passing behind him, he turned quickly, and in the same movement, put his hand across the guy's mouth, and eased the syringeful of midazolam-3 into his neck.

He struggled, and Jericho held him firmly against the seat, moving him down behind the bank so that they weren't obvious to the two at the front.

The alarms went off.

Contrary to what they'd hoped, all hell broke loose.

50

As soon as the fire alarm sounded, another alarm went off. A different siren, more insistent, strident, piercing.

The two men at the front of the ops room, stood quickly, looking around.

'What the fuck?' shouted one of them loudly.

Jericho approached them, gun raised. Neither of them seemed particularly perturbed.

The fire alarm dimmed in volume a little, while the other raged on.

'Reported fire in Sector C,' said Badstuber, her voice steady, clipped, speaking into the small microphone. 'Fire in Sector C. All personnel make their way to the elevators in Sectors A, B, D and E. All personnel to take elevators to Level Zero. That's Level Zero, all personnel.'

'What the fuck is this?' said the same guy.

'Turn around,' said Jericho. 'Don't touch anything. Hands on your heads.'

A moment while he could see them debating whether or not to get into a fight, then they turned. Jericho put the gun in his waistband, took a syringe in either hand, took a second to consider where to inject them, then lowered his hands, and injected them at the same time in the buttocks.

They both flinched, jumped round, looked ready to fight. Jericho backed off, whipped the gun out, the men were paused on the brink, somewhere between action and indecisiveness, and then in unison they stumbled, they fell.

'What's the other alarm?' Jericho shouted at Badstuber, while waiting over the two men, ensuring they stayed down.

She didn't bother shouting in reply, instead making a hopeless gesture, then she indicated the CCTV relays showing on the screens.

People were already starting to move. However, that included security guards, scores of them, now running along corridors.

'Incoming,' she said.

'You can secure this door?' asked Jericho, having moved next to her, confident the two guys were out.

'Yes. And the others. And that one there,' she said, indicating a door to the left, 'is an elevator direct to the surface. Though I'm not sure I'd want to get stuck in it.'

'What else are you doing?' asked Jericho.

'I've managed to get into a different part of the system. A different password. Look at my memory here, that's pretty good, right?'

She was looking at him, smiling.

'I mean, three years ago I was full-on menopausal, and I couldn't remember what I had for breakfast.'

'What are you doing?' asked Jericho, struggling to not enjoy Badstuber's flippancy, keeping a straight face, hoping he could keep her focused.

'Oh, right, yes, you asked a question. Accessing files, sending them to myself, and to Stuart. I mean, Detective Inspector Haynes. And to a couple of people at the FIS. There are some I trust, though I should be careful.' She was talking almost to herself, her voice barely audible. 'And when I have got that fully underway, I need to find how they have access to nuclear codes, if they really can hack the system. And maybe one of these other passwords will work for that too.'

Badstuber decisively pressed a button, and in an instant the more insistent alarm went silent, and now there were distant sounds, carried through the earth and along corridors.

And then, footsteps in the corridor. Shouting, and then banging at the door.

'Dammit.'

Jericho turned away and walked quickly to the cabinets on the far wall. The weapons store.

He really didn't want to have to kill anyone else, but he had to keep them at bay until Badstuber had finished what she was doing. And there was going to be so much information there, who knew how long that would take.

He lifted a Glock, and an L110A2, a 5.56mm light machine gun. Then he put the machine gun back in place. He needed a couple of weapons, but he wasn't going to stand there like some action hero, indiscriminately discharging hundreds of bullets. He lifted another Glock, they were both already loaded, he stuffed another couple of cartridges into his pockets, then he turned back to the door.

A louder thump against the door, and then the first gun shot.

A pause, Jericho stood ready at the side of the door, both guns held before him, a sudden feeling like this might be the end. He was about to be met by fifty men with weapons, and they weren't coming to negotiate.

Another loud thump, and then another hail of gunfire.

Badstuber leaned into the microphone.

'Facility self-destruct,' she announced, 'has been set for three minutes. Now two minutes, fifty-eight seconds and counting.'

Her voice did not echo inside the room. Jericho's eyes swept the CCTV cameras. It was apparent she'd directed the announcement only to the corridor outside.

There was a pause.

Badstuber's fingers fluttered rapidly across the screen.

Faintly, from the corridor, the sound of the countdown. Agitation, and then several of the men turned and ran. Some shoving, a punch thrown, more men turned away.

A boot against the door, then three of them started firing, as their number thinned out.

'This is fun,' said Badstuber.

She was still rattling across the keyboard, Jericho's part in the drama reduced to waiting for something to happen, a guard at the door.

'There must be gas masks,' said Badstuber. 'And gas, obviously. Try another cupboard.'

Jericho smiled ruefully, shook his head at himself. She was making a better job of being guard than he was.

He went through the next three cupboards. More weapons, then a cupboard of grenade launchers. What was the point in them down here, he wondered? And then, the last cupboard on the right, longer, slightly thicker, the one he'd mistaken for likely holding heavier and more dangerous weapons, contained fifteen gas masks in three rows, and thirty cannisters of tear gas.

'Bingo.'

He lifted the gas masks, and quickly ran around, fitting them to the three men he'd just drugged. Then back across the room, and he handed Badstuber the next mask. A glance at the CCTV of the corridor, then at the door. There was a little give in it, and a bullet whizzed into the gap, and then a volley of them, all pinging well wide.

They shared a look, they slipped on their masks.

With the gap in the door, the sounds louder from outside. Gunfire, shouting, the fire alarm, the relentless, but false countdown.

Another large boot to the door, it buckled further.

Jericho tossed the first cannister towards the door, then the second. Thick smoke filled the air, immediately finding its way through the gap.

A clearly audible shout of, 'Fuck it!' and the guards outside split into two factions.

Some turned and fled. Those remaining opened fire with everything they had at the door, accompanied by coughing, angry shouts.

A series of bullets riddled the chair next to Badstuber. Jericho cursed, started firing at what he could see of the gap in the door as the room filled with smoke. He couldn't see the monitor to see if he'd hit anyone.

One gun spent in a matter of seconds, onto the second. The uproar of firepower from the corridor reduced, as someone was hit, or backed off, or succumbed to the smoke.

And then a figure in the smoke, something pulled around their face, running into the room, firing indiscriminately.

Jericho stood, took one shot, stopping him in his tracks.

A tug at his sleeve, and he turned, ready to fight.

Badstuber. Her eyes, through the smoke and on the other side of her mask, said, 'Come on,' she put her arm around his shoulder, and as best they could, they limped towards the door at the back, where the elevator was waiting for them. The door opened, clean air and silence, and they entered, pressing themselves against the side, as Badstuber pressed the button for the surface.

Gunfire did not follow them.

And then the door was closed, and suddenly they were

speeding upwards, through the earth and through the mountain.

Badstuber removed her mask, and Jericho followed.

'You all right?' he asked.

She was breathless with the thrill of it, the rush of it, rather than the short run to the elevator, and she slumped down onto the floor, back against the side wall, left leg propped out in front of her.

She felt no pain.

'Oh, yes,' she said, laughing.

'You're still high?' asked Jericho.

'God, yes. That was better than sex,' she said, then she laughed again. 'No offence, but I just saved the world. Or, you know, maybe.'

She smiled at him.

'What did you do?' he asked, having to stop himself laughing at the rush she was feeling, the brightness of her eyes.

'Sent every file I could find, as I said. That's still running, by the way, but I thought we should get out. It was getting hairy.'

'Good call.'

'There's a division of the Swiss army on the border with Chad. I had already alerted them to the...' Her brow furrowed, something innocent in her look. 'I have absolutely no idea how long ago that was. How long have we been down here?'

'We don't know.'

'Right. Well, at some stage I said they might be required in the DCA. Hopefully they were waiting for, you know... the thing. They have Apaches. They're good helicopters.'

'One of the best.'

'Yes. They should be no more than half an hour away. I locked the alarm, to make sure it continues for at least forty-five minutes. And... what was the other thing I did. Sent the files, called in the army... oh, I know, I disabled, and recoded the links they'd made to nuclear weapons systems. That was another one of those passwords I remembered. And by the way, that man, Merrick, Stanley Merrick, he was exaggerating the control he had. They didn't have *control* over the nuclear arsenals of the world. Nevertheless, I think, you know, I think they would've had enough to set the ball rolling.'

She smiled stupidly. He wondered if she would remember this feeling when the drugs had worn off.

'Don't tell me you brought peace to the Middle East in ten

minutes?' he said, and she laughed again.

'Don't be silly.' She smiled, and he asked the follow up question with raised eyebrows, and she added, 'Well, that's the maybe. All that,' and she waved her hand upwards, 'all the silliness and the stupid wars... we're going to need the grown-ups to step back from the brink, that's all.'

'Not too many grown-ups,' said Jericho.

'Exactly.'

'Maybe if they get eyes on how much they've been getting played by this guy.'

'Maybe,' she said. 'Maybe, maybe, maybe.'

She rested her head back against the side wall, and closed her eyes.

Jericho watched her, keeping an eye on the passage of the elevator. This was a two-stop lift. Bottom and top. And he was waiting for it to slow and stop when it wasn't supposed to. And yet, he knew. It wasn't going to happen.

This, at last, was the moment when the tables had been turned. Except, of course, it wasn't him who had done all the work to bring down the Pavilion. That had been Stanley Merrick. He'd destroyed it from within, he'd sucked up all its power, and he'd planned global destruction on a whim, to see how the earth would look in a few decades' time.

And then it had been Amanda who'd made all the inroads into Merrick's empire, and Badstuber who'd been able to see it through.

He checked the number of rounds left in the Glock. He had two more cartridges jammed in his pockets.

But he felt it already. He wasn't going to need the gun. When they reached the top, and they were nearly there, they were just going to be two more people to add to the list, and they could wander around with everyone else, with an air of not being entirely sure what was going on, while waiting for the arrival of the Swiss military.

This part of the story, the turning point, was over.

51

There was a chill breeze coming in from the east, ruffling the waves on the Dornoch firth. The sky was blue behind a busy thoroughfare of clouds. To the north, there was a huge dump of rain over Helmsdale, and another far out to sea.

Jericho and Haynes were walking along the beach adjacent to the golf course, aiming to turn up over the dunes, on to the links on the fourteenth hole.

Merrick was out there, playing a round on his own, though he was accompanied by a caddie. The caddie had not been provided by the club, and they assumed he was security. Haynes had come surreptitiously armed, just in case.

The world was still burning, of course. Israel was at war with everyone. Ukraine was still fighting off the invaders. India and Pakistan remained on the cusp of all-out war. And on and on. There was nothing that two people in a bunker far beneath the mountains of central Africa could do about that.

But Badstuber had done just as she'd said she would. She'd disseminated as much information from the Pavilion files as she could, and left it to the grown-ups.

So far, it seemed, the grown-ups had been paying attention, though no one could count on that continuing.

There were a few other people on the beach, and Haynes was wary. A lone woman. A dog walker. A couple who seemed to be together, the woman bent low over shells in the sand, taking photographs from various angles on her phone, the man watching for a while, then wandering off, bored waiting for his wife.

'We're good,' said Jericho.

They'd been walking in silence, since they'd parked at the golf club and talked to the pro about Merrick's likely whereabouts on the course.

'We're good?' said Haynes,

'You're looking at these people, wondering if any of them are Merrick's security. I don't think so. He's grown complacent, and what happened in DCA makes no difference to that. In fact, given that we find him here, I suspect he might not even know yet.'

'Surely…?' said Haynes.

'Well, he might, but if he does, this fits in with who he is just as much. He's held such dominion over his own people, and the world, for so long, he wanders around happily, and he won't fear a detective inspector from the Metropolitan Police turning up to arrest him. He'll be thinking he'll be out in time to finish his round before tea.'

Haynes shook his head, muttering, 'Asshole,' quietly into the day.

It had been a little over twenty hours. Jericho had at least slept on the plane on the way home, but that aside, there had been no time for it, and he was tired.

They had coordinated with the Swiss military on their arrival, Badstuber happy to put all her trust in Lieutenant-Colonel Árbenz. He and his men had then taken over the facility. Strangely rudderless, Merrick's people had not put up any more of a fight.

Without a word, they turned together and started walking up over the dunes. They could see Merrick, bent over a putt on the fourteenth green. He was wearing the same clothes as he had been the first time Jericho had met him, in Dornoch Cathedral, three years previously.

The caddie, standing a little to the side, noticed them first, and he straightened, said something to Merrick.

Merrick, having put his first putt two and a half feet short of the hole, turned and looked over his shoulder. He watched them for a moment, said something to the caddie, and then leant back over his ball. It lipped the hole, and came to rest an inch to the left. They could see the small shoulder slump, then he stepped forward, tapped it in, picked out the ball, and then turned to face Haynes and Jericho as they walked up onto the green.

Haynes, wanting as little of a scene as possible, looked off down the fairway. There was no one immediately waiting to play to the green, but a fourball was at the tee.

'Mr Merrick,' said Haynes. 'We need to have a chat.'

Merrick looked between the two of them, glanced along the fairway, and then nodding, walked with them from the green, in the direction of the fifteenth tee.

They walked in silence, bar the blowing of the light breeze, the lonesome cry of a gull, and the high-pitched twittering of the skylarks. They came to the tee, and they stood at the back. And now, having established their position and where this was going to play out, the men eyed each other.

'You,' said Haynes, indicating the caddie, 'don't do anything dumb.'

The caddie stared deadpan.

'Detective Inspector Haynes, Metropolitan Police,' said Haynes, showing his ID. 'Mr Merrick, you are under arrest for the kidnap and imprisonment of Robert Jericho and Ilsa Badstuber. The charge sheet when it comes will be long, but that's all we need for now. The likelihood is they'll still be reading out the list when you die an old man in prison.'

Merrick didn't manage to keep the smirk from his face, and he made no effort to hide the head shake.

'What have you done?' he said to Jericho.

'You really walked away from that cave and didn't look back?' said Jericho. 'You had no contact with anyone there?'

Merrick looked like he was about to answer, then he checked himself.

'What cave?'

Another stare around the four, though neither Jericho nor Haynes got the impression the caddie was about to try to heroically save the day.

'I didn't do much,' said Jericho. 'My wife had provided agent Badstuber with a list of codes, the meaning of which she wasn't entirely sure. Turned out they provided access to all your systems. She shut you down. And I don't mean, she shut down your facility in the African desert. That's still operational, though it's now controlled by the Swiss Army. She shut down, and revealed, all your contacts. Governments, police, spy agencies, NGOs, the UN, big business, museums, cornershops selling Irn Bru and cigarettes.' He paused. He was enjoying the look on Merrick's face, despite the fact he was trying to remain dispassionate. It was all in the eyes, however, a fire of outrage. 'You relied too much on Hammersmith, and once she was dead, you had to act quickly to plug the gap. You likely thought you could get to the end of all this,' and he indicated the clear, liquid light of the Scottish north-east, as representative of the world at large, 'without having to put so much trust in anyone else.' A long pause, and then, 'You couldn't.'

Merrick took a step closer to Jericho, a finger jabbed into his face.

'I fucking know people, you clown.'

'We know,' said Jericho. 'And we know which people. We look forward to seeing the strings you try to pull.'

He looked back along the course, the fourball behind now making their way along the fairway towards them.

'We should go down onto the beach to make our way back,' said Haynes. 'They're expecting us at the local station to formalise the arrest.'

Merrick sneered, head shaking.

'I'm an American fucking citizen,' he said.

'Your embassy consular is being informed as we speak,' said Jericho. 'Your phone will likely ring shortly. That'll be Deborah Azinger. She's your insider there, right? The nominal Pavilion representative to the Court of St. James?'

Jericho couldn't help the dark smile. Merrick scowled again. He looked sharply at the caddie, a silent conversation played out between them, then Merrick took an ugly, deep breath, and shook his head.

'This ain't over, numbskull,' he said.

'You know,' said Haynes, keeping his voice light in the likelihood of it making Merrick even more annoyed, 'as far as you being free to walk around goes, I think it just might be.'

52

They arranged to meet back in Lausanne, two weeks after they had taken the last elevator ride together. Badstuber had had to have a long, and complex operation on her foot; there had been three days of debrief with her agency, as she passed on everything she'd unearthed about Merrick and the Pavilion; and she'd wanted to spend a long weekend with her three children in the mountains.

Jericho had passed everything onto Haynes, and left him to it. As far as he was concerned, the job was done.

Perhaps there would be remnants of the Pavilion still out there, lurking in the shadows. One day the call would go out, the ancient practitioners of their peculiar evil would reassemble, and a faux-Tarot card would arrive in the post. Jericho's post, and Badstuber's post, and in the post of everyone else who had worked to bring the Pavilion to its knees.

Or perhaps not.

Merrick was in custody, and there was little doubt he should remain there. Badstuber had unearthed all the evidence they needed. But the world is as it is, and money talks, and Merrick had money, and Jericho would not be surprised if he learned one day that he'd been allowed out.

He checked back into the Imladris Hotel at the lakeside the day before Badstuber arrived, this time a suite two floors higher, with its own private balcony looking out upon the lake.

The following day he'd been out for a walk in the low hills surrounding the town, and she'd arrived earlier, surprising him.

When he returned to the room, he found Badstuber on the balcony, sitting at a small table, her left leg, with a boot around the foot, propped on a seat. Bottle of Dom Pérignon already open, glasses poured.

He approached her, they stared silently at each other, then he lent down and kissed her softly on the lips, his right hand touching her face.

He took the seat to her right, and together they looked across the lake to the mountains, white caps against a late afternoon blue sky. They lifted their glasses, they clinked in a silent toast, they took a drink.

'How's the foot?' he asked.

They looked at her foot. She had metal pins in each toe, another three in the foot.

'A bit stiff, thanks,' she said, with a sad smile.

'You have a nice time in Grindelwald?' he asked.

'Perfect. They were all pleased to see me for once.'

'As they should be,' said Jericho. He lifted his glass and toasted her again. 'Their mother saved the world.'

'I don't think so.'

'Really? That's what you said.'

'How d'you mean?'

'In the elevator. You said you'd saved the world.'

'I didn't say that.'

'You did. Given the security levels at that place, there's probably video evidence.'

She looked a little troubled, and turned away, head shaking.

'I was not myself.'

'You were amazing,' he said. 'I know you were working off all the details Amanda had found for you, but you knew your way in, you didn't hesitate, you flew round that system at a hundred miles an hour. I really didn't see that coming. So, be modest or not, but if you hadn't done what you did, you and I at least wouldn't be here now, and who knows how many other people.' A pause, then with a small shrug he added, 'Maybe nobody would be.'

'I could not have done anything without you.'

He smiled a thank you, they drank, they returned once more to silence, looking out on the cool lake, a slight breeze blowing across the top of the water.

'We made a good team,' she said after a while.

'We did,' said Jericho.

Their fingers found each other, and rested lightly together. In the middle of the lake, the Evian ferry puttered through the water, the sound travelling for miles. The sky spoke of a chill, clear night, the moon a slender white curve against the blue.

There was still plenty to worry about out there in the world, but for that moment, that evening, neither Jericho nor Badstuber had to worry about it.

'When d'you need to be back at work?' asked Jericho sometime later.

'I may be called in for interview, but that aside, I have two months off. I thought I might take a small villa in the Dolomites.' A pause, and then, 'You are welcome to join me.'

They drank champagne, they felt the cool mountain breeze on their faces.

'I'll check my diary,' said Jericho after a while, and Badstuber smiled.

Printed in Dunstable, United Kingdom